Just when you thought it was safe to go fishing...

SNAP

Steven Bredice

Typeset by Jonathan Downes,
Cover by J.T.Lindroos with thanks
Layout by SPiderKaT for CFZ Communications
Using Microsoft Word 2000, Microsoft , Publisher 2000, Adobe Photoshop CS.

First published in Great Britain by CFZ Press

CFZ Press
Myrtle Cottage
Woolsery
Bideford
North Devon
EX39 5QR

© CFZ MMXII

All rights reserved. Without limiting the rights under copyright reserved above, no part of this publication may be reproduced, stored in or introduced into a retrieval system, or transmitted, in any form or by any means (electronic, mechanical, photo-copying, recording or otherwise), without the prior written permission of both the copyright owners and the publishers of this book.

ISBN: 978-1-905723-86-7

For Tara

Acknowledgments

The author gratefully acknowledges the support, insights and kindnesses of James Scarola, Mitchell Cohen, Alfred Bredice, Peter Gora, Bill Isham, Paula Mills, Paul Kayhart, Laura Walker, Meg O'Donnell, Dan Bouchard, Brett Campbell and Jonathan Downes.

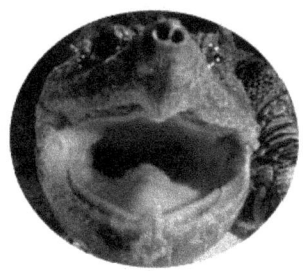

Contents

Prologue	....	7
Kryptos	....	11
Zoon	....	67
Logos	....	159
Epilogue	....	177

CRYPTOZOOLOGY n. (Gr. *Kryptos*, hidden, *zoon*, animal, *logos*, study or knowledge) The study of hidden animals, including species taxonomically known through the fossil record but believed to be extinct, and those outside the taxonomical record but for which anecdotal evidence exists in the form of myth, legend or undocumented sightings.

--Wikipedia

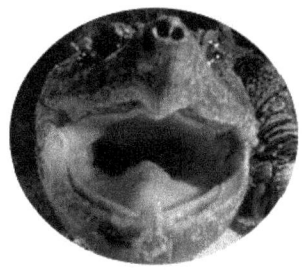

Prologue

The sound of their footsteps reverberated off the stone walls as they walked down the dimly lit corridor. The ring of keys dangling from the guard's belt jingled a little with every other step he took. The psychiatrist walked a half-step behind, uncertain as to which cell housed the inmate he had come to see. The psychiatrist carried a leather satchel. The guard carried a beat-up wooden chair. As they neared the end of the wing, a man's voice could be heard. "Move, already," the man was saying. "Will you?"

The guard stopped, turned to the psychiatrist, and said, "He's at it again." The psychiatrist nodded. The guard reached for his key ring, fiddled with it for a couple of seconds, then inserted one of the keys into the old-fashioned lock. The door unbolted with a crisp mechanical click and swung open. Inside there was a wizened old man sitting before a checker board. Opposite him was an empty chair. The old man was talking to the chair's invisible occupant.

The guard held up his hand to signal for the psychiatrist to wait, then addressed the old man.

"You gentlemen have got a visitor," he said.

"Excuse me?" the old man replied, looking over from his checker game. He wore a puzzled expression on his face. Pretending not to notice, the guard placed the chair he had been carrying upon the floor inside of the cell. Then he indicated that it was alright for the psychiatrist to come in and sit down on it.

"I'll leave you three alone," the guard said, aiming a knowing look at the psychiatrist. He raised his hand, palm open, fingers extended, to signify five minutes. The psychiatrist was disinclined to defer to the suggestion of an underling. Beyond that, he had come on a special mission. He held up his index finger to indicate one hour. The guard shrugged, stepped outside of the cell, closed the door behind him, and walked off down the hallway, footsteps echoing and keys chiming.

The psychiatrist turned to look at the inmate. "I'm Dr. Robertson Abercrombie," he said, holding out a manicured hand. "From the Canadian federal government."

"George Mapolis," said the inmate, grasping the doctor's silky palm within his own. It was a lonely, shabby extremity that George offered his visitor in return for such a fine one. A one-armed man has trouble handling nail clippers, and his remaining hand is typically rather calloused. "What kind of a doctor are you?"

"I'm a psychiatrist."

"Ah. I see." George let go of the doctor's hand. He glanced around the cell, looking past his visitor as if he were searching for something that had just that instant proven to be useful or relevant, but was now misplaced. He obviously registered the doctor, in his tweed jacket, blue double-knit Oxford shirt and Tartan-plaid tie, as an obstacle in his field of vision.

"Seen enough of us over the years?"

"Something like that."

"You've been here since what, 2010?" the psychiatrist shot back. "That's a long time, Doctor. Or should I call you Professor? Forty-something years."

"Forty-five years, three months, two weeks, five days, fourteen hours, twenty-nine minutes and, " George paused to glance at his wristwatch, "thirty-eight seconds. And just 'George' is fine, Doctor."

Dr. Robertson Abercrombie, determined to maintain control over the situation, fixed the prisoner, George Mapolis, with a hard stare and said, "You saw a monster on *Le Lac Perdu*."

Suddenly, George is at a loss for words. Suddenly, he is lying on his back, staring up into a starless sky, clutching a canoe paddle like a newborn baby to his beating breast, shivering and whimpering and waiting for the next sickening *bump* to come against the bottom of the boat. He is counting the seconds until dawn and praying to God he's numbered the days correctly - and that the float plane will actually be coming at first light.

There is a monster circling around in the coffee-dark waters below, a monster that has already killed, and wants to kill again. This is what happens when a fishing trip goes horribly wrong. The people feed the fish, instead of the other way around. It isn't pretty.

There is blood all over the boat. George's blood. It is as if someone has uncorked a couple of bottles of Burgundy and poured them out onto the deck. Blood-stained gear is strewn haphazardly about. Lockers and hatches have been flung open and tangled piles of line, life jackets, spent flare cartridges, and other such things lay in jumbled heaps, all soaked and sprayed in George's blood, like red wine.

The monster has been stalking the boat, appearing and then disappearing in the fog, diving underneath it, then ramming it from below, over and over again. It is less interested in damaging or capsizing the vessel than in terrorizing its occupant and drawing out his torment. It is waging psychological warfare.

And so, in this, the darkest hour before the dawn, on a desolate lake a thousand miles into the Canadian wilderness where there is not another soul, literally, to be found now that everybody else is dead, there is mayhem in the air.

kryptos

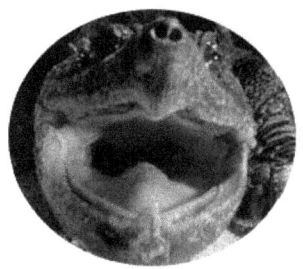

Chapter One

Regardless of George's deeper motivations, and putting aside the question of whether he withheld material information from the others beforehand, there were factors in play here beyond scientific curiosity or the need for academic validation or a hoped-for personal salvation. Or even the pernicious influence that the darkness of the beast can exert upon a distracted mind. A lot could nowadays be said or written about it all, in hindsight, but the outing, or expedition, or whatever it was, was never designed as a monster hunt.

It was a fishing trip.

And nothing more.

The flight in had been like flying into Shangri-La, over rugged, snow-capped mountains of Himalayan proportions spreading in successive ranges as far as the eye could see. Indeed, the breathtaking beauty of the place must have had some sort of an enchanting effect on them, looking back on it now. The lake itself appeared as a shimmering mirage sprawled across the basin of a huge meandering valley that lay hidden amongst the towering peaks. They were amazed at its size.

The pilot brought the plane in low over the water and gave them an aerial tour. He pointed out a few of the best places to fish and some prominent landmarks, then took them in for a water landing near a little cove where a small cluster of rustic buildings was situated around a modest stretch of beach.

There was a wooden dock, where two boats and an old canoe were tied up. They unloaded their gear and bade farewell to the pilot, then watched as the float plane taxied out of the cove, came around into the wind and took off with an angry roar. It made a big bank turn and headed off to the south, growing smaller and quieter until it became a silent speck in the sky, and then disappeared.

"Well, boys, this is it," George said with no small quantum of pride. "The Lost Lake."

Everyone just milled around on the dock, taking in the view. "It's beautiful, George," Peter Gordon finally said.

"It's so . . . wild out here," Nate Peterman added.

"We must have been in the air for three or four hours, and did you even notice a road or a house down there?" Jack Pelham asked. "We're probably, what, hundreds of miles away from anywhere."

"This really is the life out here," Danny Farnsworth said. "With absolutely nobody around to bother us. For five whole days."

"It almost seems too good to be true," Bill Isley observed.

Bill couldn't wait to start fishing, so he pulled together some tackle and went down to the dock while the rest of them set up the camp. As he helped haul gear up to the main lodge, George, for the first time in a long time, actually felt happy. He was where he wanted to be, where he needed to be, among trusted old friends in this pristine environment, far removed from the troubles of his existence back home in the States.

Maybe this experience was what George needed to get his life back on track.

The lodge was comfortable in a primitive way, and Peter came back to report that the little cabins were perfectly adequate as sleeping quarters. They had plenty of liquor, and there was even a refrigerator with an ice maker powered by a little gas-fueled generator. They brought with them a supply of food sufficient to round out the meals of freshly caught fish they planned on eating during the week, plus bacon and eggs and coffee for breakfasts.

"We are six very lucky gentlemen," Nate said.

"George, we really have to hand it to you," Peter put in. "We've all been looking forward to this but it's even better than I could have imagined."

"You did good, George," Bill said.

"You guys have no idea," George said. "The privilege is all mine, believe me. But before we get started . . ."

George went over to a duffel bag and reached inside. He pulled out a picture in an 8-by-10 frame. It was a portrait of their friend Tim, taken during their senior year in high school. His piercing blue eyes seemed so lively and his face wore its familiar goofy grin.

"I can't believe he isn't here," Jack said. "Tim would have been in his element. He tied flies so beautifully."

"He understood fish," George said. "He sure drank like one. I miss him."

"I know," Nate said. "I know."

George placed Tim's picture on the mantle. They all stood there for a moment, left to their own thoughts. Suddenly they became aware of a commotion down on the dock. Jack looked out the window. "Hey, guys," he said, "Bill's got a fish on!" They all ran out of the lodge and down the path toward the dock. Bill was wrestling with his pole, which was bowed sharply over and wobbling violently back and forth. He had something big on the line.

"Jesum Crow, Bill!"

"I know! Unbelievable, isn't it? It hit the line so hard, and *voom*, off it went!"

"Let out some slack," Nate advised. "Bill, let out some slack or you're going to lose it."

Peter ran and grabbed a big net on a long aluminum pole. They all stood around and watched intently as Bill tried to maneuver the fish toward the dock without snapping his line. But every time he got it close, it would start to struggle and flail, and he would have to let out more line and start all over again.

Finally Bill was able to drag his catch up to the surface, and to their surprise, what they saw was not a fish, but a huge snapping turtle. Its spiny green shell was maybe three or four feet in diameter and its pointed, scaly head was easily as big as a man's. It thrashed around furiously in the shallows, fighting to free itself, digging in against the bottom on thick, muscular legs ending in leathery webbed feet with sharp curved talons.

"Whoo-hoo, turtle soup!" Danny hollered. There was a wild look in his eye that struck George as being a little creepy. The more time George spent around Danny the less he felt he knew, or completely trusted, him. The two of them kept an uneasy distance from one another, Danny nursing some obscure grudge against George, and George harboring an almost visceral antipathy toward the dark streak in Danny's soul.

Bill continued to struggle with the turtle, and eventually it dawned on them that they were never going to get it up onto the dock, so they moved over to the beach and after a long tug-of-war managed to drag it onto the shore.

The process of opening the turtle's shell was crueler, and rather more dangerous, than any of them had expected, or cared to recall. The poor thing writhed frantically as they struggled to hack off its head. Turtles are well-defended animals and, ironically, that means there is no humane way to dispatch them. Danny almost lost a couple of fingers in the effort.

"They say a turtle contains seven kinds of meat," he informed the others as he methodically pursued his gruesome work. "Pork, beef, mutton, chicken, duck, lobster and fish."

Upon finally severing the creature's head, Danny heaved it onto the beach. To their astonishment, the decapitated turtle continued to work its jaws and blink its eyes as it lay there bleeding in the sand. Scout, Bill Isley's chocolate lab, ran over and started growling and barking, unnerved by the preternatural sight. Bill grabbed him by the collar and pulled him away from the turtle's bolt-cutter jaws. They put the head in a five-gallon plastic bucket and sealed the lid. Thumping and bumping sounds continued to emanate from the bucket for several hours.

"Kill a turtle and it will live until the sun goes down," Danny said. "It's an old wives' tale. It's also supposed to bring bad luck. Unless you intend to eat it."

When it was all over, the aroma that rose up from the fire pit and wafted out over the lake gave reassurance that their effort, however unsavory, would be well-rewarded. George discovered that a couple/few of Peter Gordon's signature Martinis not only washed away the guilt, but sharpened the appetite quite nicely.

"This," Bill said, "is really living."

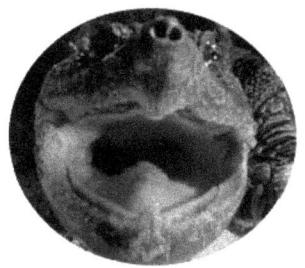

Chapter Two

When did the first sign of trouble appear? That was a good question. If someone held a gun to his head, George probably would have singled out that confusing moment when he'd discovered the footprint in the mud. Until then, he was just another member of a fishing party innocently enjoying the solitude of an isolated lodge on an unspoiled lake. And so as the turtle soup began to simmer, he had gone off by himself for a casual stroll along the shoreline when he quite literally stumbled across it, the outline of a reptilian foot clearly imprinted in a deposit of grayish silt not very far from the camp.

The footprint was remarkable in two respects. The first was its clarity. Since the muck was exceedingly fine and very damp, it had accepted the impression of the weight-bearing extremity with great accuracy, and then preserved it intact. Triangular in shape, the track displayed a deep heel and a broad ball behind four webbed toes, each tipped with a robust claw. It was obviously stamped into the ground with great force, being nearly two inches deep.

Size was the footprint's second remarkable characteristic. By George's rough measurement, it was more than two feet long and equally as wide. He could have put his boot into the toe prints, and the six-inch-deep holes left by the claws were practically as big around as silver dollars.

He could only stare at the sight in amazement. George struggled to conceptualize what sort of animal could have left such a trace of its passage upon the earth. He had to wonder: Could the legends be true? Then somebody called out to him from the lodge. George snapped back to attention. Their dinner of turtle soup was ready, apparently. Obeying the beckoning voice, he wheeled around and began retracing his steps in the direction of the lodge, where the savory smell of cooking turtle meat was rising into the breeze.

Surprisingly, when he turned his back on the footprint, a tingling sensation crept down George's spine. Despite himself, he quickened his step a little. Then his inner scientist took over. As he strode along the water's edge, George contemplated the meaning and magnitude of his discovery. He had acquired some prior awareness of the lake's reputation, but this had by no means conditioned him to expect such a find. It was a stunning development. From a scientific standpoint, George realized, he was obligated to document the evidence. He would have to return to the print later, with a camera and something to put inside of the footprint for scale. There was significance here. Proof of this sort might even vindicate George's politically incorrect interest in the field of cryptozoology, and quiet his critics in academia. His publisher would certainly be excited. Meanwhile, George decided he would keep quiet about his find for the time being. There was no need to inform the others. Not yet, at least.

As he ate his bowl of turtle soup, all George could think about was the footprint. Danny offered up some more gloomy adages about turtles and curses. George did his best to keep up with the small talk but at the first opportunity, he pulled away from the group once again, meandering casually up the path toward the lodge. Inside, he went straight over to his duffel bag and pulled out his digital camera, which he slipped into his pants pocket. Then he looked around for something to use for scale. In a kitchen drawer, he found an old wooden ruler. He tucked it inside of his shirt.

He went over to the window and looked down on the others as they milled around on the dock, talking and laughing together. The existence of the anomalous footprint was now a secret standing between George and his friends. They were unsuspecting. Which made him feel isolated from them. Like an outsider. His main concern, however, was to return to the site of the big track while the light was still good. He would have to do this without attracting the attention of the group. Perhaps he could slip out the back door and circle around to the site of the footprint through the woods, snap a few pictures and return to the lodge undetected. Then he could walk back out the front door and return to the dock by way of the path. He would come up with a reasonable excuse for his absence and all would be well.

The twilight was beginning to gather as George picked his way through the trees. He moved away from the camp on an arc that took him to a spot on the waterfront a little beyond the patch of mud where he had originally found the print. Then he followed the shoreline back until he located it again. George pulled out the ruler and placed it in the middle of the footprint. He took some pictures, then changed the camera's settings and recorded some video. He felt a secret thrill. Now he had the evidence he needed. George pocketed his camera, looked around somewhat furtively, and then withdrew back into the woods.

Quietly, he retraced his route through the forest, emerging a few minutes later from the woods behind the lodge. He went in through the back door, closed it behind him and walked back over to the window. As he passed by the mantle, he noticed Tim's face, smiling down on him. Down below, the scene was much the same as when he had left it. So he opened the front door and sauntered down the path to rejoin his friends. He told them he'd been to the outhouse. No one seemed to care.

If an interest in cryptozoology and a little bit of pre-trip research qualified as a basis for personal culpability, it ought in fairness to be acknowledged that George's actions, and omissions, were not the only causal agencies at work in relation to the expedition to *Le Lac Perdu*. As far as George was concerned, it was a conspiracy of circumstances beyond his control that even brought them here in the first place. Like spousal abandonment. And the suicide of a close friend.

The experience of coming home from work to a dark house and a scrawled note instead of a stiff wife and a loving drink coincided with Tim's sudden . . . passing. By all rights Tim should have been hoisting a cocktail on the dock along with the rest of them, but he had shot himself in the mouth. He was a doctor who had gotten hooked on drugs. Somehow he had wound up in a standoff with the police inside of his ex's apartment. It was the explosive crash at the end of a long and painful downward spiral.

George's marriage, on the other hand, had ended with a whimper. Sometimes, he dreamed about her, but mostly his sleep was dreamless, representing long black gaps in the stream of his thoughts. On awakening, a few sweet seconds of blankness would bleed through the membrane separating sleep from consciousness, a grace period before George's identity began to reconstitute itself. Then would come the feeling that something was amiss. There was something to be sad about, some unfinished emotional business to be picked up again now that the sleeping was over. Finally he would remember what it was.

She was gone. Nothing had been the same since the miscarriage. One day, she called. George hadn't been answering the phone, but he happened to be shuffling past the hall table and without thinking, he'd picked up the receiver and held it to his ear. He didn't say hello. He just listened to the static on the line and stared at the pattern in the wallpaper.

"George," she said, "is that you?"

George hesitated. His chest tingled as if the blood in his aorta had turned to butter. He tried to speak but nothing came out. He thought about hanging up, but finally said, in a voice hoarse from disuse, "It's me."

There was a long pause. The line crackled and hissed. Then he heard her disembodied voice ask, "Is everything alright?" No, George thought, everything is falling apart at the seams. But thank you for asking.

"Yeah," he lied, "everything's fine."

"George, I—"

"Where are you?"

"How can you be so damned—" she stopped abruptly, and then modulated her voice to a much slower cadence, speaking to him as if he were a small and somewhat slow child. "I'm having some papers sent to you in the mail. They're basically self-explanatory. I really don't want to make a big legal fuss. You can keep the house if that's what you want."

Her voice broke. "I don't want you to be angry with me." George could feel her crying silently at the other end of the line. Neither of them said anything for a long while. Finally the phone went dead with a hollow click.

It had been a mistake to seek solace, and no small measure of carnal pleasure, in the arms, and then in the bed, of one of his students. The whole affair had been destined from the start to end badly, and so it did. The cumulative pain and loneliness of these various developments had inspired George to make some calls, and the calls resulted in the idea of a private reunion of a few wiser but sadder high school friends, and somehow fishing became part of the concept, and the next thing George knew he was researching all-inclusive Canadian fly-in destinations.

As the plan evolved the destination migrated ever further into the northern wilderness. Eventually, in a place called Nunavut Territory, he'd found a large lake with, incredibly, only one outpost, consisting of a main lodge and several housekeeping cabins and a couple of boats that had been ferried in by heavy-lift helicopters. They would have the whole lake to themselves, boats, tackle and gear included. It would be just the six of them for the entire week, not even any guides or staff. And it was available for the whole summer. No one, apparently, wanted to travel so far north when, if you were willing to put up with only a little human contact, you could still catch your limit of trophy fish in an unspoiled environment, and be several hundred miles closer to the 50th Parallel.

So the price was right. And George wanted to be truly alone with his long-lost buddies. He did not want to hear another boat or see the smoke from anyone else's campfire. He wanted to know that the lake was theirs completely. Absolute, purifying isolation was what George needed in order to make this journey back to himself these 30 years later. He had looked forward to it, this reunion with a boyhood that had slipped away unnoticed one fleeting second at a time, as winter gave way to spring and spring became summer. The thought had given him a little piece of happiness to take out and polish during the long, dark hours he was laboriously linking together as the grieving wore on.

Plus, in researching new ideas for a follow-up to his first cryptozoology book, George had found references to interesting legends connected with the northern lakes of Canada; legends concerning gargantuan specimens of known aquatic animals. He had begun compiling materials and found *Le Lac Perdu* mentioned among lakes where such reports, by 18th-century fur trappers, had come from.

As far as George was concerned these stories made for interesting speculation but were probably either traveler's tales or instances of misidentification. Nevertheless his collection of maps, sketches, statements and historical references continued to fatten as the trip approached. He decided he would bring these documents along and sort through them by the lake, make some rough notes, and maybe run a few ideas by his old friends.

Snap

After dinner, they gathered around the bonfire with Tim's portrait. They took turns holding it while pouring out their best liquor for him. Later on, over tumblers of single-malt inside the lodge, they plotted their next day's fishing activities. Hovering over a map, they decided that three of them, Nate, Peter and Bill, would take one of the boats southward and use downriggers to troll for lake trout. George, Danny and Jack would take the other boat across the lake and explore the various bays along its easterly shores. The boats would return to the lodge at sunset. They would compare notes, realign the personnel on each vessel and plan new excursions based on the day's results.

It was time to relax with cigars on the porch. They went out and sat in Adirondack chairs and puffed and sipped and chatted. Looking out over the broad black expanse of the water, they could see the firmament reflected upward in its dark, subtly undulating surface. There was not a cloud in the sky and the stars stood out bravely in the crisp night air, which was chilly even in the middle of June this far to the north. In the silences they could hear waves lapping now and then against the shoreline. Here and there came the enigmatic splash of a big fish jumping in the windless darkness. There was so much life in these waters.

"You know," Peter said, "it's pretty amazing that a place like this has just this one, single camp, don't you think? It's weird."

"*You're* weird," Danny said, and they all laughed.

George rotated his tumbler and savored the merry sound of the ice as it swirled around and around in the glass. He was glad now, to be among his oldest friends here in this place of immaculate solitude. The very darkness, profound as it was, seemed to wrap itself around him like a warming cloak. The conversation of his companions, gathered on either side of him, meandered and flowed along, soothing as a babbling brook in George's weary ears. He closed his eyes and allowed his mind to drift upwards and away into the crisp air of the Canadian night.

It was incredibly peaceful up here, so far to the north of his familiar landscape of worries. Someone made a joke and there was laughter. Then there was a lull in the conversation. The aroma of fine cigar smoke played inside of George's nostrils. He settled groggily into his enfolding chair and experienced a tentative sense of, at long last, peace.

Just then, a roiling sound rose up offshore, and after a half-second's silence, there came a sharp, flat smacking *boom* immediately followed by a roaring splash of amazing proportions, as if an object of immense weight had been dropped onto the water from a great height. The sound of the spray falling back onto the lake's surface lingered for several long seconds. There was more loud splashing and then the sound of bubbles breaking in the water before everything became quiet again.

"Oh my *God*!" someone yelled. "What in the ever-loving *hell* was that?"

Somebody else dropped their glass onto the wooden deck of the porch with a sickly clunk. There came the sound of Adirondack chairs scraping against the floor. The bottom dropped out of George's gut and the space that was left filled up with a heavy, liquid, primordial sense of absolute dread. Something of his dinner welled up from deep within his gut and he swallowed it bitterly back. He wanted to get up but his legs were rubbery.

Panicked voices surrounded him and someone ran inside the lodge, the screen door closing behind with a loud smacking sound. Then the door creaked back open and George saw Bill Isley emerging with something in his hand. Bill scrambled down the porch steps and ran toward the shore. He raised his arm as if to fire a pistol and then a powerful beam of light raked the water, moving unsteadily back and forth. The light found a patch of boiling, greenish froth where the reflected stars had been just a moment before. A choppy wake was coming toward them from out in the middle of the cove.

"My God, I think I saw it - did you see it? The shape?" It was Nate's voice, but an unnaturally high-pitched version of it. "It was . . . huge!"

"Bill, get away from the water!"

"Shut up," Bill snapped.

He held one hand up toward the porch to signal for silence while he played the beam of light over the water with the other. Whatever it was, it was gone now, although a moment later its wake arrived and broke against the shoreline in noisy waves. Then all was quiet once more. Bill came back up from the beach.

"Where's the bottle?" he asked.

"I'm going to bed," someone else said. "This didn't happen."

George got up and went to the railing and tossed the contents of his stomach over the edge, into the night.

It smelled really bad.

Later, George slept fitfully. He was sharing a cabin with Danny, an assignment he had made deliberately, hoping maybe that some camaraderie would develop between them. And yet, perhaps predictably, Danny was not interested.

Danny had never liked George. There was forty years' worth of history between them; what had turned Danny against him had happened in the first few, when they were still boys. But the two of them had so many close friends in common that they were forced to spend time together, rubbing against each other the wrong way, year after year.

When George had asked him which bunk he preferred, Danny, rather than deferring the choice like a good sport, picked the better one, near the window, throwing his duffle bag on it to stake his claim, even. Promptly, Danny pulled out a beautiful new pair of lumberjack boots in brown leather and began odiferously smearing them with mink oil, his face frozen in a satisfied grin as he worked.

"Well, those sure are nice boots you have there, Danny," George had said.

Danny looked up from his swabbing and locked eyes with him. "Envious, George?"

"A little, I guess," said George, forcing a smile.

"Naturally."

Apparently there would be no reconciliation. Instead, Danny would be at the ready for the entire week, waiting for opportunities to tweak George with his passive-aggressive commentary. But George wasn't going to let it ruin the whole trip. It was just Danny being Danny.

Now, on the evening of Day One, having brushed his teeth in an only partially successful attempt to wash away the bile-tinged aftertaste of the turtle soup he'd up-chucked on the porch, George lay down on his little bunk and stared up into the darkness. The adrenaline had subsided and now he was drained. The cryptozoologist in him wanted to hover over the evening's events and ponder down upon them. First the footprint in the muck and then the big splash in the cove. But the person in him was simply too exhausted.

A last thought did wander toward the contents of the leather satchel full of the research materials that he had brought along. It was on the desk. When he had the chance, he would go through it and find those references to *Le Lac Perdu*, and also look for any other reports out of the Nunavut Territory in general. He seemed to recall that there were some.

When sleep did come, George dreamed of Tim. At first, the setting was Tim's bedroom at home. Their senior year they had often spent their school nights together like this. Tim put on some *Blue Oyster Cult* – 'Don't Fear the Reaper'- and they smoked pot. Then the scene shifted and they were on the lodge's front porch. Tim wanted to go for a swim in the starlight. Thinking of the big splash, George was trying to talk him out of it. But Tim was already taking off his clothes. Before George knew it Tim was trotting down the steps and then he was running naked through the night toward the water.

"Tim, no!" George had screamed in the dream.

But Tim was gone.

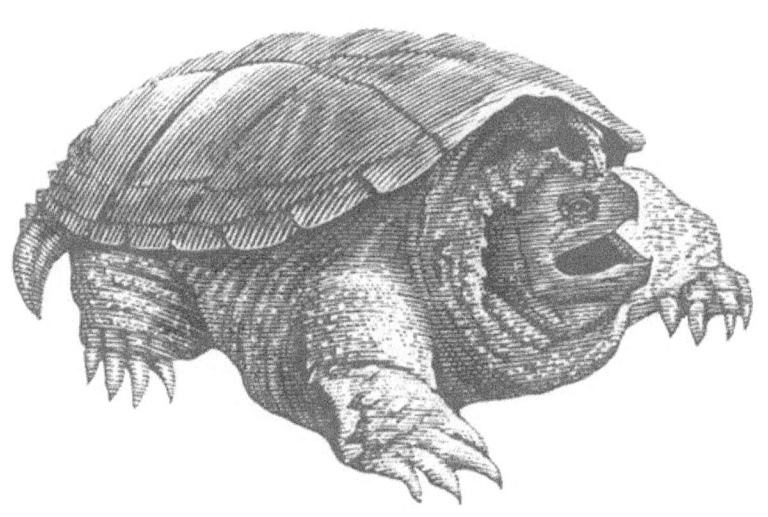

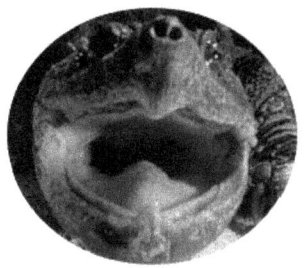

Chapter Three

Day Two began auspiciously enough. After breakfast, Nate, Peter and Bill set off in the smaller boat to do some downrigger trolling in a promising area south of the camp that they had identified the night before. George took Jack and Danny with him in the bigger of the boats, and they headed across the broad lake toward a likely bay on the opposite side. About an hour later, they pulled in between its enfolding spits of low-lying shoreline. Finding it to be tranquil they anchored up and began to fish.

"Cooking that turtle in the shell over the campfire last night was a nice touch," Jack observed as the line from his last cast settled lazily down onto the greenish surface of the water.

George sniffled, then said, "Turning that big mother into soup in the first place was a nice touch. It's good to have a chef in the group. Right, Danny?"

Danny, reclining in the prow with his hands clasped behind his head and a tattered Red Sox cap shading his face, let out an insouciant sigh. "Indeed, George," he said, "it was a good idea of yours to invite me. Showed leadership skills on your part. Team-building. Delegating. Like you do in the department."

Thanks, Danny, thought George.

This was supposed to be a vacation. George didn't need to be reminded of the fact that his professorship at the State University was in some jeopardy following his authorship of an embarrassingly successful book that, to his dismay, was sold in the cryptozoology section rather than with the works of mainstream science. He was, after all, coming up for tenure. Being branded a "cryptozoologist" spelled academic doom. It didn't seem to matter that his was a scholarly analysis of the quality of the evidence which, while respectfully acknowledging a number of deeply interesting questions, was quite far from being speculative.

The whole situation was complicated by the object lesson in bad judgment that was his Quixotic involvement with a nubile co-ed named Laura Harding. She was a student in his freshman aquatic biology class. It was held in a large lecture hall and Laura always sat in the front row.

She had obviously taken a shine to George, as had several other attractive young women in the class, each of whom were making this apparent from various stations around the theater in the form of steamy eye contact combined with the body language of attraction.

In Laura's case, that meant maintaining an equestrian posture, breasts thrust forward, knees and ankles closed together primly, as if she were riding her seat rather than merely sitting on it. She took no notes but rather kept her hands clasped in front of her, fingers knitted together, palms pressed flat upon her writing surface as if it were in danger of floating off into space unless she held it down. She gazed steadily up at him with pretty eyes that were attentive one moment and dreamy the next.

There was nothing about her demeanor to overtly suggest that her receptivity was anything beyond academic in nature, but whenever George's glance did stray her way the sight of her put him in mind of an unfurled flower blossom willingly exposed for pollination. He found, initially to his pronounced discomfort, that if he allowed his gaze to linger upon hers for any length of time, it would set in motion an inconvenient physiological reaction that required him to withdraw behind the blocky speaker's podium while she followed him with what he feared was a look of curiosity, and maybe amusement.

As the semester began, George was still living in his marriage, and, while he had to admit there was a little thrill connected with the thought of these twice-weekly lectures, there was nothing more to it than that. Laura wasn't even the only female student who was exhibiting the pathology. A couple of them, wearing short skirts without panties, gratified themselves by slouching in their seats with their carefully groomed private parts brazenly on display for him. These girls, Amy Somers and Quinn Porter, he found most uninteresting. To him, there was nothing erotic about such promiscuous behavior. While Laura was also partial to short skirts and flimsy footwear, her shapely buttermilk legs were always positioned in a perfectly modest arrangement, and her demure interest in him had a sweet and innocent quality that he found appealing in its way.

As the term wore on, Laura's interest in him only seemed to intensify. George's wife had been out of the house for about two months by this point, which meant there was one less reason not to allow himself to want this pretty young student. He tried unsuccessfully to convince himself that Laura was perhaps not really very far different in her heart of hearts from Amy or Quinn, but, insanely, as the weeks passed, it seemed as if he were beginning to care for her.

"Hey, I think I've got a bite!" Jack sat up and looked eagerly into the water. He jerked his pole upwards and back. The top two feet of the pole was bent downward, straining against the line. "Wait a minute. I think it's just a snag . . . or is it?" The corners of Jack's lips were pursed into a puzzled frown. He tugged some more against his unyielding line. There was no give whatsoever. Like a snag.

Then the line started to move. Jack's eyes were like bright blue flames. George followed their gaze. Sure enough, the thing Jack had hooked was moving toward the mouth of the bay and into the broad lake, taking drag off of his reel with a noisy whine. Jack was now straining to keep his grip on the bending pole, leveraging its cork-covered butt against his belly as the big game line tightened up. He hung on so firmly that the boat was even coming around some under the pull, as if they might be led out of the bay under tow.

"Jack, let out some line," George was saying. "Let out some line before it snaps. Danny, haul up the anchor, would you? I'll start the motor."

"This is one heck of a Lake Trout, or . . ." Jack let his thought trail off.

"It won't be a lake trout," George said as he tried to get the motor to turn over. "Not where you were casting, near those weeds. More like a pickerel or a northern pike. But one of those guys would try to go under a log or something. They wouldn't head for deeper water . . ."

By now, the boat had been brought around a full 180 degrees and was on a course straight out of the bay behind whatever was on the end of Jack's taut and straining line. The thick monofilament was draining from Jack's reel even with the drag set as tight as he dared to keep it. He had about two-hundred-and-eighty feet spooled up but about half of it was now out.

George steered the boat to follow the fish. He kept on having to give more and more throttle to keep up with the demand on Jack's line as the fish moved with incredible speed, and purpose, toward deeper water. They followed it out of the bay and onto the broad lake, Jack using every bit of skill to play out the line, yielding up as little of it as he could without allowing it to snap under the strain. Arms working, he maintained an uneasy balance in the well of the boat as it cut through the heaving swell.

He was obviously excited, but also vaguely disturbed. As were Danny and George, in the silent contemplation of the measure of this thing that was taking so much heavy-duty line so effortlessly. It was only a matter of time before the line ran out, and what then?

"Keep her steady, George," Jack said.

George maintained a little forward pressure on the throttle as he peered through the windshield. Even Danny was now sitting up. In fact he was somewhat aggressively angled out over the prow. Their apprehension was forgotten. The chase was on.

"How are we doing on line, Jack?" Danny shouted hoarsely back against the wind.

"Running out any minute, now. Wait a second . . ."

"What is it?" George asked.

"It's . . . stopped."

George looked over at Jack. His pole was straight and the line was completely slack. George cut the throttle and the engine settled into a throaty burble as they became inert in the water, rising and falling on the gentle swell. Jack reeled in a few clicks, paused, and then reeled in a few clicks more. The engine continued to idle boisterously. The sound of Jack's reel turning click by click was like the sound of a clock ticking. Water lapped and splashed choppily against the hull of the boat.

Then, suddenly, the line gave a rough jerk downward, reversed direction and started pulling hard and fast astern of them. Jack turned his body to follow his rod as it spun 180 degrees around. Reflexively, George threw the engine into reverse to follow the line, and as he did so he became aware of two things at once: The line had gone slack again, and Danny had been pitched from his perch on the prow and thrown headlong into the water.

Danny was certainly in sight, bobbing in the waves off of the bow, but he was being drawn quite briskly away from the boat in some sort of cross-current. And when George had cut the engine after realizing Danny had fallen overboard, it had stalled. Now George was cranking the starter, but it wouldn't turn over. He was looking into Danny's eyes, which were wide and almost pleading. The distance between them was steadily opening up. George glanced over at Jack. The line was still slack. Tentatively, Jack started reeling some in. George looked back over at Danny.

"Danny," he said, "start swimming."

But Danny, in his boots, was struggling just to keep his head above the wind-driven chop. He wasn't making any progress in the current, hardly even slowing his rate of separation from the boat. Seeing this, Jack put down his pole and picked up a paddle. George kept trying to get the engine to turn over.

Then it happened. At first George doubted his eyes. But a harder look confirmed that there was something big moving under the surface, a brackish-green shadow speeding through the water off their starboard gunwale, maybe six or eight feet down. It moved with astonishing speed, like a torpedo. And its sheer size was beyond comprehension. It was of oceanic proportions, comparable in size to the boat itself.

George and Jack traded glances.

"What was *that*?" Jack asked. "A submarine?"

"I don't know," George said, giving the starter a last desperate crank, "and I don't intend to find out."

As if on cue, the engine rumbled to life.

George engaged the propeller and gave throttle.

"Hold that paddle over the port side for Danny to grab onto!"

George turned the wheel and gunned it, making for Danny's bobbing form. He scanned the water for a sign of whatever it was that was stalking the gloomy depths beneath them. Danny was heaving just off the port bow now. George throttled back into neutral and then put the engine in reverse to slow the boat. Jack leaned over the side and extended the paddle.

"Danny," he yelled, "Grab on!"

Danny, beginning to grow weak in the chilly water, could barely grip it, but he did, with what looked like the last little bit of strength he had left. George put the engine in neutral and rushed forward to help Jack. Together they drew the paddle in, bringing Danny alongside. George reached down and grabbed Danny by the belt, and Jack did the same. They hauled him up.

Just then the water began to boil and swell underneath them. The boat listed away from this upwelling wave and then, at the very instant that Danny's feet cleared the rail, the surface broke, revealing a cavernous black opening that before their disbelieving eyes became a gaping mouth framed within a primordial set of sharply beaked jaws. Incredibly, this gargantuan maw continued rising straight up out of the water where Danny had been floating. It was followed by a broad, mottled green collar of leathery skin, a pair of even wider armored shoulders and finally a glistening brownish breastplate that expanded symmetrically into a roughly oval shape. Water cascaded down upon them as the hulking shape reared overhead until it was literally towering beside them, blotting out their view of the lake.

When the monster reached the apex of its trajectory it seemed for one horrifying instant that it would come crashing straight down upon the boat, crushing them and swamping their vessel. Instead it began gradually arcing backwards away from them. Slowly tumbling, it landed on its back, crashing into the water with a resounding shockwave of sound that slammed into their bodies with visceral force, concussing their eardrums and rattling the fillings in their teeth.

The creature's huge flat underbelly, a mosaic of yellowish plates of shell the size of paving stones, slowly submerged beneath the water and then the boat rose mightily up on the emanating swell, sending George and Jack tumbling onto the deck with Danny, who lay there shivering and spent.

Struggling in vain for mental clarity, George clawed his way instinctively toward the helm. He reached for the throttle lever but pushed on it clumsily. This caused the boat to lurch ahead in the water with a throaty roar. George went reeling sternward, lost his balance again and fell hard, hitting his head against the transom.

The boat flew forward, its hull slamming against the waves. George pushed himself up onto his hands and knees and started crawling uphill on the planing deck in an effort to regain the helm. But the vessel, bounding rudderless at cruising speed over the rough waters, was see-sawing wildly. It was all he could do to reach for and then cling to the tubular metal stanchion that supported the pilot's seat just aft of the center console. By degrees, George pulled himself up just enough to grasp the throttle, which he pulled back sufficiently to bring the boat under rough control. Only then was he able to regain his footing. He got behind the wheel, wind and spray blasting him in the face. Jack and Danny were still flopping around on the foredeck. Finally back in control of the boat, George turned around to look toward the receding patch of water where the creature had attacked. It could easily have snatched Danny bodily within its jaws, severing him at the torso. But there was no sign of it now. He checked the fish finder. Nothing. George brought the boat down to idle speed. Jack was back on his feet now. Danny, soaked and chilled in his drenched clothing, was curled up on the deck, arms folded against his chest. He looked like a discarded puppet.

"Danny, go get inside the head and take off those wet clothes," George told him. "There's a blanket down there. Try to warm up."

Danny gave him a sick look but complied.

Jack found his pole. The line was slack. He reeled it in. At the end of the line was a heavy-gauge steel leader. It had been cleanly severed, as if by a bolt cutter. Jack held the end of the leader between a thumb and forefinger and stared at it. "I guess I'm done for the day," he muttered. George looked around briefly, got his bearings, and turned the boat toward the camp, on the lake's far shore.

The horizon seemed like a mirage, a destination that retreated even as they moved, an elusive, unreachable coast against which they made only minimally incremental, barely discernable progress. The wind and the current had been with them on the trip out, but on the way back in they were working against both. It was maybe two hours later when they finally entered the enfolding shoulders of the pine-grown cove that sheltered their little cluster of cabins from the weather of the broad lake. From over by the lodge, a hearty campfire was throwing sparks up into the evening sky as they put-putted across the placid cove and up to the dock. And as they did so, a question cropped up in George's mind. What, he wondered, would he tell the others?

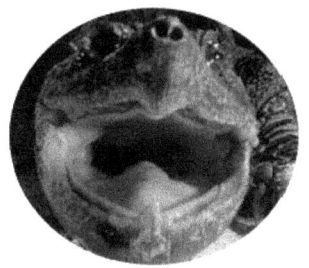

Chapter Four

Le Lac Perdu. The "Lost Lake". Discovered in 1679 by an expedition of French fur traders, The Lost Lake marked the farthest reaches of their northwesterly explorations. A huge ecosystem supremely rich in biological resources is what they reported finding. Their descriptions portrayed a bountiful fishery that supported numerous species of aquatic mammals coveted for their luxurious pelts, along with the herds of elk, deer and moose needed to supply their intrepid sorties.

A reliable supply of fresh meat not only ensured the sustainability of their daily exertions in this frigid and inhospitable environment, but also supported their commercial operations. For every pelt there had to be a trap and for every cleverly laid trap there was bait, bait which not only needed to be acquired but also to be freshened regularly until it was raided by one of the desired species of fur bearer. These in turn needed to be harvested before being scavenged by any of the many opportunistic carnivores that ranged the lake's winding ribbons of boulder-strewn shoreline.

Forty two miles long and seven miles across at its widest point, *Le Lac Perdu* was situated just south of the sub-Artic tree line. It lay cradled in a steep V-shaped trough of granite that had been gouged out 15,000 years earlier when the North American Laurentide ice sheet receded back toward the Arctic Circle during the waning of the Wisconsin Glacial Episode. The lake itself was formed as the result of melt water pooling at the rim of the retreating ice in the wake of this glacial scour. Steep, rugged mountains rose up on either side, their ridgelines making a jagged 360-degree silhouette in the skies above and around the lake's surface. This meant that the lake bottom dropped off at a correspondingly steep angle, so that the water might be 40 or 50 feet deep within just a few yards of the shore. Farther out, depths would reach several hundreds of feet and in some places, the lake was literally unplumbed.

There were only a handful of islands, most of them jagged up-jutting promontories of rock with a few scrubby pines that were given over to colonies of waterfowl, who used them as nesting grounds. Only a couple of these islands were accessible for any practical purpose worth the risk of bringing a boat ashore among the submerged rocks that surrounded them. The largest of these was Black Island, a kidney-shaped patch of forested acreage that was roughly a mile long and half again as wide. Black Island's inside shoreline was sandy in spots, graveled in others, but relatively level. Toward the island's center, the land rose steadily up to an exposed promontory edged by a crescent-shaped line of rocky cliffs towering over the water in sheer walls along its outer circumference. The other major island was somewhat smaller and a good deal lower in elevation.

Lost Lake was sustained by several tributaries. From the north, a river delivered an influx of fresh water, while numerous smaller streams and rocky brooks flowed down from the surrounding mountains. In addition there were springs from which welled a supply of cold water borne of aquifers deep under the ground, churning up silt from the bottom and giving the lake its characteristic dark color. At the lake's southern end, it grew shallower, until the broad waters gave way to marshes and swamplands where another series of streams and brooks discharged its outflow. Along the miles of undulating shoreline in between there were several large bays and numerous small coves, a few of which were situated along less steeply angled terrain.

It was in one of these inlets that their rustic little outpost was located. The sole manmade structures on the entire lake, they were accessible only by float plane. As George guided the boat into the cove, he could see and then smell smoke wafting across the water from a lively orange campfire, which popped and crackled and threw zig-zagging sparks up in the air. The others were already back, cleaning the fish they had caught and getting the camp set up for dark.

When they neared the dock Nate Peterman trotted out to catch them. Jack tossed him a line and George cut the engine.

Nate's face grew concerned.

"Where's Danny?"

"He's in the head," replied George.

Jack opened the door to reveal Danny, sitting, wrapped up inside the blanket, on the closed lid of the toilet. He reached in and helped Danny up onto the deck. Danny in his blanket and bare feet looked like the bedraggled survivor of some shipping disaster as he emerged from the little compartment recessed underneath the boat's center console.

"What happened?" Nate wanted to know.

"He fell overboard," George told him. "He needs to get warm."

By now Bill and Peter had realized something was amiss. They stopped cleaning fish and came down to the dock to help out. Together, they got Danny out of the boat and aided him in making his way up the path and into the lodge.

Nate waited for them to get inside then turned to George and Jack and asked for an explanation. The two of them exchanged looks. "First, some drinks," George finally said.

Nate bit his tongue. "Sure," he replied. "Coming right up."

Standing by the fire with their tumblers in hand, George and Jack looked tired and defeated. Firelight and shadow played across their drawn features as the lid of nightfall closed down on their little clearing at the water's edge. Eventually Danny emerged from the main cabin, fully clothed now but still wrapped in his blanket, clutching a fifth of whiskey in his hand. Peter and Bill returned to the fish-cleaning table and quietly resumed work on dinner. They spoke softly between themselves while the others stood silently around the fire, staring into the flames, each lost in his own private thoughts. Finally Nate came over to George and asked, "Can I talk to you for a minute?"

With a little nod of his head Nate invited Jack to come with them. Together the three of them walked casually down the path and out onto the dock. They stood around in a small circle, staring at their feet. Danny remained by the fire, alone and seemingly oblivious, taking the occasional pull from his whiskey bottle. The silence was broken only by the occasional splash as fish rose here and there around the dock to feed.

"So are you guys going to tell me what the hell happened out there today, or what?" Nate asked.

"Danny . . . fell out of the boat," George said.

"We saw a monster," Jack blurted out. "A monster. It was awful."

"Okay," Nate said, eyeing George expectantly, "I'm listening."

George told Nate the story of what had happened to them that afternoon on the lake. He related the details matter-of-factly, without embellishment or emotion, as if he had been a detached observer rather than someone who had directly experienced the event and lived through the terror it had inspired. He didn't mention the footprint.

Nate silently took it all in, occasionally raising an eyebrow or cocking his head, but accepting George's report as he related it. When George was through, Nate spent a quiet minute staring off into the darkness.

"Alright," he finally said. "And you, Jack, what did you see?"

"I don't know, Nate," Jack replied, "but whatever it was, it was huge, every bit as big as the boat. It must've come 10 feet out of the water. It was going after Danny. It was greenish . . . and brown."

Nate locked eyes with Jack, then George.

"What you're describing is a giant . . . turtle."

Neither of them contradicted this statement.

"Is that what you're telling me, you saw a snapping turtle as big as a . . . Volkswagen?"

"I'm not prepared to say that," George replied.

"You just did," Nate said.

George couldn't disagree. Large, predatory turtles were, indeed, known to science. The alligator snapping turtle, an ugly and fiercely armored reptile with big claws and large, sharply beaked jaws capable of snapping a man's forearm, were known to exceed 200 pounds with shells several feet across. A decomposing carcass had been found in the southern bayous back in the 1970s. At first it was mistaken for a dead boar, it was so big. George recalled having seen a grainy black-and-white photograph of the animal in a textbook way back in his graduate school days.

But the thing he had seen rearing up beside the boat, intent on taking a full-grown man from the water, was of a different scale altogether. It was simply incredible. And yet he had seen it with his own eyes. It had indeed been a giant snapper.

What conceivable evolutionary mechanism could have accounted for this creature's existence, he wondered. It could have been a mutation. Or an undiscovered species in its own right. Or an evolutionary throwback, a surviving example of some gigantic prehistoric creature that was a scaled-up version of a known present-day species. Like the giant beaver, an 800-pound animal known to have actually existed in North America but only from the fossil record.

This turtle, however, would somehow have evaded extinction and continued to live and breed in isolation here in this huge, unfathomable, remote body of water that was hardly ever visited by humans. This was far-fetched but not theoretically impossible. Generations of scientists once believed the coelacanth had been extinct for 65 million years until a living specimen was hauled up by fishermen off the coast of South Africa in 1938. The megamouth shark, a plankton-feeder that grows to be up to 18 feet long, was only discovered in the Pacific Ocean in 1976.

Tonight, George would open up his briefcase and delve into the papers and books he had brought along in connection with his ongoing cryptozoological research project. But first he wanted another drink and something warm to eat.

The three of them headed back to the fire, where the day's catch was now poaching over the coals along with baked potatoes wrapped in foil and a big cast-iron frying pan full of asparagus drizzled in olive oil. Peter pulled together a round of Martinis and everybody but Danny, who continued to nurse on his whiskey bottle, drank at least one. George had three.

Danny didn't want his dinner and Jack only picked at his food but George ate ravenously. Bill and Peter were still unaware of the whole story behind the day's events. At Nate's suggestion they waited until Danny had staggered off to a distant corner of the lodge before filling them in. Both of them were frankly skeptical.

Peter eventually waved them off, wanting no more to do with the conversation. He withdrew into a corner of the lodge with a book. For his part, Bill said he needed physical proof, or to see the animal with his own eyes.

"What about that turtle we killed," George asked?

"And where's your dog, Bill?" Nate wondered aloud.

It was a good point. Scout, Bill's chocolate lab, had gone missing.

Peter, looking up from his book, suggested he was roaming around in the woods, chasing deer perhaps, or even running with the wolves that could be heard howling in the distance now and again. He argued that any number of other possible fates could have befallen the dog. Drowning, maybe. Or he could have been killed by a more conventional predator, like a bear or a fisher cat or even a big northern pike for that matter. Then he stuck his nose back in his book. Bill furrowed his brow and gathered his mouth into a tight little frown.

Nate was adamant that given the fact of George and Jack's report, plus the big splash in the cove the night before, these rationalizations were even more speculative than the notion that Scout had been taken by the big snapper while running around on the shore or swimming in the cove.

Despite a nagging concern over the welfare of his dog, Bill remained unconvinced about the turtle, and decided to call it a night, pointedly remarking that things would probably seem different tomorrow in the light of day when they were all sober again.

"Well," George said, "you may be right and I hope you are but as of now I have no intention of going back out onto that lake. I'm done fishing."

"We have three more days left," Nate said. "What the hell else are we supposed to do around here for three whole days? I intend to get my money's worth. You know, George, this whole trip was your idea."

"Exactly," Bill agreed. "I really can't believe you're going to bail on the rest of us."

"It's not my fault," George said. "I had no idea this would happen."

"Nothing has happened," Nate said, a note of exasperation in his voice. "You saw something big in the water. That's why we're here, to catch big fish. The bigger the better. Bring 'em on.

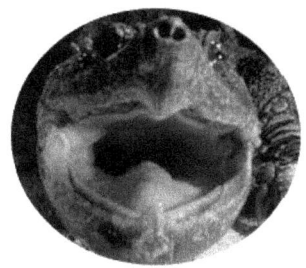

Chapter Five

The defining moment in George's relationship with Laura occurred after class one day, when he was packing up his materials. He looked up from his satchel and saw that she was standing right in front of him, quietly waiting for him to notice her presence. She wore flip-flops, a short but not immodest denim skirt and a white tee shirt that was certainly not tight, but was nevertheless quite form-fitting. Such good posture she had. It struck George that there was nothing Laura could possibly wear that would be unflattering, and the only sight capable of diverting attention from her slender and beautifully toned figure was that of her striking face.

Having only seen her from the stage, he was taken aback by the sight of her features close up. Her lips were delicately drawn upon a pair of crisply dimpled cheeks. Her chin was squarish but exquisitely feminine. She had an aqualine nose that had once been broken, which slightly diminished her beauty but vastly enhanced her charm. She was heavily freckled, but her complexion was flawless, as if her skin were made of parchment. But most striking were her blue eyes, which sparkled to an almost dazzling effect, as if she were full of stars. He found himself, momentarily, at a loss for words.

"Professor Mapolis," she began, rescuing him from the awkwardness of the moment, "I'm Laura. Harding. Laura Harding. I'm sorry. I'm nervous." Her voice had a slightly raspy tone, which gave it a sultry quality that contrasted provocatively with the freshness of her overall physical appearance.

"Hello Laura."

"I've read all of your books, both the textbooks and the cryptozoology ones, and I really love them." That voice. It was captivating.

"Well thank you."

"And your lectures. They're brilliant."

"That," George replied, "is a very lovely compliment."

"But what I really want to talk to you about is this." Laura held out a five-by-eight-inch index card with a tack hole in the middle of it. On it, he recognized his own blocky handwriting. It was his posting for a graduate research assistant, which he had placed on a bulletin board in the biology department the day before.

"I'd like to apply for the position."

"Your enthusiasm is encouraging, Laura Harding," George said. He smiled. "But I have to tell you, the position is only open to graduate students."

"Without exception?"

"Well, generally, yes."

"So there are exceptions, then."

She was persistent. And self-possessed beyond her years. He liked it. Which meant he had to put an immediate stop to the madness. His professionalism, maybe even his integrity, was at stake. Ironically, he couldn't let her have the job, for her own sake.

"It depends on the nature of the project."

"May I ask, what is the nature of this project, Professor."

"That's the problem. I'm not sure that even describing it to you is in your best interests right now, academically speaking." He realized she was having none of it. "I mean, there are certain levels of study that ought to be completed before you become exposed to certain . . . theories and perspectives."

"Well, I'm sure certain individuals are insufficiently versed in the fundamental principles of scientific inquiry to responsibly venture into the cryptic realm of these theories and perspectives, but certain others might have the psychological, emotional and intellectual wherewithal to withstand the challenges they pose to our conception of the known, and the unknown, universe."

"Very good. Actually, that sounds vaguely familiar."

"It should. You kind of wrote most of it. *The Myth of the Beast.* Providence House, 2003. Page 231. About two-thirds of the way down."

George looked at her sideways.

"Photographic memory?"

"Photographic memory," she replied. "I retain everything I read."

"I bet it feels more like a curse than a blessing sometimes."

"True. And it's kind of cool that you get that. But the point is, that's a useful characteristic to have in a research assistant. For your new cryptozoology book."

George glanced around the room. He lowered his voice a little. "Who said anything about a cryptozoology book?"

"You went about not saying it very thoroughly."

"What are you, nineteen going on forty-two?"

"No. I'm twenty-two. I was in the Peace Corps before coming here. Why do you ask, are you an ageist?"

"Are you applying for a job?"

"Not with an ageist."

"I'm not an ageist. I'm sorry."

"Are you a classist?"

"I hope not."

"Then you ought to consider my application, despite my membership in the freshman class. Look, let's at least discuss this over a cup of coffee."

"I can't. I have my symposium in forty-five minutes." All of a sudden she looked like she wanted to cry. He softened. She had read all of his books, after all, even the cryptozoology ones. "I'll tell you what, why don't you come along with me. We'll see how you handle . . . certain concepts." She recovered her demeanor and gave him a smile that seemed ample reward indeed for such a small kindness.

The symposium, an informal monthly gathering of graduate students and a few senior underclassmen, went on at the *Village Pub & Brewery*, a cellar bar with mahogany wainscoting and stone floors where it was always dark, no matter the time of day. It was a place where both the locals and the University population mingled in relative comfort, and its layout allowed for the group to take over a small parlor separated from the main taproom by a post-and-beam threshold.

The group was created to give interested students a forum for the exploration of topics in science that were not covered by the University curriculum, which is to say topics that were ignored, impolitic or downright forbidden. Naturally, cryptozoology was chief among them, and George, by virtue of his popular writings and his relative accessibility, was their luminary. The ready availability of good beer bore no inconsiderable influence on the proceedings.

People were beginning to assemble around a large square table in the middle of the room when George walked in with Laura. One of the grad students, Marsha Mullins, turned her head so sharply at the sight of them that George thought for an instant that she had been slapped. Marsha's face registered a trace of annoyance and then broke into a big happy smile.

"Hi Professor Mapolis," she said, coming straight over to them. "I was just taking drink orders."

"I'll have a Sammy." George turned to Laura. She nodded. "Make it two."

"They're going to want to see your I.D.," Marsha told Laura.

"She's fine," George said. "She's with me." He introduced them. Marsha, a doctoral candidate who wore her graying hair pulled back in a tight pony tail, simply squinted at him. "Okay," she finally said, and went off to the bar.

George and Laura sat down and the group began to assemble at the table around them. Marsha handed George two beers and took a seat on the opposite corner next to her friend, Beth, who was in the master's program. The two of them began whispering to each other.

"We left off with a discussion of the methodology used to document Sasquatch footprints, and the analytical approaches being applied to the data," George began. "Kyle was telling us about the skeptic's position on the validity of the casts and photographs."

"Thank you, Professor." Kyle was a senior biology major in the undergraduate program who tended to think in rigid, literal terms. He was a brilliant taxonomy student and a promising candidate for graduate work, but the very traits of mind that enabled him to perform meticulous technical functions seemed to inhibit his ability to exercise any scientific discretion in his broader thinking. So deep was his reliance on accepted methodology, and the accompanying fear of any idea that might render some of his learning obsolete, that scientific dogma had become for him a citadel to be defended from intellectual infidels rather than a collective work of art in progress.

"I was saying," Kyle continued, "that there hasn't been enough rigorous analysis of the purported field data for us to draw any meaningful scientific conclusions as to the validity of Sasquatch. It's a known fact that there are hoaxers out there walking around in big wooden feet. If Sasquatch were out there, people would be reporting it. Sasquatch is a legend."

George nodded sagely. He might disagree with Kyle, might even find his viewpoint to be crabbed and condescending, but if countervailing ideas couldn't be freely expressed, and respected, here in this forum, how could he complain about the close-mindedness of the University establishment? He was about to solicit comments from the group when Marsha spoke up.

"Laura," she said, why don't you tell us what you think?"

The room became silent. Taking their cue from Marsha, everybody swiveled their heads in Laura's direction. Beth actually giggled a little. It was unusual for one student to call another out. Laura was a stranger to the group. She was young, obviously no graduate student, nor even an upper-level underclassman. There was a palpable air of expectation, and George was just deciding that he ought to intervene when Laura spoke up for herself.

"First, it's a known fact that people *are* reporting seeing Sasquatch," she began. "Second, we can't cite the lack of rigorous analysis of the field data as a reason not to go ahead and actually perform rigorous analysis of the field data. Working scientists ought to do what scientists do, develop a hypothesis and test it, but they're afraid of seeming frivolous. And some of the work *has* been done. For example, when plotted on a graph based on size, the thousands of casted or photographed prints form a perfect bell curve, identical to a natural distribution. Third, the casts display pressure ridges consistent with a flexible foot supporting a great weight, along with anatomical features such as dermal ridges. They are all individual, and none resembles any of the fake wooden footprints proffered by people who want to be publicly accepted as 'hoaxers'. There is a basis for formal inquiry into the question by the academy."

Nobody said anything.

"Kyle," George finally interjected. "Any thoughts?"

Kyle sat there, staring into his half-empty glass of beer, lips pursed a little, and shook his head no. Out of the corner of his eye George caught Beth sliding a note over to an annoyed-looking Marsha. Rob Sterling, a doctoral student, was still looking across the table at Laura with a wry smile on his face and a twinkle in his eye. Everybody shifted around a little in their seats. "Okay," George went on, "let's have Wendy's report on the Loch Ness Monster."

It was around seven o'clock when the symposium finally broke up. A few students lingered over their drinks, casually chatting with George. By about seven-thirty the last of them had straggled off. George invited Laura over to the bar. They took a pair of seats in the corner and ordered a couple of whiskies.

"I have to tell you, I'm impressed, Laura Harding," he said, raising his glass. "You're good."

She clinked her glass against his and they each took small sips. An hour and another round of drinks later, George knew a lot more about his promising young student. Her parents were physicians. She loved to sail. She lived off campus, in a house she co-owned with her boyfriend, a singer-songwriter in his thirties with a day job as a coffee-house barista, three kids and an intrusive co-parenting ex-wife. She also learned a lot more about him: How a chance encounter on a hiking trail with a hairy, man-like creature had led him to become fascinated with the subject of unknown animals and related paranormal phenomena; how he had amassed the tremendous body of research that informed his books; how he had actually written them; and his private thoughts about the topics they covered.

He formally offered her the research assistant's position and she formally accepted. They talked long into the night and before either of them knew it, last call was being announced. George looked around. They were practically the only people left in the bar. Her place was just around the corner. "Come on," he said, rising to help her from her seat, "I'll walk you home."

After seeing Laura home, George wound his way back through the darkened streets of Barrington toward his own house on the other side of the University. Under a brooding midnight sky he followed the now-deserted pathways that vivisected the campus greens, flanked on their various sides by imposing stone buildings in the Georgian style. These august architectural symbols of authority and tradition still inspired in George a sense of awe.

He thought about the first time he had walked this route as a bona fide faculty member, and how he'd been similarly humbled at the sight of these same buildings. He had been so innocent then, genuinely eager to pass along his enthusiasm for learning to coming generations of students and grateful for the opportunity to pursue his own research under the aegis of this venerable institution. Now he was on the verge of a forbidden involvement with one of his students, a rank betrayal of the values he had once been so deeply honored to serve. It would be unethical and he resolved to make sure the relationship never strayed beyond the proper bounds of teacher and student.

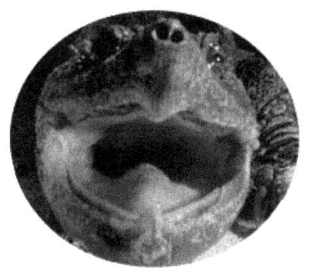

Chapter Six

George had in fact known of the Nunavut Territory's reputation as a hot spot for reported sightings and encounters with monstrous animals, which was an ulterior motive behind his decision to select this particular province as their destination. While he never actually expected to see such a creature he had thought there was an off chance that he would come across some useful and interesting information from a researcher's standpoint. Certainly a field visit to the area would have provided him with descriptive material for a colorful chapter about the geography, natural history and biology surrounding the strange reports emanating from this remote part of the world.

Although he'd had no reason to believe that he was putting everyone else in danger when he organized the trip, after the attack on Danny, he decided it might be best not to make too much of his prior knowledge of the lake's history. Or to even mention it at all. The same, obviously, went for the images contained in his digital camera. No, the main concern was getting everyone out of this place safely.

Unfortunately the float plane was not due to arrive for three more days, and there was no way to contact the guide outpost, since there was no radio in the camp. Remoteness, along with atmospheric conditions in the region, made one next to useless. Cell phones were also out of the question. There wasn't even any air traffic overhead.

George had been warned about all of this before they booked their reservation. He had meant to mention this to the rest of them ahead of time but it had slipped his mind, with so many other details that he had to attend to in order to make the trip happen. This too was something George decided he would keep to himself for the time being.

All of this made George a little uncomfortable. He took inventory of his numerous little deceptions. Suddenly it seemed like he had so many guilty secrets to keep from this group of his closest friends. But there was really nothing he could do about it, he told himself. They simply couldn't know the whole truth. Bill had already lost his dog, and Danny had been subjected to a terrible physical and emotional ordeal. It would be natural for them to look around for someone to blame and George would be that someone, he was certain of it.

But they were six men living together in a confined space under circumstances where their survival could be at stake. They would need to be able to trust and rely upon each other implicitly over the next several days. George was convinced they were in danger, grave danger perhaps. And it was possible their situation might get even worse. At that point their anger might turn into rage and maybe even violence. Besides, he rationalized, some sort of lame confession would serve no purpose except perhaps to soothe his own conscience, which, when he thought about it, actually seemed selfish rather than altruistic. Only a part of him accepted this as a legitimate moral choice, though. Even if the group's collective welfare was best served by George's silence, he couldn't help but notice that it coincidentally served his own interests quite nicely as well.

How, George wondered, had he gotten himself into this position? In small increments, he realized. An omission here, another one there and before he knew it he had concealed some important pieces of information that when taken together constituted a rather significant deception.

George felt queasy in his gut and suspected he looked a little pale. He wondered if anyone would notice. If they did he would just chalk it up to the attack. That would sound plausible. And then he realized that he was preparing another lie. As if it were second nature to him. George was in too deep. He needed to learn the truth about the Nunavut Territory and *Le Lac Perdu* without revealing that he was aware of any reason to make such an inquiry, let alone that he had deliberately brought along the materials necessary to write a book on the subject.

They made drinks and settled into a poker game. Bill dealt a hand of seven card stud. George had a pair of aces in the hole with a three of diamonds showing. Peter opened for a buck and Bill raised him, with George seeing the bet. It went around and George got a king. Now he had two aces down and king-three up.

"So do you believe in Bigfoot?" Bill asked.

"I think that we have some evidence for its existence, yes," George replied. Nate had a nine and ten of spades showing. He couldn't possibly have the straight flush, though. Right?

"Witness sightings, footprints, castings showing dermal ridges," George continued. "These things are hard to ignore. But at the same time, they don't constitute anything like the level of proof science requires. And rightly so. We need a body. But I'm open-minded about the possibility that there's an unknown primate living in North America."

When the bet came around again, Nate raised and George began to think about folding. Until he got his next up card, which was another ace. He looked around the table. Bill, despite his early raise, had folded but Peter, who had opened, was hanging tough with a jack-nine-seven showing. Maybe he had a pair in the hole. Regardless, the question now was whether he had three of a kind, or was going for the straight.

George played it cool. Large, hairy, manlike creatures, he said, were being seen all over the country, not just in Washington or Oregon but also in places like Pennsylvania, Ohio, Florida - and even New England. When Nate picked up the eight of spades, suiting up with the nine and ten, George pushed the conversation forward to disguise his disappointment.

"They look into the windows of houses, throw rocks at people who invade their territory, all sorts of things like that," George said. "They make terrifying noises in the night, they use big branches to beat on the trees, and they come into camps when people are asleep, and look around."

Then George got a second three, giving him the full house. Nate had picked up the ten of spades and George's intuition told him he either had four cards to a straight flush or three of something, most likely tens. Since Nate had the higher pair, he bet and George decided to let the poor bastard go through another round thinking he had the boss hand with his three tens. George would wait until the next round to raise, when Nate, heavily invested in the pot and willing to throw in good money after bad, would overplay his hand and donate to George's pile of chips.

"But don't they also disappear?" Bill asked. "Into thin air, I mean. I read that somewhere."

"Well, I'm of what we call the 'flesh-and-blood' school, which means I think that if they exist, they exist as living, breathing animals," George explained. "In other words, primates, or perhaps even feral humans. But some people do believe they're paranormal."
"Meaning what?" Peter asked.

"Meaning, like Bill said, that they might be inter-dimensional, I guess, for lack of a better word. Beings that appear *in* our world but are not *of* our world. Or psychic manifestations of some sort. The Tibetans, for instance, believe that certain thoughts can take on a physical form. Others theorize that they're entities or apparitions that assume animal or quasi-animal form, but result from complex psychosocial factors, rather than a paranormal explanation, and can be explained in scientific terms."

Legends of a hairy man were handed down in literally every Native American tribe in the United States, who spoke of interactions with groups of Sasquatch, including the exchange of goods. However there were also tales of abductions. Indian women would be taken as mates by male Sasquatch, and Indian men would be taken by the females, according to lore. Often, the purpose of these abductions would be for cannibalism. Stories abounded of Bigfoot snatching people up, smearing pine tar into their eyes and carrying them around in rugged woven baskets slung over their shoulders. Children would often go missing under suspicious circumstances.

These transgressions resulted in a declaration of war by the Indians, who according to one story trapped a family of offenders in a cave. They gave the Sasquatch a last chance to show their changed intentions but they failed the test and so the Indians set a fire in the cave, killing them all. The cave's walls are blackened, reportedly from the smoke, to this day.

"There are also reports of Bigfoot being seen in association with UFOs. Appearing in columns of light and then disappearing in the same way. So it's a complicated phenomenon."

When Nate got his down card and made a big bet with his pair of tens showing, George figured he had him. Nate had a full house. George's full house, aces over threes, would beat Nate's boat of tens and whatever else, but Nate would follow him on a merry chase before it was all over.

George raised the limit, and then, surprisingly, Peter came in over the top. Neither Nate nor George had been paying attention to Peter's hand and it turned out he had picked up another jack somewhere along the way, plus he had three cards to a straight showing.

"I thought Bigfoot was a hoax by some guys with wooden feet strapped to their boots," said Danny, who sat off by himself, wrapped in a blanket.

"Well, people do hoax some of these things, it's true," George said. "But why should the existence of a hoax invalidate the possibility of the real thing?"

"What about Champ?" Bill asked.

"Oh, well, that's another complicated phenomenon," George said. "The Lake Champlain Monster also goes all the way back to Native American legend. There's even a description of a sighting in the journal of Samuel de Champlain himself."

In more recent times, the monster, described as a large sea serpent, had been seen by numerous eyewitnesses, including a ferry boat full of people who all gave their story to the waiting media when they reached the dock. George had personally interviewed witnesses to five other sightings.

"Something is in that lake, I'm convinced of it," he said. "These people were completely reliable. But again, until we have tangible proof, it's another mystery for us to wonder about."

Everybody had by now folded except for George, Nate and Peter. They bet and Nate was called.

"I've got 'em," he said, turning over a pair of tens for the full house.

"So have I," George retorted, flipping over his pair of aces to reveal his bigger boat. George reached out toward the large pile of chips in the center of the table. "Watch and learn boys," he said. "Oh - and show us your cute little straight, why don't you, Peter, just for our amusement."

Unfortunately, Peter had four jacks, and the entire table erupted into uproarious laughter at George's expense.

"Peter, you sandbagging son of a bitch!" he said.

"So George," Jack wanted to know, as Peter raked in the pot, "what made you decide to write a book about all of this stuff?"

"Because it's grossly under-represented in the literature," George said. "In fact, it's been almost ignored. It's forbidden territory. I couldn't resist."

Peter held up his glass. "To forbidden territory," he said, and they all joined in the toast.

"Well, I hope it works out for you, George," Danny said. "You're up for tenure what, this year? Next year?"

"Next year," George said.

"Are you worried?" asked Danny as he came back into the room.

"No, Danny, I'm on vacation," George said with a smile, raising his glass. "And I'm trying to have fun."

Danny, conceding the point, held his glass toward George's and they drank up. They all sat there around the poker table, no one quite knowing how to fill this awkward little break in the conversation. Nate stepped in.

"To our lovely wives," he said, "and our beautiful children."

"Here, here!" said Jack.

When the poker game was over, people started turning in for the night. After the last of them finally straggled off to bed, George snuck back to his cabin. Being careful not to wake Danny, he retrieved his briefcase of materials and quietly slipped back out the door.

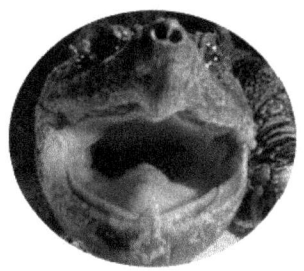

Chapter Seven

It was actually a cheery yellow light that glowed through the windows of the lodge and George was grateful that he could find his way back along the path from the cabin without the need of a flashlight. Once inside, he threw a few more logs on the fire and doused all but one of the oil lamps, which he brought over to an old, gravy-colored wooden desk where there was an antique swivel chair. The fireplace was on one side of the room and the desk was on the other. The space in between receded into shadow.

He sat down, opened his briefcase and began to go through its contents. He had amassed quite a stack of documents, mostly in the form of photocopies, gathered over the course of the past several months from a number of libraries, academic collections, museums, government repositories, and other similar sources. His research spanned three and a half centuries and encompassed the vast and desolate reaches of the northwestern Canadian wilderness. He had journals written by the region's original explorers, their maps and sketches, old manuscripts containing first-hand accounts from members of later expeditions, reports taken by rangers in the field, information collected by the provincial governments, old newspaper stories, oral histories of the region's native tribes, and so forth. He seemed to recall that somewhere in this pile of papers there was a clue about the mystery of the Lost Lake.

Laura had been responsible for assembling most of this research. Over the weeks following the symposium, they spent many hours together in close quarters, ensconced in an isolated alcove on the second floor of the library where George had commandeered a large table, which they had covered with numerous piles of books and papers. She had proven to be an excellent amanuensis, retrieving citation sources from the stacks, verifying references, conducting literature reviews, hunting down obscure manuscripts and so forth. Her photographic memory enabled her to provide George with referential support and even direct quotations, perfectly accurate down to the punctuation marks, from widely assorted authorities practically on demand. In addition, she was a stimulating conversation partner with whom George could test, develop and refine his ideas.

None of his feelings for her had subsided during this period. On the contrary, George's resolution to keep his hands off Laura was sorely tested as the days passed, and he distinctly sensed that this feeling was a mutual one. Laura might come up to him from behind, put a hand on his shoulder and lean her head in to softly ask a question or relay an answer, a stray lock of her fragrant hair brushing against his cheek. A slight sideways turn of his head would have transformed the encounter into a kiss, and in these moments they were neither teacher and student nor lovers, but denizens of some netherworld residing in between the two states. The yearning he felt for her intensified until it became an ache deep inside of his heart.

He was slowly and inexorably succumbing to temptation, and in the process, beginning to rationalize his behavior. The code of academic ethics to which he had been struggling to adhere now seemed like a cold, dead creed. The Platonic ideal existed only as an intellectual construct rather than a living reality, and it could neither displace nor compete with the yearnings of the human heart. Loving Laura might be fraught with risk but it no longer seemed quite so clearly wrong.

These were their lives, and this was their world. He examined the reasons why he had originally framed the matter in a moral context to begin with. Was there really a power imbalance at work here, or was it chauvinistic in general and condescending to Laura in particular to presume that she stood on a lesser footing than he by virtue of their social positions alone? Was it fair to her to suggest she needed anyone's protection from him? By what right of entitlement had the academic establishment appropriated for itself the power to impose boundaries on *her* relationships, and what she did with her body? Who were they to tell Laura that her feelings were invalid, or that it was wrong for her to want to sleep with her aquatic microbiology professor?

Generally speaking, cryptozoology recognizes source material from the realms of myth, legend and folklore, along with undocumented sightings reported by eyewitnesses in historical times. Mythology, the most remote and least credible of these categories, deals with utterly fanciful creatures dreamt up by the human imagination. Having attributes that cannot possibly exist as described, they are fictitious inventions that clearly have no basis in objective reality. While they are presented as having an ostensible basis in history, mythological beasts really serve to express the world view of a people, or to explain a practice, belief or natural phenomenon. Examples include such creatures as fire-breathing dragons, gargoyles, mermaids, unicorns, basilisks, the Manticore and the Phoenix.

Legendary beings are slightly less implausible. Legends are stories coming down from the past that are popularly believed to have some basis, albeit unverifiable, in historical fact. Unlike mythological creatures, creatures of legend could at last theoretically exist from a biological point of view. They usually resemble some known species but typically have exaggerated characteristics such as great size, suggesting a biological relationship to an actual animal whether it be existing or extinct. Sea serpents, lake monsters, relic dinosaurs, thunderbirds and big, hairy manlike creatures such as the Sasquatch fall into this category.

The boundary separating legend from folklore is less distinct than the boundary between folklore and myth. Folklore is defined as a traditional tale, usually preserved orally among a people.

Less remote than either myth or legend, folklore describes widely held notions that are nevertheless unsupported in fact. By implication folklore, unlike legend, deals in stories of recent enough origin that they may be traced back across the generations to a living individual or group of individuals who claim to have actually experienced the events described. Thus the same animals that live in legend are prime examples of folkloric animals as well. They populate native stories and "traveler's tales".

Reports of undocumented sightings might be viewed as contemporary folklore. Unconfirmed, but not theoretically unverifiable, they usually bring creatures of legend or folklore forth into the modern day. As often as not the sources of these reports are rational, educated people of all social stations, including those who are relied on in their daily lives for their ability to perceive, recall and accurately relate information, and who would be expected to have a strong social disincentive to make a false or incredible report. Sea serpents, lake monsters, relic dinosaurs, thunderbirds and hairy manlike creatures, in addition to appearing in legend and folklore, are "seen" by contemporary humans from all walks of life.

The Loch Ness Monster, Champ and Ogopogo are but a few examples of lake monsters that have reportedly been observed and even photographed by typically reliable witnesses.

Sasquatch, Bigfoot and the Yeti have also been seen by credible individuals, and numerous casts of their footprints have been analyzed in scientific detail by credentialed academic experts in primate anatomy. Truly intriguing prints are usually spaced far apart and impressed deeply into the ground, suggesting a huge stride and immense weight. Tracks stretching for miles have been found by good witnesses in remote areas where no hoaxer would reasonably expect his work to ever be discovered.

In the Congo, reports of a huge, dinosaur-like animal, known as Mokele-Mbembe, have persisted for decades. There are also undocumented modern reports of relic specimens of animals known to have existed as recently as the last glacial period, which ended about 12,500 years ago. The paleontological record of the Pleistocene in North America includes megafauna such as the giant beaver, *Castoroides Ohioensis*, along with the Mastodon, the Wooly Mammoth, the giant sloth, the flat-faced bear, the Dier wolf and the saber-toothed tiger.

Thunderbirds, predatory raptors with wingspans reportedly reaching 25 feet, are occasionally reported today. These monstrous birds bear a striking resemblance to the *Argentavis magnificens*, a feathered, flying creature which was easily that large. Its biggest feathers would have measured about five feet long and eight inches wide. *Teratornis merriami*, whose skeleton was discovered in the La Brea Tar Pits, had a wingspan of about 16 feet and weighed 170 pounds. It is known to have lived as recently as 10,000 years ago, coexisting with modern humans.

In the 1970s, a boy from Lawndale, Illinois, was reportedly picked up and carried for about a dozen feet by a Thunderbird before his shirt ripped. The attack was witnessed by his mother. In 2002, a pilot in Alaska reported flying alongside an eagle-like bird with a wingspan comparable in size to the fourteen-foot width of his Cessna.

George's snapper fell into a similar but slightly different category, assuming it was an oversized example of the present-day alligator snapping turtle and not an Ice Age relic of some sort. Sightings of giant specimens of known animals are not unheard of. In India and China, reports from remote provinces tell of ants the size of river rats, and spiders as big as terriers have reputedly been seen in the rain forests of Papua New Guinea. Accepted size limits for reptiles and invertebrates, who continue to grow slowly throughout their adult lives, are not absolute. Very old individuals could conceivably reach significantly exaggerated proportions.

In fact George's sighting was not without precedent. In 1898, a farmer in Indiana claimed that a colossal alligator snapping turtle was living in the lake bordering his land. No one ever bothered to verify his report and he eventually sold the farm. In 1948, two men in a rowboat claimed they saw the turtle while fishing. It had surfaced near them and was reportedly as big as their boat. A year later, the farm's new owner noticed that his livestock was disappearing. Chickens, and even a calf had vanished, all of them near the lake. One afternoon he saw the turtle sunning itself on the shore. Badly frightened, he called the police. When they arrived it was still there. A team of four Clydesdales was brought in and chains were attached but the horses couldn't budge it. The chains snapped and the turtle disappeared into the lake. A deep-sea diver was brought in but the lake's bottom was silty and poor visibility forced an end to the search. The lake was eventually drained, but the mysterious creature was not to be found. Unverified reports from Kansas tell about the capture of a 403-pound specimen in the Neosho River in 1937. Two specimens in captivity in Chicago in the 1990s were documented at 249 and 236 pounds. Known to have lived in captivity for as long as 70 years, they are believed to survive up to 150 years. Some living specimens allegedly have been found with musket balls embedded in them.

Known to science as *Machrochelys temminckii*, the alligator snapping turtle is a relative of the common snapping turtle, *Chelydra serpentina*. Both are carnivorous, known to eat fish, crawfish, mollusks, other turtles, snakes, birds and crabs. The alligator snapper, though, has a spiny, more aggressively armored shell and grows much larger. Although the alligator snapping turtle favors a warmer climate, one study showed that they tend to wander north as they grow larger with age, the biggest specimens being found at the uppermost end of their normal range. If an old alligator snapper in the Nunavut Territory were oversized in proportion to its location so far north, this could explain what George had seen.

George adjusted the oil lamp and pulled out a notepad and a pencil. The fire popped and crackled in the hearth. He settled into his chair and began reading.

The Nunavut Territory, covering one-fifth of the Canadian landmass, was officially separated from the Northwest Territories in 1999. It comprised the major portion of the Canadian Arctic Archipelago. The Territory's mostly Inuit population of around 29,000 was dispersed over about 746,000 square miles of land interspersed with 62,000 square miles of water. Baffin, Devon and Ellesmere are among its largest islands, with a sub-polar climate lacking in true summers. The other main climatic region, the Mackenzie River valley, where *Le Lac Perdu* was situated, had a sub-arctic climate characterized by cold winters and relatively warm but short summers.

Mining was the territory's dominant industry. Fur trapping was its oldest. The region has supported a continuous native population for about 4,000 years. Its written history began in 1576, when Sir Martin Frobisher made the first recorded European contact with the Inuit, their word for "people", while leading an expedition to find the Northwest Passage. This initial encounter ended badly, with both sides taking prisoners, who perished.

By the 1700s the Northwest Territories were dominated by two fur-trading concerns, the Hudson's Bay Company, based in London, and the North West Company out of Montreal. Their rival trapping expeditions were responsible for most of the exploration and mapping of the Mackenzie River drainage basin, of which *Le Lac Perdu* was a part.

The advance scouting parties sent into the wilderness ahead of these trappers came back with strange reports from the Lost Lake. It was a place held in superstitious regard by the Inuit, who refused to go there. The trapping scouts disregarded their warnings, assuming the Inuit were trying to deter them from a bountiful fur resource. Although they found the fur habitat they had envisioned, they determined the area too remote and inhospitable for reasons only hinted at. Notably the party suffered the loss of some men in what was described as a boating misadventure. A member of the party reportedly went insane as the result of this episode and was returned in irons.

While early maps of the Mackenzie River valley depicted *Le Lac Perdu* in a roughly accurate sketched outline that even included its biggest islands, it began to appear only in the form of a written notation on later maps and eventually it vanished from the maps entirely. Although the reasons for this were never directly referenced, the cartographers' omission seemed odd to George in light of its reported fur resources, especially considering the general rush to harvest the beaver pelts that formed the province's unit of currency.

Thirty "made beaver pelts" could buy a keg of rum. Ten weasel skins bought an "Ordinary Riding Horse, or eight buffalo robes. Four buffalo robes were worth one scarlet Hudson's Bay blanket. Five buffalo robes fetched a bear-claw necklace. With such a high demand for pelts and a fierce competition for the best trapping grounds ongoing amongst rival companies, there should have been a strong financial incentive to press into the watershed of the Lost Lake. But it remained a forgotten, and, George guessed, perhaps even taboo, subject from the late 1700s on.

Before George was through with his reading, he had written out a dozen pages of notes in longhand on his pad. It was clear from the historical record that their lake was more than merely isolated, it was a place in the world cursed among the native people and shunned by the Europeans boldly roaming the rest of the region in search of lucre. This was where they had been dropped off and, come to think of it, rather abruptly abandoned, hundreds upon hundreds of uninhabited and untraversable miles removed from even the most rudimentary and far-flung outposts of human civilization.

George looked around inside of the lodge and recalled how, when he was booking the trip, he had asked about its construction. A portable gasoline-powered saw mill had been helicoptered up to a clearing at the location, he was told. A workman was left behind to carry out the job of milling some of the felled trees into beams, studs and planking, then constructing the lodge, the cabins and the dock. This was back in the 1960s.

George was curious about why this colorful piece of information was not mentioned in the outpost's advertising. It turned out that when the helicopter crew returned at the end of the summer, they found a neat little cluster of rough-hewn but well-constructed wood-frame buildings, a sturdy dock and a well-maintained saw mill, just as expected. However the workman, a French-Canadian lumberjack named Jacques Fortin, was not to be found. A hard drinker and habitual brawler who for these reasons usually worked alone, it was assumed that he had gone for an evening swim to cool off after a hot day at labor and drowned, maybe while drunk.

If it were true that Jacques Fortin had disappeared during a swim, it was quite possible that instead of drowning, he had been killed and eaten by the turtle. But without a body or the remnants of one there would be no reason to suppose anything besides a prosaic explanation. Even with some sign of predation, the outpost's owners would have had no incentive to publicize it.

George wondered whether, during his summer alone on the lake, Jacques had observed or experienced anything unusual or disturbing. If so, he might have realized the danger he was in, the possibility of his own death, and the fact that the returning crew might have no indication of the reason. He might have wanted to leave them some sort of clue or warning, but he would have also wanted to avoid coming off as a crackpot in case he survived the summer. So he would have hidden his message somewhere, most likely in the lodge itself. In fact, in the event that Jacques had interacted with the monster before his death, this was really a very likely scenario.

George got up and began examining the cabin's interior. He looked for any sign of a false front in the walls or a likely place in the floorboards where something could have been secreted. It took about fifteen minutes for him to find it. At the base of the fieldstone fireplace he had built, Jacques had laid a piece of trim into place but had neglected to nail it down. This contrasted with the straightforward but careful carpentry evident around the rest of the place. It was definitely odd, and exactly what George was looking for.

George took out his pocket knife and used the blade to pry up the loose board, revealing a supporting stud running beneath the floor parallel to the fireplace. In the space between the stone and the wood a writing tablet had been wedged into place. George reached down and picked it up. He replaced the floorboard and held the little notebook in his hands. He hardly dared to open it. He finally brought it over to the desk and sat back down under the lamplight with it, uncertain whether he wanted it to be full of writing or entirely blank.

Jacques scribbled in a crude cursive hand, his pen strokes making deep impressions in the paper as if the unaccustomed act of using it to shape irregular letters into misspelled words was a task associated with great effort. Equally clumsy was his style, but George guessed it accurately conveyed the colloquial ways of speech of a Francophone of meager formal education and a concrete turn of mind getting along as necessary in English. Given the extent to which Jacques had gone to produce and conceal the little volume, George could only assume that its contents would be rather grave.

Jacques began with an entry dated July 10, 1963, which recorded the sound, and a shadowy glimpse, of a large creature moving around near shore after dark. He had been frightened enough to write down a little prayer for his safe deliverance. A few days later, he picked up his pen once again to relate another sighting, this time during the middle of the day, when a large aquatic animal had surfaced near the mouth of the cove. It had a long neck and he wasn't sure whether or not it was some sort of lake monster. Again, he wrote a prayer.

On July 18, the writing was even more erratic than usual and as George read on, he discovered that the reason for this was that the entry was written during an actual attack. Jacques was cowering inside one of the cabins as something lurched around outside, snapping trees and sending vibrations through the ground with its footsteps. Terrified, he had peered through a window to see a huge beast on the prowl. He had retreated from the sight and was furiously scribbling down what he thought were his last words. He lapsed into and out of English now, describing in an idiosyncratic combination of the two languages the animal's menacing activities.

In the morning, when he finally gathered enough courage to venture outside, Jacques found swaths of devastation where the animal had been, along with numerous gigantic clawed footprints leading from, and then back down to, the shoreline. By this point, he was about two-thirds of the way through the project, with two more cabins plus the dock still left to build. He was now convinced that he was being visited by the devil, and prayed for the courage to continue with his work and the grace to do so in safety.

Far from casually swimming in the lake, Jacques was by now avoiding it at all costs, forsaking even bathing, much to his annoyance. The last entry in his grim diary concerned his misgivings about completing the dock, which apparently entailed getting into the water and wrangling the two final pilings into place, then framing in the supporting beams and finally laying the decking. He wrote that his hope was to be finished well before sunset, in time to barricade himself inside of the lodge for the night. He prayed for deliverance from the devil. After that, there was no more writing.

George closed the book and sat for a long minute, staring off into a darkened corner of the room. Clearly, whatever Jacques had seen and described so fearfully was the same thing that had gone after Danny, and the source of the footprint he had come across during his walk along the shore. He revisited his decision to keep the print a secret from the others, but decided to do nothing about it for the time being. His scientific curiosity was aroused now. He would see what the future held. So he freshened the lamp wick, picked up his pen and set about adding a summary of the contents of Jacques Fortin's journal to his thickening collection of notes.

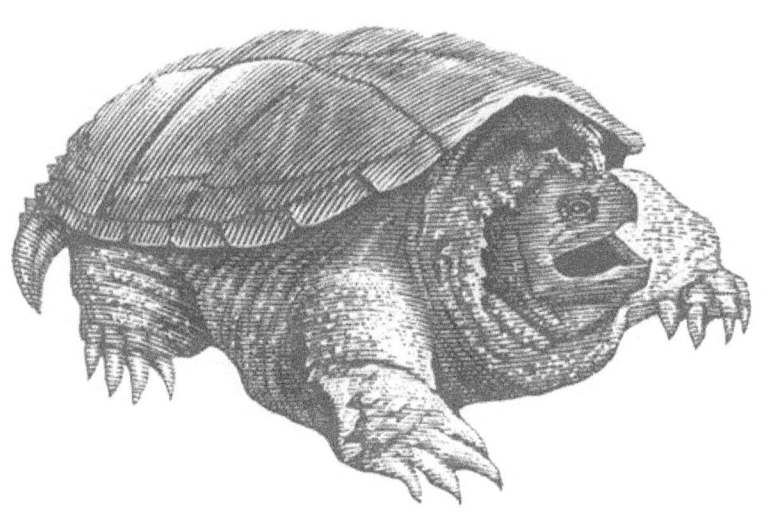

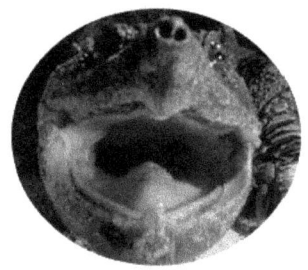

Chapter Eight

Bill Isley lay on his bed, wondering when his dog was going to show up. He tried hard to come up with a good reason not to be worried, but he was unsuccessful. Until Scout came back, Bill wouldn't be able to get any sleep; it just didn't feel right. Bringing Scout up to the lake had posed quite a little logistical challenge. Getting him across the border was not a problem, and flying him out of Montreal was a manageable inconvenience, but when they had arrived at the guide outpost near Whale Cove, he found out that the dog's weight would have to be subtracted from his allotment of gear for the flight up to the lake on the float plane. Big male chocolate labs tip the scales at around 100 pounds, which meant that Bill had to leave behind most of his baggage.

But it was a compromise he made willingly. It seemed like an important thing to do. Bill had had Scout since he was a puppy. He had picked him from a litter with championship bloodlines nine years earlier. The second biggest of the males, Scout had a blocky head, a fat, wagging otter tail, webbed feet and an especially intelligent sparkle in his eye. Bill raised him diligently and trained him well. He was a good dog and Bill wanted to give him the life he deserved, which meant making sure Scout got plenty of time in the woods and on the water. But there was no use denying that Scout was nearing the end of his prime and Bill was becoming acutely aware of his dog's mortality. Bill had had labs before, and they usually lived to be somewhere between 12 and 14 years old. The last couple of these years were spent in decline. Before Scout began to show signs of diminishing vitality, Bill wanted him to have this one last grand experience in the wilderness.

And Scout, by all indications, seemed to be making the most of it. He had thoroughly enjoyed himself on Day One, gallivanting around the camp with his wet pink tongue hanging out. He kept bringing sticks over to people, campaigning tirelessly for them to throw them out into the cove for him to retrieve. He would run out onto the dock and hurl himself off the end, landing in the water with a big splash. He would dog-paddle out and fetch the stick, flinging his tail out of the water to assist him in making a sharp turn back toward shore. Then he would chug back in and repeat the process. With six men available to take turns throwing the stick for him, he managed to keep himself gainfully occupied in this manner for hours on end.

On Day Two, Bill had brought him along in the boat with Nate and Peter. He was happy he did. Scout seemed to think fishing was an immensely entertaining endeavor, and he spent the day lit up with innocent excitement. When they returned to camp, Bill began to clean their day's catch of fish, and Scout meandered off to do some exploring around the perimeter of the cove, and that was the last Bill had seen of him. Bill thought back on the discussion in the lodge. Surely, the talk of a giant turtle in the lake was nonsense. Nevertheless, he found himself wondering when Scout was going to show up again. He wasn't worried, but he was concerned. And so he lay there listening expectantly for the sound of Scout's soft scratch at the door.

Bill was sharing a cabin with Jack, who had gone to bed immediately and was now snoring lightly. It was quite dark, and very quiet.

After about an hour, Bill decided to get up and go outside. He wanted to take a walk around the camp and see if Scout was out there. So he quietly got to his feet and slipped out of the cabin, leaving Jack asleep inside. Once outside, Bill noticed the glow of a light from the lodge, and he walked over for a look. Through the window, he could see George inside, sitting at the desk, hunched over a pile of books and papers, making notes. He was working on his book, apparently. Bill decided not to disturb him.

Bill wandered around the camp with the aid of a flashlight, hoarsely whispering for his dog. For some reason, he did not want to sound a general alarm yet. Scout's absence, and its effect on him, seemed like a private matter for the time being. He wanted to avoid becoming the focus of everybody's sympathetic concern. Surely Scout would come back and everything would be alright. Then, Bill would be able to enjoy the rest of this vacation.

Bill went down to the beach. He shone the flashlight around the shoreline and out over the water but there was no sign of Scout. He noticed that there was a canoe tied up at the dock, and he went over and checked it out. Sure enough there was a paddle in the craft. Since Scout wasn't sniffing around the campsite, it stood to reason that he was probably cavorting along the shoreline like the water dog that he was. Bill decided to go looking for him.

Bill untied the canoe and got in. He pushed off from the dock and began paddling. The waters in their sheltered little cove were black but as smooth as glass. The moon glimmered through a bank of clouds, casting a subdued glow that enabled Bill to vaguely make out the shadowy contours of the nearby shoreline. Quietly, he pulled himself along over the water with smooth paddle strokes.

"Scout," he whispered.

"Scout?"

Nothing.

Snap

He kept paddling.

Then Bill heard what sounded like a splash. It seemed to have come from somewhere behind him. He stopped paddling and listened for a moment. The sound didn't repeat itself. He started paddling again, and calling Scout's name, a little louder now.

"Scout," he called.

"Scout!"

He paddled some more. Then he heard it again, the splash, only this time it came from somewhere in front of him. Also, it was a little louder, and more suggestive of something sizeable making a disturbance on the surface. Bill froze. He tried to make out any sort of shape in the waters ahead. Surely Scout was somewhere out there, rooting around in the water for a fish, or maybe even taking on another one of those turtles that seemed to populate the cove. This was a startling thought. A snapping turtle the size of the one they had eaten could easily clip off one of Scout's forelegs with its fearsome jaws.

Bill turned on his flashlight and directed its beam in the general direction of the splashing sound. But Scout was nowhere to be seen. Perhaps it had just been a big fish rising up to strike at something on the surface. He turned off the light and sat there in the canoe, floating on the water, listening some more. After a while, he resumed his paddling, tracing out a course parallel to the outline of the cove, periodically stopping in order to scan the shoreline with the aid of his flashlight.

"Scout," he called.

"Scout! Scout, come!"

And then Bill heard a sound that sent a cold chill down his spine. Something *very* large was moving around in the cove, he realized. Immediately he was overcome with a sense of dread. He suddenly felt vulnerable and exposed in his little canoe, floating on the glossy surface of the water with only a thin strip of fiberglass beneath him. It occurred to Bill that a full five minutes' worth of paddling separated him from the safety of the dock.

Bill was no longer thinking about Scout. Instead, he was preoccupied with whatever it was that was responsible for the noises he was hearing in the water around him. He was nagged by the recollection of the violent disturbance they had heard in the cove the night before. Now, it seemed like a bad idea, getting into the canoe and going out on the lake in the middle of the night without telling anyone. He thought of Jack, snoring in his bunk. Maybe he would wake up, notice that his cabin mate was gone, and decide to come looking for him.

He realized it was time to turn back.

Bill brought the canoe around and started paddling toward the dock. By now, his only concern was making it back to the camp and returning to the cabin, and the warmth and safety of his own bed. Whether or not it made any sense, Bill decided that he needed to get off of the water immediately. His daughter, Kate, was going to be married in the fall, and as he paddled, he thought about how much he was looking forward to walking her down the aisle on his arm. The thought of Kate's wedding, and his desire to be there for her, made him paddle even faster and harder.

By the pale moonlight, Bill could discern the outline of the dock across the water. He had about 75 yards to go. The canoe glided smoothly along through the darkness. Everything was quiet except for the little rippling sounds made by his paddle. His arms were starting to get a little tired but he pressed ahead, determined to reach the dock as quickly as possible.

Bill was not quite sure why he was feeling so anxious. Really, there was nothing to worry about, he told himself. He still wasn't buying the idea of a giant turtle. Surely it was a product of George's eccentric fascination with fantastic creatures, coupled with his overactive imagination. Now he was letting his own imagination get the better of him. Once he got back on dry land, everything would be okay. Then he heard another splashing sound.

It came from somewhere in the expanse of water between him and the dock. He stopped paddling. Some sort of a shape seemed to be lurking just under the surface a few dozen feet off the end of the rickety wooden structure. He struggled to discern its shadowy outline, but he could not make it out. He got his flashlight and aimed it at the spot.

Incredibly, the beam picked up a pair of large red ovals glowing over the surface of the water. At first, Bill was confused. This was a difficult observation to explain. He tried to figure out what he was looking at, but no plausible explanation occurred to him. Then an implausible one came to mind: He was looking at a pair of reflecting red eyes, and they were the size of footballs.

Bill immediately turned off the flashlight and picked up his paddle. He brought the canoe around and started paddling away from the eyes - and the dock - as fast as he could. But a minute later, when he heard another splash off the canoe's bow, he stopped. This was all wrong. Shining the light toward the source of this new noise, he saw, with a deepening sense of dread, that the eyes had somehow reappeared on the other side of the cove. Whatever it was must have submerged and swum right underneath his canoe, resurfacing in front of him, only closer now.

There really was a giant turtle in the lake, after all.

And it was stalking him.

Bill found himself fighting off a growing sense of panic. He thought of the others, safe in their cabins, and wished with every fiber of his being that he were back there with them. He had to get back on land, he realized. Otherwise, someone else would be giving his daughter away on her wedding day.

Suddenly the canoe seemed small and flimsy, unstable and slow. Bill couldn't remain where he was and yet there was no way he would be able to outrace the turtle back to the dock. His only hope was to head directly for the shore, right away. He started paddling. Then it occurred to him that the turtle might try to intercept him like before. He stopped paddling again, and picked up the light.

As he suspected, the eyes had moved. Now they were floating between him and the shore. Bill sat there in his canoe, transfixed by the pair of red ovals reflecting back at him in the beam of his flashlight. Not only was the turtle blocking his way forward but it was also positioned so that it would be able to cut him off along the diagonal - whether he tried to head for the dock or for another spot on the shoreline.

He had been outmaneuvered.

It was checkmate.

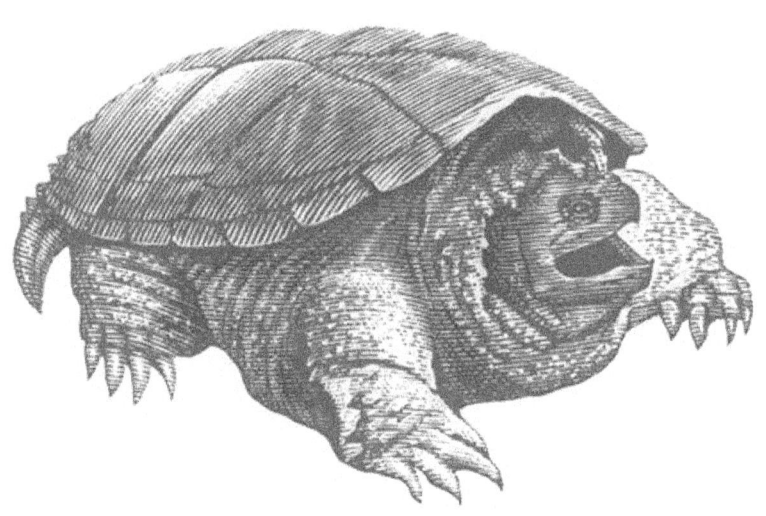

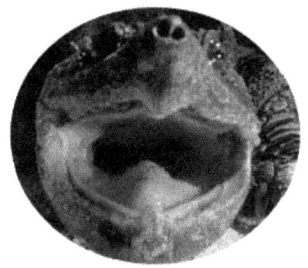

Chapter Nine

By the time the spring semester drew to a close, the impasse between professor and student had become a familiar presence in George and Laura's daily lives together, and this enabled their friendship to deepen even as they skated on top of the other feelings they were busily suppressing. They both knew, however, that in reality it was only a matter of time. They were a sexual accident waiting to happen.

On the final Thursday night of the term, the Biology Department feted its faculty research assistants. George waited for Laura in front of the Science Building. She was a couple of minutes late this evening, which was a bit out of character. Just when he was beginning to grow anxious she appeared at the top of the hill. She wore a short dress that was cinched at the waist, and thickly heeled, square-toed shoes that accentuated her leggy appearance. Aware of his gaze she concentrated on picking her way down the sloping path on her heels without suffering an embarrassing fall. This gave her gait an oddly halting cadence, as if she were being led to some serious proceeding by an invisible escort.

George had forgotten his wallet so they went up to his office. Her cell phone rang while they were there. She spoke a few brief words and hung up. She put her 'phone down on corner of the desk and pulled George over to her by the lapels of his suit jacket.

"Here," she said, straightening his tie. "There." She said when she was finished.

He smiled, leaned in and gave her a little peck on the cheek. "Come on," he said. "Time to go."

The reception was a slightly stiff affair. George was grateful for the open bar. He left Laura and went to get them drinks. On his way back, a scotch in each hand, he ran into Phil Richardson, the department's chairman, along with Dick King, a professor who was interested in the assistant chairmanship, which was currently vacant.

"I like the look of your assistant, George," Phil said, giving him a little nudge with his elbow.

"I'll bet those legs go clean up to heaven."

George was at a loss for words.

"That raises an interesting question, Phil," Dick said. "Which is, what are we going to do?"

"What do you mean?" George asked.

"She's gorgeous," Dick answered, as if the significance of this point were so obvious as to be self-evident. George tried to identify the reasons why Dick saw this as some sort of a problem, but couldn't think of any that were not in some way either insulting, if not vaguely threatening, to Laura, himself, or the both of them.

"Well," George said, "we could throw acid in her face."

He flashed them an enigmatic smile and begged off. He returned to Laura, who was already being chatted up by Seth Boynton, a good-looking and supremely suave upperclassman who had left a trail of broken hearts through the freshman dorms that year. He was in the process of explaining, in his easy way, that Laura's status as an off-campus resident must be why he had never encountered her until this very night. Laura looked a little flushed and George's heart began to pound. For a moment, he wasn't entirely sure whether the age difference between himself and the Seths of the world counted for or against him in her book.

"Oh, there you are," she said when he pulled up. "Seth, this is Professor Mapolis."

"Hi Seth," said George, awkwardly standing there double-fisting the whiskies. Mercifully, someone started clinking a spoon against a water goblet, signaling that it was time to be seated for dinner. George handed Laura her drink, walked her to their table and helped her into her seat. They were sharing a table, to George's chagrin, with Phil Richardson and Dick King and their assistants, a couple of bookish graduate students, plus Harriet Spencer, an unhappily married biochemistry professor, and her own research aide, who was none other than the dashing Seth Boynton himself.

Seth had unsuccessfully tried to jockey himself into position to sit beside Laura but had to settle for a seat opposite her, which provided, George knew, the consolation prize of a direct view of her beautiful face. Just as his annoyance began to bubble to the surface, he felt Laura's hand, moving slowly back and forth along the crest of his thigh muscle. He discretely reached under the table and held his hand there, palm open. She took it, interlaced her fingers with his, and gave it a long, gentle squeeze. Looking across the table at Seth, George sensed that he was not getting what he'd hoped for in the way of eye contact from Laura, as his youthful attention was already beginning to stray around the room.

George and Laura held hands under the table for most of the evening, reluctantly breaking contact only during dinner and dessert. The proceedings were far from exciting but George found himself not wanting them to end, ever. He felt an incredible and strangely familiar sense of peace as they sat together, for the first time, as a couple. Mindful of the necessity of discretion, he could not say for sure whether this impaired or enhanced the thrill of the moment. It did lend to it a slightly melancholy air, but there was something delicious about this feeling, as if the need for secrecy only intensified the emotional connection running between the two of them.

On the way out of the reception, Laura remembered that she had left her cell phone in George's office, so they walked back to the Science Building to retrieve it. With the lights of the party receding behind them, George reached out for her again, and they strolled, hand in hand, across the lonely, darkened campus, past the imposing buildings that had not so long ago stood as monuments to an ethos he now no longer wished to be controlled by, or even reminded of.

George let them into the building and they took the elevator back up to the fifth floor. George unlocked the door to his office and pulled Laura inside. The instant the door was closed they embraced, and, cupping her chin in the crook of his hand, he leaned into her face and kissed her on the lips. She reciprocated, gently at first, but then she turned her head and found the tip of his tongue with the tip of her own, and they began exploring each others' mouths together, gently, but with barely restrained passion. Standing there with their bodies pressing into one another, George could feel the electricity between them, and his hands tingled as he ran them softly up and down her curves and then around to the small of her back, which was exposed by the party dress she had on.

After this extended, writhing kiss, she pulled herself away just a little and began loosening George's tie. She pulled apart the knot and untwisted it, then began working on the buttons of his shirt. She exposed his chest and brought her face into the nest of hair on his sternum. She placed the palm of her hand over his heart, and locked eyes with him. They began kissing again and as they did he began working on the buttons of her dress. When he was done, she shimmied her shoulders a little and the dress fell to the floor, forming a puddle of fabric around her feet.

She stepped out of the dress and immediately dropped to her knees wearing only her shoes, panties and bra. Gently, she rubbed the area of his trousers against which he was straining, then unzipped his pants, unbuckled his belt and pulled open his boxers. She slipped them down a little, cupped him prayerfully in her hands then placed her mouth over him. They stayed like that for a while, just savoring the way it felt both physically and emotionally to be connected in such a way.

After a long while, she released him and stood up. She pulled him over towards the desk and sat on it, leaned back, and spread her legs for him.

"Is it safe?" He asked.

She replied by placing a hand on each of his buttocks and drawing him up and inside of her. She began to lose herself in the sensuous experience of being opened up so very completely and then taken, really taken, by, she now realized, the only man she had ever really wanted. The room began to swirl and the only awareness she had was from the waist down, where all hell was breaking loose. Her final lines of defense in tatters, she gave up trying to control things, and in the next instant there was a warmth coming from somewhere deep inside of her and she knew, but didn't care, that she had given herself completely over to him.

It was at this moment that her cell phone rang. At the time it seemed of no consequence. She flailed an arm instinctively toward it, knocking it off the desk and onto the floor. It occurred to George to wonder not only who had been calling, but also, for whatever reason, whether the 'phone had inadvertently been flipped on. Meanwhile Laura's panting had been replaced by staccato cooing noises which in turn gave way to a series of high-pitched utterances that became increasingly more shrill and profane until the ragged tone of her voice and the uncharacteristically promiscuous things she was now screaming reached a slightly disturbing but mysterious and wonderful crescendo. They climaxed together, clutched one another tightly, then sank down onto the surface of George's desk, exhausted, and fell asleep.

Zoon

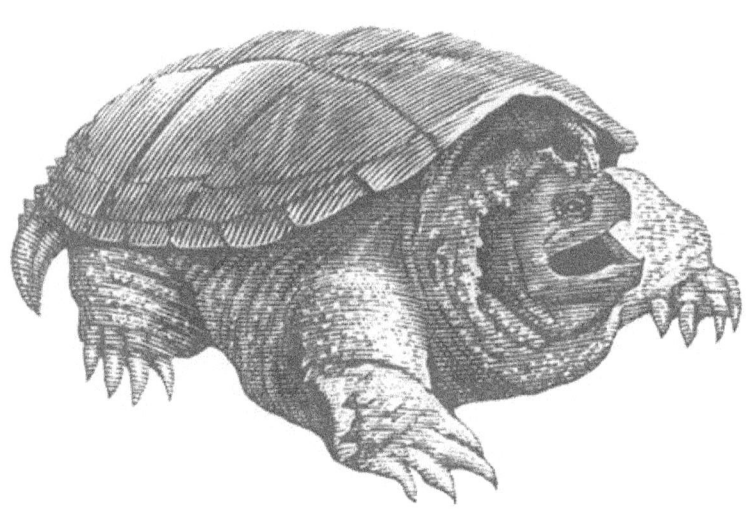

Chapter Ten

It was 5 a.m. and Nate Peterman couldn't stay in bed any longer. He had been tossing and turning all night, feverishly dreaming about fish. For the past hour or so, he had lain awake, waiting impatiently. He wanted to be out on the water in time for sunrise, in time to catch the beginning of the morning feeding cycle, in time to catch a big one. Or maybe even *the* big one.

Before leaving on the trip, George had suggested that they each contribute twenty-five dollars to a pool, which would be awarded to the person who caught the biggest fish. Just as Ahab had nailed a cold coin to the mast of the *Pequod*, George nailed the bills comprising the prize money to a post inside the lodge. Nate had his heart set on winning this bounty. The hundred-and-fifty dollars was of little consequence, but the competitive challenge had captured his imagination. He wanted to be the one who ripped the money off of the pole. He would use it to buy rounds for everybody back in Iqaluit, where their return flight to Montreal was scheduled to originate at the back end of the trip.

He got up, lit a lantern, and put on his clothes. Peter was still asleep. Nate went over to his bed and gently rustled his arm.

"Rise and shine, Peter," Nate said. "Are you ready for some fishing?"

"Um, yeah," Peter said groggily. "Sure."

"Then let's go."

Peter got up and sat on the edge of his bed in his boxer shorts, rubbing the sleep from his eyes. "Do you mind if I get dressed first?"

"Not at all. Take your time and I'll get our gear together," Nate told him. "I have a feeling we're in for one incredible day on the lake!"

"Hmmm," Peter said, still not fully awake. "Yeah. Hopefully."

Peter began getting dressed, slowly. Nate could hardly stand it.

"As soon as you're ready we can get going," Nate reminded him.

"What's the rush?"

"I want to be out there by sunrise."

"Obviously." The comic stylings of Peter Gordon, professional funnyman. "What about Bill?"

"Oh," Nate said, "he's in with Jack. You know those two. They're a couple of sleepyheads. He can hitch a ride on the other boat. The *S.S. Wannabe*. You, on the other hand, are hooked up with a serious fisherman. I want to get going. Come on man, they're biting!"

"Okay, okay. Here I come!"

Carrying their fishing gear, they walked down the still-dark path to the dock and got into the smaller, faster boat. Neither of them noticed that the canoe was gone. Nate started the engine and they cast off, putt-putting toward the mouth of the cove under a grayish but gradually brightening sky. When they cleared the cove, Nate brought the engine up to cruising speed and they headed briskly off over the waves in a southeasterly direction.

According to their charts, there was a sunken island a couple of miles from shore. After about 45 minutes, the contours of an underwater mountain appeared on their depth finder and Nate pulled back some on the throttle. He watched the screen until it indicated that they were right on the edge of a submerged precipice. Then he turned off the motor.

At first light, the big fish could be expected to rise from the inky depths in a spot like this, where they would have access to the aquatic life along the margins of the shoal's thriving ecosystem. Nate decided that live minnows would present well since they would closely mimic a typical species of prey native to the reef. They baited their lines, cast them into the water and settled in to wait.

"You realize the bounty is mine, don't you, Peter?"

"Something like that."

"As George would say, watch and learn, Peter. Watch and learn."

They sat there, observing their lines floating on the calm surface of the lake. The light of dawn lay flat on water the shade of tobacco. A faint mist rose into a brightening sky, where billowing linen-colored clouds hovered. There was no breeze in the air. They were within sight of a couple of strips of discernible shoreline but the horizon was mostly water laid out against the distant backdrop of the mountains.

"So what do you think of this giant turtle business?" Peter asked, after a minute.

"I don't know," Nate replied. "Do you think it's possible?"

"No."

"They must have seen something. They seemed pretty freaked out."

"I'll bet it was a prank. They're probably back there laughing their asses off right now. If there really were things like giant turtles and Bigfoot, people would be talking about seeing them."

"But they are, apparently," Nate said, and they both chuckled. "Seriously, though, it's an awfully big planet."

"That it is," Peter said. "That it is. But it sounds to me like George is getting to you with all of his talk about mysterious monsters."

"I suppose."

"He likes a good campfire tale. There's nothing wrong with that, but sometimes he blurs the line between reality and imagination. In case you haven't noticed."

"George has always been a bit of a fibber," Nate conceded.

"I don't think he's dishonest. It's more like he's . . . selectively accurate."

"He lives in a fabricated reality."

"Right," Peter agreed, "they're not lies, they're engineered representations."

"Synthetic truths."

"Exactly."

"Anyways," Nate said, "what would it take to convince you that there are such things as monsters?"

"I suppose I'd have to see one with my own eyes."

"So you don't believe the eyewitnesses, unless the eyewitness is you."

"You could say that, I guess. Like I said, I'd need to see one for myself."

"Have you seen Pluto with your own eyes?"

"No, but Pluto could be a hoax."

"Did you see the look on Danny's face last night?" Nate asked. "That wasn't the look of somebody who was pulling a prank."

"Well, you heard what George had to say," Peter replied. "If it wasn't a hoax, then it was probably a case of mistaken identity."

"By three of them? And they're pretty experienced fishermen. I mean, George is an aquatic biology professor. You would think they would be fairly reliable observers."

George, Nate knew, had been developing his own cryptozoological taxonomy, a method for classifying the various sorts of possible explanations for the reported phenomena that would permit the conclusion that at least some of these animals must, of logical necessity, be real. He was working on a theory modeled on the pyramid, with cases of mistaken identity forming the base, hoaxes forming the middle section and valid, if unverified, sightings of real-life monsters forming the capstone. The presumption was that the most probable explanation would reside toward the bottom of the pyramid, assuming there were more sincere witnesses than hoaxers, and, in turn, more hoaxers than valid reporters. As investigation and analysis moved a particular case further up the pyramid, it would tend to compel the conclusion that the only remaining explanation, upon the elimination of all of the possible ones, would be the one that was "impossible".

"Well," Nate said, "if we eliminate a prank, and we give them credit for actually knowing what they were looking at, that leaves—"

"Hey, I think I've got a fish . . ."

"Whoa!" Nate said.

Peter's pole was jerking sharply in his hands, doubling over on itself, while his reel gave up drag with a metallic whine. He started playing the fish, which was putting up a strong fight.

"Keep her steady, Peter," Nate said. "Don't try to pull it in yet. Let it run. Tire it out."

Nate got the net and stood ready with it, watching Peter work his tackle. However, the fish was nowhere near ready to give up.

"Damn, that fish has got a lot of fight in it," Nate said. "Are you getting tired?"

"I am," Peter said. "My arms are aching. This thing is strong."

Peter walked back and forth along the rail, following the fish as it struggled in the water. By degrees, he managed to bring it closer and closer to the boat, reeling in and playing out line as needed in order to keep the fish from snapping it or shaking off the hook. Only when it began to tire would he be able to bring it within the reach of Nate's net.

Peter wrestled with the fish for perhaps a half an hour before it finally came to the surface, and when it did they immediately realized that it was a northern pike of trophy proportions.

"Wow, Peter," Nate said, "nice fish!" He tried to reach it with the net but he couldn't quite get to it. "Try and bring it a little closer."

"It doesn't seem to like the boat," Peter replied. "I think I need to tire it out some more."

"Wait a minute," Nate said, "let me grab hold of the rail so I can lean out."

"Just don't fall in," Peter said. "I don't know how to run the boat, remember."

"You worry too much," Nate said with a laugh as he craned his body out over the water.

"After all, we could be back in the cabin right now, sleeping. Aren't you glad you decided to get out of bed? Seriously, where else would you rather be than right here, right now?"

Before Peter could reply, the unthinkable happened: Up from the water directly underneath Nate's outstretched body rose a huge greenish form. It was the turtle. Peter wanted to shout a warning but it was already too late. Breaking the surface with a splash, the monster emerged from the lake and continued rising upward, deftly snatching Nate in its great, gaping jaws before returning gracefully back into the water with his body crosswise in its mouth.

For one pained instant, Peter found himself looking down into Nate's upturned face. Nate wore a stark expression of surprise, which softened into a look of sad resignation as the animal dragged him slowly down under the water and off into the murky depths. Aside from a few bubbles of air rising sporadically to the surface, there was absolutely no trace of either of them now. Everything was eerily calm and quiet. The serenity felt surreal in light of the macabre event that had just taken place.

Peter stared in disbelief at the spot where the animal had just submerged with the body of his hapless friend. Nate, who had been so keenly alive only a moment earlier, was simply gone, as if someone had made him disappear with a *snap* of their fingers.

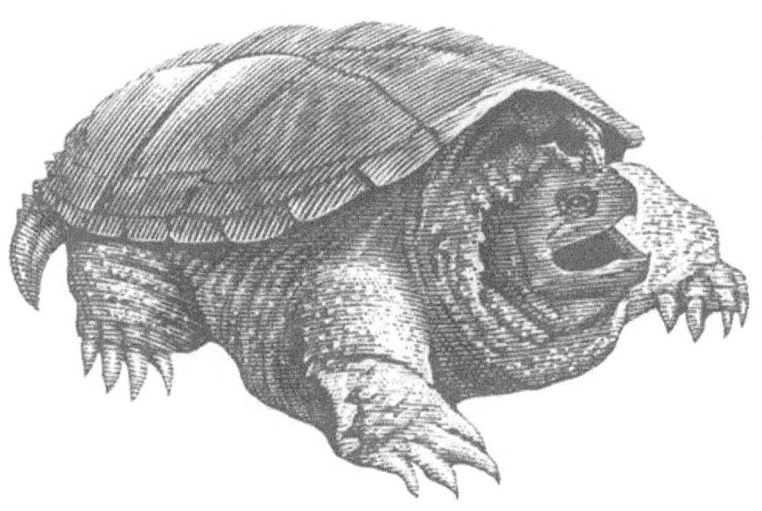

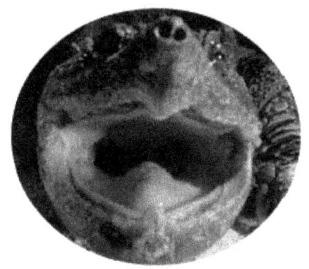

Chapter Eleven

When George woke up later that morning he discovered that Nate, Peter and Bill were already gone. According to Jack, Bill must have gotten out of bed early, leaving without waking him. The cabin shared by Nate and Peter, meanwhile, was empty, and the smaller of the camp's two fishing boats was not at the dock. Apparently the three of them had set off at sunrise for another day out on the lake. Jack and Danny, on the other hand, were not very interested in fishing. They were tired and demoralized and wanted a day off.

George knew the feeling. He had no desire to go out on the lake either. Today, or ever again. In light of what he had heard, seen and read over the past couple of days, he had a pretty good idea that something monstrous was swimming around in those tea-colored waters - and a sick feeling that the chances of another encounter were not necessarily remote. He felt a sense of dread just thinking about such a possibility. Even the thought of having to be on the water in the float plane a couple of days from now unleashed butterflies in his stomach.

In the lodge, George got himself a cup of coffee and took it over to the window, where he stood for a long time, staring through the panes of glass at the lake's inscrutable, undulating surface. Close to shore, the waters were smooth and dark, impenetrable to his gaze, revealing no information about what was concealed below. Further out, the silvery expanse of the broad lake was choppy and flecked with whitecaps, while the irregular mountains jutting up along the opposite shoreline were slate-colored in the flat northern light. It was a scene composed of monochromatic halftones, little slivers of black and white and silver and gray, beautiful, but beautiful in a cold, hard way, like a diamond.

In this light, so lacking in warmth, George realized that he, personally, did not matter out here, that he had no value, only a role, and that the role was defined by where and how he fit into this ecosystem and its vast unsympathetic food chain. Everything in this place was eating something else, or being eaten by something else. Like the horny snapping turtle they had caught and eaten the other day. George had cut its gullet open out of scientific curiosity and it had been full of other animals. Now it had, in turn, become something filling their own stomachs.

It wasn't kill or be killed, it was kill *and* be killed. It was nice to be an apex predator, though,

George thought with a smile. He would rather be eating the snappers instead of the other way around. Immediately he was struck by the absurdity of this notion, given the circumstances. It very nearly *had* been the other way around, for Danny at least, which was in fact why George was standing here looking at the lake through a window and thinking about these things in the first place. George's smile disappeared. He had always taken it for granted, being the king of the world. This must be what it felt like just before being deposed by an unwashed mob of angry subjects.

In a sudden flash it all became clear. Nate and Peter and Bill had brought along live bait to lure big fish, but what if the big fish themselves were lures? Thinking they were the predators, George's friends could become prey even as they stalked their quarry, just like the lake trout and the pickerel and the northern pike that confidently attacked the bait writhing on their hooks.

Queasy with dread, George wished that he had never eaten that turtle soup. That ill-considered meal had somehow inserted them into the lake's merciless cycle of life and death. He just knew it. It was as if the drain plug had been pulled from his gut. He felt an urgent need to tell Jack and Danny about this, to explain his startling realization that this beautiful lake with all of its coveted fish was not what it seemed, that it was really a baited trap cleverly and cruelly laid for them, ready to spring closed and exact a cold-hearted but deserved revenge upon them for their hubris and greed.

And then it hit him that, unless he was willing to show them the pictures in his camera, or perhaps Jacques Fortin's journal, they would think him insane, and probably rightfully so. He himself did not know whether he was thinking rationally. Even before leaving on this trip, his mind had not been right. He had been rattling around in a dark, empty house for weeks, trying to process the decampment of his wife and the violent death of his friend. Besides, he was picking up the feeling that Danny was already suspicious. A breathless warning about all of this natural beauty actually being a predatory deception would only seem like callow, self-interested pandering. The photographs would be positively damning.

Danny and Jack had to remain unaware of the danger. Not just so that George could keep in the clear, but also for the sake of their own protection. He *couldn't* warn them, because if he did, it would actually make them *more* suspicious of him. In that case they would see his warning as a ruse, disregard or even flout it, and thereby expose themselves to even greater risk—which would in turn be magnified if they proceeded to become angry and confrontational toward *him*. Telling them the truth would be wrong. The *right* thing to do would be to protect the others by deflecting them from the full knowledge of their predicament.

He immediately felt a lot better about his ostensible moral dilemma. In fact, he now saw with gripping clarity that it was no dilemma at all. It was as if the scales had fallen from his eyes, this realization that being "good" would really lead to a bad result, and that being "bad" would not lead to a good one. George simply did not, in this situation, enjoy the luxury of being able to behave ethically.

He would need to tread carefully in order to manage to avoid sliding down the slippery slope of rationalizations that might lead a weaker or less enlightened person to stop being deceptive. Perhaps the first few truths would only be small ones, but then it would become easier and easier to weave individual little strands of accurate information into a larger tapestry of honesty. And then what?

George turned away from the window and got himself another cup of coffee. He held the steaming mug in his two hands and sipped from it cautiously. He felt a little claustrophobic, confined here in the lodge with Jack and Danny and his burdensome secret. The three men on the lake had better make it back all right. If they didn't, he would be in serious trouble.

George did not want to seem preoccupied, but was simply unable to make casual small talk with Jack and Danny, unsuspecting as they were of the concern he was privately harboring. He needed an excuse to avoid meaningful conversation. It was too early to take a nap. Holing up in his cabin under the pretense of working on his book was not an option, since it would only draw unwanted attention to the idea of monsters. There were a few books lying around, but they were all horror novels. One of them was about a man-eating shark. He picked it up, dropped it on the floor as if by accident, and then, in a moment when no one was looking, kicked it underneath the couch.

What George needed was a more innocuous pretext for holding himself aloof. He began pacing around the lodge, casually examining the little knick-knacks and curios that lay scattered about as if he found them fascinating. Out of the corner of his eye, he monitored the others, trying surreptitiously to figure out whether or not they were paying any attention to his nonchalant meanderings. He had the uncomfortable feeling that Danny, his sullen cabin mate, was discretely observing his activities.

In the living room, George came across a framed copy of a familiar poem hanging from a nail on the wall:

If

By Rudyard Kipling

If you can keep your head when all about you
Are losing theirs and blaming it on you;
If you can trust yourself when all men doubt you,
But make allowance for their doubting too;
If you can wait and not be tired by waiting,
Or, being lied about, don't deal in lies,
Or, being hated, don't give way to hating,
And yet don't look too good, nor talk too wise;
If you can dream - and not make dreams your master;
If you can think - and not make thoughts your aim;

> If you can meet with triumph and disaster
> And treat those two imposters just the same;
> If you can bear to hear the truth you've spoken
> Twisted by knaves to make a trap for fools,
> Or watch the things you gave your life to broken,
> And stoop and build 'em up with worn out tools;
> If you can make one heap of all your winnings
> And risk it on one turn of pitch-and-toss,
> And lose, and start again at your beginnings
> And never breath a word about your loss;
> If you can force your heart and nerve and sinew
> To serve your turn long after they are gone,
> And so hold on when there is nothing in you
> Except the Will which says to them: "Hold on";
> If you can talk with crowds and keep your virtue,
> Or walk with kings - nor lose the common touch;
> If neither foes nor loving friends can hurt you;
> If all men count with you, but none too much;
> If you can fill the unforgiving minute
> With sixty seconds' worth of distance run
> Yours is the Earth and everything that's in it,
> And - which is more - you'll be a Man my son!

Sipping his coffee, George stared at the poem, pretending to contemplate it, in order to buy himself some more time to perfect his strategy of deception. Maintaining a nonchalant façade required a lot of mental effort when you weren't devious by nature. It was going to be a long day.

Despite a promising beginning, this vacation was in danger of becoming a major personal disappointment. There was too much tension in the air now. Moreover, the excitement he should have been enjoying with this new discovery was tempered by the moral inconvenience, and danger, of the situation. Plus, his plan to spend some time organizing his cryptozoology research was, ironically, being interfered with by the appearance of this real-life monster. Now, his attention was being diverted by the responsibility of looking out for the safety of the group, which felt burdensome. Meanwhile, although he had made the discovery of a lifetime, without a body, he had no conclusive proof. The photographic documentation was certainly probative, but even this would, he knew, be subjected to endless analysis and debate. The working assumption would be that it was a hoax, in accordance with the familiar paradigm. His own report as a first-hand observer would be seen as self-serving, if it didn't completely destroy his academic standing. Jack and Danny could back him up, but as his longtime friends, their corroborating testimony would probably be discounted.

The best he could hope for would be to organize a return trip to the lake with a team of scientists and the proper equipment. Of course, the odds were they would never find anything in such a big body of water. A lot of people's time and money would be wasted. George's academic credibility would be completely destroyed. There was simply no winning.

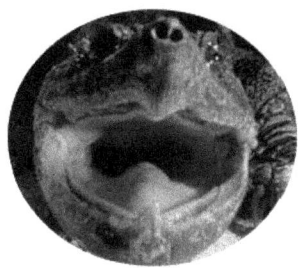

Chapter Twelve

Peter backed away from the rail and staggered over to the helm, where he grabbed onto the wheel for support. He could not believe it. And yet it had actually happened. Nate had been eaten alive in front of his very own eyes. He sat down and cupped his head in his hands and stayed that way for several long minutes, afraid to look up. The sun beat down on the nape of his neck, causing beads of sweat to form along his shoulders and run down his back. The breeze had yet to stir, and the heat at mid-day had become stultifying. His shirt was getting soaked.

The temptation to completely surrender to the fear was almost irresistible, so Peter forced himself to focus his mental energy on identifying concrete steps he might take to confront his predicament. Not knowing what else to do, he put on a life jacket. An inexperienced sailor, he was a weak swimmer as well.

He suddenly realized how dependant he had been on Nate's boating skills. He felt incredibly vulnerable without him around to handle the vessel.

He couldn't call for help since there was no radio on board. So he decided to try and operate the craft himself. However, the key was not in the ignition. He looked around for it, but it was nowhere to be found. Then he had the realization that Nate must have put it in his pocket. It was gone forever. The revelation that he was truly stranded settled heavily into the pit of Peter's stomach. His only hope was that the others would come looking for him. Eventually. Right now, though, the men back at the camp would have no reason to even consider him overdue. Peter decided that he needed to find a way to signal the fact of his distress to them. He located the vessel's flare gun, figured out the directions, and fired off a round. The flare shot up into the sky and exploded.

He scanned the westerly horizon, looking for any sign of a response. None was forthcoming. Fifteen minutes dragged by. He sent up another flare. A few minutes later, he shot off a third, and then a fourth, before realizing that he was wasting his ammunition. Clearly, the flares weren't visible from the camp. They would only be useful once a search was under way. His best bet would be to save the rest of them until after it got dark, when they would be more likely to be noticed from any sort of a distance.

Snap

The boat drifted along, dead in the water, as the sun climbed higher and higher in the sky. Cotton candy clouds stood out crisply against a bright blue backdrop. The water sparkled in the sunshine and the surrounding mountains provided panoramic views in almost every direction. Finally, there was a light breeze, and the cooling air smelled sweet and pure.

Peter scanned the water, looking for some sign of Nate. But there was no trace of him. He had been missing for a couple of hours now, and Peter had to reluctantly assume that he had either been drowned or eaten. Most likely eaten. It was too horrible for him to contemplate. Peter still couldn't believe it. His friend had been picked off like a dangling piece of bait at SeaWorld. The sight of it kept replaying itself in his mind. It felt like a bad dream. But there was no escaping from it.

Nor was there any escape from his current predicament. Peter was surrounded by water for miles in every direction, suspended in hundreds of feet of it, floating on it, rising and falling as its surface undulated beneath the boat's heaving hull. The sheer expansiveness of it was intimidating. Everywhere he looked, he saw waves. Land was only visible thanks to the height of the mountains, but they were so far away that they appeared only as indistinct irregularities along the margins of a watery horizon. He was hopelessly at sea.

He had no idea where he even was on the lake, since he had been adrift for seven or eight hours by this point. The sunken island had disappeared from sight within the first twenty minutes. From then on, since there were no discernible landmarks of any use this far offshore, he had no way of tracking his course. All he knew was he was heading generally southwest, away from the camp and toward the broadest section of the lake.

Peter's situation was dire, and it was getting worse instead of better. He started to think about the possibility of spending the night on the water. He rummaged around the boat and gathered up all of the consumables on board. There were four bottles of water, a cooler half-full of mostly melted ice, three cans of beer, a hunk of cheese, and a couple of packages of beef jerky. Turning his attention to the issue of gear, he found a flashlight, a multi-tool, a coil of rope, a blanket and another box of flares. With this, he had essentially done all he could to prepare for nightfall, which struck him as a depressing thought.

He decided that he would ration himself one of the beers, which he opened with a satisfying poof. He took a sip from the can and felt the cool, clean liquid wash against the back of his throat. Dehydrated and on an empty stomach, he felt light-headed after two sips, and a little tipsy before half of the can was gone. Which was nice.

When the beast ultimately reappeared, it was after the passage of a long hour, and the consumption of a second beer. Peter spotted it in the form of a submerged shape planing toward the broad side of the boat like a torpedo, ephemerally visible in the random shards of sunlight that managed here and there to penetrate the water's heaving surface. Propelled by swift, muscular strokes of its big webbed feet, the animal plowed through the murk, encasing itself in a shimmering, teardrop-shaped vortex of displaced water that distorted its outline as it moved. Peter noticed with surprise how the turtle's algae-glazed shell imparted a phosphorescent tinge of green to this underwater wake.

The boat rose perceptibly on the displaced water that welled up as the creature passed underneath it. The rising and falling sensation made Peter a little nauseous. A minute or so later the turtle came back around and made another run under the boat, rocking it some more. It returned again and again, seemingly picking up speed with every pass, and making the vessel rock with greater force each time. Finally, it took a prodigious run at the boat, as if to ram it. At the last minute, however, it darted up, erupted from the surface and launched itself completely out of the water, becoming fully airborne.

Peter had no time to think. As the turtle flew through the air at him, its great beak gaping, he dropped to the deck. Incredibly, the turtle sailed right over his head, clearing the boat entirely and hurtling into the water on the other side with a thunderous splash. Peter picked himself up, and saw to his amazement that the turtle had already vanished. A few minutes later, it resurfaced about a hundred yards away and turned around for another run at the helplessly drifting vessel. When it was within 100 feet of the boat, it submerged once again. Peter followed its underwater wake as it closed rapidly upon his little bobbing craft. Realizing it was lining up for another launch, he made for the shelter of the head enclosure. Although the doorway was less than a dozen feet away, it felt as if he were moving through wet cement. His arms and legs were rubbery and awkward.

Then the turtle broke through the surface again. Airborne once more, it flew straight at him, this time with its huge beak agape. Peter reached for the door and opened it, but he was not in time. Before he could make it inside, the turtle belly-flopped onto the deck of the boat, driving its port side down into the water. Immediately, Peter lost his footing. Flailing his arms and legs, he fought desperately for purchase on the steeply sloping deck. But the fiberglass panels were slick with spray and there was no way for Peter to stop himself from slipping feet-first toward the turtle's waiting, wide-open mouth.

An agonizingly long second later he found himself lying spread-eagle on the animal's big lower jaw, looking up at a shadowy triangle of yellowish palette and a silhouette of horny beak darkly framed against the bright blue sky. All he could do now was to wait for this massive overhanging jawbone to come down and crush him. In this drawn-out moment there was enough time for Peter to realize that he had one last chance to roll out of the animal's mouth. But he was paralyzed with fear, too scared to do what it took to avoid the very fate he dreaded. Realizing this too late, he strove nevertheless to make a move, but his opportunity had passed him by. Decisively, the turtle closed its mouth. In the process, Peter was severed cleanly just above the nipple line. It was more or less like he'd imagined it would be - a sensation of extreme pressure rather than one of pain - except for the crisp snapping noises made by his breaking bones, an effect which caught him a little by surprise.

Satisfied with its work, the colossal reptile sank back into the water with Peter's dismembered torso and lower extremities captured in its mouth, leaving his head, still attached at the shoulders, to topple back into the boat. The vessel recoiled as the turtle's weight was removed, and it began rocking violently from side to side. The next thing Peter knew, he was lying face up on the deck, his arms spread wide. He was a decapitated head nestled in the shredded remains of a life vest, connected only by the collarbones to a pair of numb, rubbery limbs, twirling like a top, awash in his own blood, staring up at the sky as it spun around and around in his field of vision.

It struck him that it was another beautiful day on the lake. Then his brain shut down for lack of oxygen. An instant later Peter found himself hovering over the boat, looking down on it from above. His truncated corpse was spinning and slipping and sliding around in the bloody deck wash as the little craft rocked violently from side to side in the churning wake. The turtle was nowhere to be seen.

He observed the scene with a casual detachment, strangely at peace with the situation. Mercifully, it was over. Nothing left to see. He turned toward the light.

Chapter Thirteen

It was four o'clock in the morning when George woke up from his post-coital sleep. Laura was still sprawled across his desk, her legs dangling off of it, her arms akimbo, her hair lying in a tangled pile around her placid face, a few gossamer strands crossing her closed eyelids. George pushed himself into an upright position. He pulled his clothing back on. Through the window, he could see the fog was beginning to lift over the campus.

Walking around the desk, he noticed Laura's cell phone lying there on the floor. It had somehow opened up in its fall off of the desk. He picked it up. It was active. He held it to his ear. On the other end of the line, he could hear someone breathing.

"Hello?" He said into the receiver. "Hello?"

The breathing sounds stopped and the line became silent.

"Hello?" George said. "Hello."

The line went dead. George ended the call. He looked over at Laura. She was still asleep on his desk. He returned his attention to the telephone. Without quite knowing why, he deleted the last number from her incoming calls list. Then he closed the telephone back up and replaced it on the floor.

He went back over to Laura. He stared at her for a while, admiring the beauty of her facial features as she slumbered. Then he began to gently stroke her hair.

"Baby," he said. "Baby?"

She began to stir. Her eyelids fluttered and then opened. She looked up at him, pulled herself into a sitting position, turned her head back and forth to take in her surroundings and then, to George's great relief, revealed by her facial expression that she was happy to discover the circumstances under which she was waking up.

"Hi sweetie," she said.

"Good morning, Laura Harding," he replied.

"You know, I almost feel like I need a new name," she replied. "If I'm not mistaken, I'm a different person today than I was yesterday."

"And . . ."

"And, I love it!"

He pulled her to her feet and they embraced, kissing and stroking one another. It was George who put an end to things. "We should clear out of here," he said. "Before people start showing up for work."

"Office hours are over, Professor?"

She had clearly meant it as a joke, but it struck a little too close to home.

"Something like that," he said.

They became full-time lovers. She found ways to spend some nights, and even a few weekends, at George's house. When they couldn't sleep together, they arranged to meet there in the afternoons for sessions of love-making followed by long, cozy naps in one another's arms. Meanwhile, their research project continued, and as it did, the lines between work and play became completely blurred. They discussed cryptozoology in bed, and stole time for making out while doing their research in the library. Their lives were becoming defined by their relationship to each other, but neither of them really cared.

Tim's ghost showed up one night, when George was in the middle of making love to her. George looked up to see him standing there, in khaki-colored chinos, a pressed Oxford shirt and shiny loafers, raising a Martini in his honor.

"Nice going, George," Tim said. "She's hot. You've got a rare look of, I don't know, what, excited contentment, or is it contented excitement, on your face? Go on, old boy, give it to her."

George looked down at Laura. She was lying there smiling with her eyes closed, breathing deeply, in a state of deep relaxation. There was nothing to indicate she was hearing Tim's voice.

"That's right, George, she can't hear me," Tim was saying. "She can't see me, either. Only

Snap

you can. Isn't that special?" Tim stole the next thought right out of George's head. "And no," he said, "you're not hallucinating."

Alright, George thought, *I get it. So what brings you here, my old friend?*

"You know your *Hamlet*," Tim said. "What was the message of the ghost on the rampart?"

George thought for a moment. *There was no message*, he finally said. *He was egging Hamlet on to kill his uncle out of pure bile.*

"Oh. Maybe I'm thinking of *Macbeth*. Then again, those were witches, weren't they?" Tim said. "Okay, I might be a little confused. Cut me some slack. This takes a lot of concentration."

Proudly, he held out his arm for George to inspect. "What do you think," he asked, flexing his fingers like a piano player, "pretty good, eh? Look at the detail. The pores in my skin, the hair follicles, the vessels and tendons. Do you remember this mole?"

Yes, you've done a really good job of manifesting yourself. And it's not as if I'm unhappy you see you. But you have got to understand that this is an untenable situation. So what is it, exactly, that you want?

"This isn't about me," Tim said. "It's about you. I'm here to tell you to watch your step."

That's it?

"Isn't that enough?" Tim replied. "Listen, you're going to need me some day. But in the meantime, for God's sake, don't do anything weird."

And by 'weird' you mean . . . ?

"Unusual. Out of the ordinary."

George looked down at Laura.

"I'm not talking about her," Tim said. "Besides, she's history." George looked up to see what kind of expression Tim was wearing on his face after a remark like that, but he had already vanished.

The next time George saw Laura was also the last. She had been incommunicado for about twenty-four hours. She had not been taking his calls or answering his text messages and George had a sick feeling in the pit of his stomach over it.

Instead of coming to class, or meeting him in the library as scheduled, she showed up on his doorstep around eleven o'clock the following night. He immediately realized something was terribly wrong. At some point during the previous day, she had been badly beaten. Her right eye was swollen mostly shut and her cheek was disfigured by an awful purplish bruise. There were red marks around her neck.

"Laura," George exclaimed, "my God, what's happened? What in the world has happened? Come inside!"

"No."

"No?"

"No."

"What do you mean? What do you mean no?"

Instead of answering him, Laura raised her right hand. In it, she held a miniature digital audio recorder. She pressed Play. The sound of breathing emanated from the speaker. Then came the sound of a male voice saying "Hello?" over and over again. The voice belonged to George.

She dropped the recorder at his feet.

"Laura, I'm sorry," he said softly.

"Sorry?" She said. "Don't bother. You are deceptive. You are manipulative. You knew all along that David knew about us. But you hid the truth from me, George! All the while letting me think you loved me. Just so you could *have* me!"

Little bits of foamy white froth were collecting in the corners of her lips. Her eyes looked bloodshot and the bloom had gone off her skin. "You were using me! I gave myself to you. How many others like me do you have in your past? I shouldn't even care. I do, but I shouldn't."

She reached up to brush a stray lock of hair out of her eyes and George noticed for the first time that her left wrist was in a cast.

"Laura, please," he implored, "come inside."

"I told him I was going out for cigarettes," she said. "If I'm not back in the next few minutes he's going to hit me some more."

"Are you serious? Laura, look at me. Are you serious?"

"I'm going back to him even if he is a brute," she told him. "At least he's honest."

She turned and walked off into the night under a cold spring rain, hunched up inside of her coat, bowed over in a way that he would never have thought possible, and disappeared into the fog. He wanted to run after her, but he let her go instead. Ten minutes later, he went back and opened the door, hoping to find her standing there. But she was really gone. He sat down on the transom and held his head in his hands as the rain beat down.

He went back inside and found the recorder she had left behind. He reset the counter to zero and listened to the tape. The sounds of their love-making on the night of the reception came pouring out of the little machine. A rush of memories flooded over him and he shut off the recorder, unable to listen any more. He put the recorder back down on the hall table and went upstairs. He got into bed and curled up into the fetal position.

The next morning, a Friday, he called in sick. He spent the weekend in bed. When he returned to work, there was a little pink slip in his mailbox. It was a drop notice. Laura Harding was withdrawing from his microbiology class. The next day, George received a terse letter over Laura's signature, with a courtesy copy to Phil Henderson, notifying him of her decision to resign her position as his research assistant. No explanation was given.

George left his office early and walked over to the library. He went up to their alcove on the second floor. He found it exactly as they had left it at the end of their last research session together. George walked over to the table and placed his hand over the last book she had touched. It felt cold.

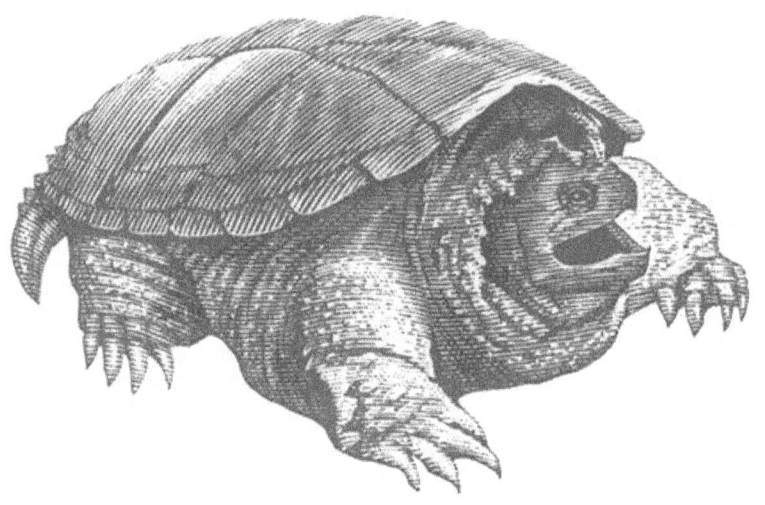

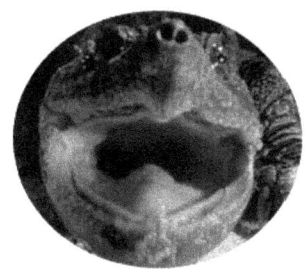

Chapter Fourteen

Around four o'clock that afternoon, the men in the lodge began to speculate about when the fishing party would be returning to camp. They were getting hungry and starting to look forward to dinner. Eventually Jack and Danny took up watch for some sign of a boat on the horizon. George built a fire and made drinks. Late afternoon gave way to early evening. It was about seven o'clock when Jack wondered aloud whether everything was okay with the men who were still out on the water.

"Maybe they're into the fish," George suggested. "They could have just lost track of the time."

This was true enough, since so far north the daylight lasted until well past ten o'clock this time of year. If nobody was wearing a watch or consciously tracking the sun and the fish were biting, the men on the boat would have no reason to even suspect they might be considered overdue back at camp.

"I'd be more concerned if it was getting dark," George added.

The point was well-taken, and it seemed to have the hoped-for effect of dampening the discussion. So they had more drinks, and passed the time waiting. When George's watch read 10:10 p.m. he was officially worried, but he didn't say anything. The longer he could deflect Jack and Danny's concerns about the men on the lake, the better. If something bad had really happened to them out there, he would be in a world of trouble. He tried to distract himself from this unpleasant thought. After all, he was on vacation. Jack, however, had noticed him checking the time.

"It's getting late, George," he said.

"Is it?" George replied. "I suppose so, now that you mention it."

"I'm worried," Jack said.

"What do you want to do?" George asked.

"Is there cell phone reception out here?" Danny wanted to know.

"No," George said.

Danny decided to check anyway, but George was correct, there were no bars on his phone.

"This can't be right," Danny said. "Shouldn't they have told us we wouldn't be able to use our cell phones up here? There's no phone in the lodge. What if somebody needed to call home?"

"I guess they figured we'd assume we would be out of touch in a place like this," George lied, recalling as he spoke these words that the brochures specifically mentioned that cell phones were useless in this region of the Canadian subarctic. "I mean, I didn't bring my phone."

"So you knew . . ."

"I guess I assumed, is more like it, Danny," George replied. "But let's try and figure out what we're going to do here."

"Well," Jack said, "we're going to have to go out looking for them."

"Slow down, Jack," George said. "Let's not make any snap judgments. We need to think this through."

"What is there to think through, George?" Danny asked. "Unless you're afraid."

"Afraid of what?"

Danny and Jack looked at George, waiting for an answer. Danny's eyes were narrow with suspicion. Jack's stare was just a confused and vaguely worried one.

George repeated the question. "Afraid of what?"

"Afraid," Danny replied, "of the thing that almost ate me yesterday. You remember, don't you, George? I'm talking about that big green . . . fish . . . that breached in the water like a whale and almost swamped us?"

"It was a turtle, Danny," George said. Then he played the academically credentialed aquatic biologist card. "And it's pretty well-known that people exaggerate the size of animals seen in the wild, especially during an attack."

"So, what are you saying, George," Danny shot back, "it was only ten feet across instead of fifteen?"

"You know what I mean."

"No, I don't know what you mean."

"Then take a guess."

Jack finally interjected. He suggested they not go out right away. They could wait for maybe another hour in the hope that the boat would finally appear. In the meantime, though, he suggested, they ought to use the time to prepare for a rescue excursion. So they refueled the boat, put a spare fuel can aboard, pulled together some tools, gathered up blankets and extra warm clothing, made a thermos of hot coffee, checked the mounted and hand-held spotlights to make sure they were operational, and threw some more paddles and lifejackets aboard. Danny also looked around the camp for things that could be used as weapons. He went to the woodpile and got the ax and the bow saw. He cut down a sturdy sapling and then shortened it down to a six-foot length, which he sharpened to a point.

Night had fallen by the time they finally cast off from the dock and began making headway toward the mouth of their little cove and, beyond it, the broad lake, only barely discernible in the darkness ahead.

The moon was shining, but it was periodically obscured by transient clouds. When it was visible they could competently search the waters around the boat without the aid of their spotlights. But when the moon was hidden they turned them on and played their piercing white beams back and forth over the wine-dark waves.

They were not exactly certain what they were even looking for. Under the best-case scenario, they would sight the other boat's green and red running lights, heading for home. If, on the other hand, the other boat was dead in the water, they might try to signal their location with a flare. Maybe they had gone ashore, in which case they probably would have lit a signal fire.

A bigger conundrum was where to focus the search. Nobody was sure whether the missing men had headed north or south out of the cove, or even which side of the lake they might be on. There were several likely destinations in fishing terms, and since the other boat had had such good luck the day before, they reasoned that their most likely choice would be to return to the same spot. The problem was they had left without mentioning exactly where that spot was, besides being to the south. However, this at least eliminated the opposite shore, and suggested that they should turn right out of the cove.

George steered the boat on a course parallel to the shore, within a couple of hundred feet of the waterline, so that the spotlight Danny was casting to the starboard side reached the land. Jack, on the port side, swept the beam of his light back and forth toward the middle of the lake. George kept his eyes on the waters ahead.

Their plan was to follow this course until their fuel levels neared the halfway mark. Then they would come about and cover a parallel swath, in deeper waters, back northward toward the camp, where they would refuel and repeat the same pattern, this time turning left out of the cove. They had not gotten around to discussing what they would do if the other boat was still missing at that point.

As the night wore on, George found his mind wandering. He had more boating experience than either Jack or Danny, though, and the piloting could be tricky on this dark night when the moon was appearing and disappearing so unpredictably. Additionally the task required maintaining an optimal balance between speed and fuel efficiency, so that they covered as much water as possible in the least amount of time. This meant that George was stuck at the helm. He drank coffee to stay focused as the miles slowly passed.

Periodically, George cut the engines and allowed the boat to drift for five or ten minutes so they could listen for a distress call of whatever sort. But aside from the occasional splash of a feeding fish and the lapping of the waves against their own hull, there was nothing at all to be heard in the darkness.

During one of these pauses George came up with the idea of sending up a flare of their own, both as a signal to the other boat and as a means of lighting up the lake for the purposes of their search.

It was two hours later, when they were on their third flare, that Danny spotted it. The flare had reached the apex of its launch, exploded in an orange sunburst, and then begun its lazy fall when he started whooping and hollering with joy. Jack and George ran over to where Danny stood pointing with excitement towards a spot at the very edge of the flare's radius of illumination. Sure enough there was a little white smudge sitting up on the water, bobbing regularly in the chop, bathed in a warm tangerine light. When George and Danny finally saw it too, they shouted and jumped around and gave each other hugs and high fives.

George in particular felt relieved. Maybe everything was going to be okay after all. He dashed over to the helm, fired up the engine and made straight for the other hull, about three-quarters of a mile off their port bow.

"Get those blankets out," he yelled over the din of the motor as they bounded over the waves.

"Somebody go forward and make ready to toss them a line!"

The smudge was gradually growing larger beneath the flare's waning light. As they drew nearer to it, though, a sickening realization dawned upon George's racing mind: They were looking at a capsized hull. George immediately pulled back on the throttle, afraid now that there might be someone floating around in the water. Jack and Danny, wedged together against the prow, turned around to look at him against the grim backdrop that was revealing itself behind them. The sight of their hollow eyes made George's heart ache.

George simply stared past them, scanning the waves for signs of a bobbing lifejacket. The elation he'd felt a few moments earlier was but a bitter memory, a cruel reminder of the dire situation that now presented itself. Their fishing trip had become a living nightmare. There was a distinct possibility, if not a likelihood, that half of the members of their party were in mortal danger, if they weren't in fact dead already. Nate, Peter and Bill were certainly in the water. Whether any of them were still clinging to the hull was one remaining question. Another was, how long had they been wet? George refused to entertain further speculation, which gravitated inexorably toward the possibility that they'd been attacked by the monster, in which case the range of possibilities shifted from the realm of the tragic to that of the horrific.

None of them should ever have found themselves in this predicament. If only the others had waited for George to get up, he would have devised some pretext or other to convince them to take the day off, too. At the very least he would have convinced them to go out in the larger of the two boats, the one he was now piloting. Maybe then they would have managed to weather whatever it was that had flipped their smaller vessel. But he had stayed up so late reading about the lake that the temptation to sleep in had proven irresistible. This was not his fault.

George was crafting his alibi even as he pulled up to the overturned hull in the water. He slowly circled the wreck. There was no one in sight. There was not even any flotsam. He'd had no reason, he would tell them, to suspect something like this could have happened. And nobody had even believed them when they told their story of yesterday's attack. Who would have? A giant snapping turtle. Seriously.

The moon went behind another cloud. George told Jack to send up another flare, which he did. George cut the engine and they rose and fell on the silent water near the glistening upturned hull of other boat. By the flare's steady orange glow, they looked around for signs of anyone or anything floating in the water. But there was nothing to be seen.

George was in a lot of trouble now. He started the motor and began tracing out an ever-widening spiral around the capsized craft beneath the flare's dying light. In what seemed like no time at all, they had covered a roughly 300-yard radius around the wreck without seeing anything to even suggest that someone had made it out of the vessel alive. George continued driving the boat around in concentric circles until it became clear that they were not going to find anyone floating in the water. With this depressing realization, they decided to head back to the wreck, cut the engine and review their options.

Chapter Fifteen

They pulled up beside the wreck and considered the depressing sight of the capsized hull, smooth and white as an eggshell. As he stared at it, an obvious question presented itself to George's mind. He suspected that Danny and Jack were thinking along the same lines: Someone might be trapped under there.

George found himself in a delicate position. The logical thing was for one of them to dive under the wreck and find out. But if somebody besides George went in the water, Danny would hold it against him. If, on the other hand, George volunteered, it might actually help his cause. Perhaps the others would even try to talk him out of it. He could initially pretend to resist, then give in and agree that it was indeed a foolhardy idea.

So he posed a choice to them. He could dive under the wreck and make sure there was no one trapped or hiding in an air pocket. Or they could wait until first light, briefly search the area again, and then dive when it would be safer, warmer and more likely to result in the discovery of whatever was down there to be seen.

His plan backfired. Danny agreed right away that a dive was necessary, but unfortunately was insistent that time was of the essence, arguing that their only real chance of finding a survivor rather than a body was to dive right then. Jack went over the pros and cons of each position but eventually sided with Danny. If, after the dive, there was no reason for encouragement, they would return to the lodge.

Danny said something about making a radio call when they got back. George didn't bother to set him straight. Things would sort themselves out in due course, and all he really wanted to do was curl up on the deck with a blanket and close his eyes for a little while. Instead, he began stripping off his clothes. Jack turned on the fish finder and stared intently at the screen, while George pretended not to notice.

The moon had gone behind a cloud again, the night was pitch dark and George was staring down into water the color of Guinness stout. Although the idea of going over the side was physically repulsive, the wreck was drifting away. The longer he waited the further away it got. He climbed over the transom and onto the swim platform. When his feet touched the frigid water, he instinctively recoiled. But there was nothing he could do about it. He lowered himself into the water until it closed around his neck like an icy noose. He freed his hands and began treading water, gasping to catch a breath.

When George was finally able to work his lungs again, Danny leaned over the rail and handed him a waterproof flashlight. As he reached up to take it, Danny looked down into his eyes and quietly said, "Good luck, George."

George was in about 380 feet of frigid water almost a mile from shore on a dark night, but he tried to banish these facts from his mind. He could not, however, help but imagine that the monster was lurking close by, a thought that made his fingers and toes tingle as he swam. For all he knew, he might reach out for his next stroke and feel something solid in the water right in front of his face, or kick against something hard with his bare foot. He kept thinking about what it might be like to be seized within those enormous beaky jaws, which were easily capable of cutting him into pieces with one crushing snap. But he kept on swimming until at last he reached the hull of the overturned boat.

He turned on his flashlight. As he struggled to stay in contact with the rocking hull, the flashlight's beam cut erratically through the darkness over his head like a swinging yellow lance. He turned around to look for the other boat and saw that it was now about 35 feet away, and drifting. He felt vulnerable dangling in the water beside the capsized vessel, knowing that he was exposed at the waist to whatever might be lurking beneath it. So he took a deep breath and dove under the wreck.

Everything was black except for the flashlight, which glowed only dully now at the end of George's arm, throwing off perhaps a two- or three-foot beam into the murky water. But it was enough to aid him in locating the boat's centerline, where the light revealed a sizeable air bubble overhead, the margins of which expanded and contracted as the boat rose and fell in the water. George swam up toward the air pocket and broke the surface, sputtering as he exchanged the stale breath in his lungs for a fresh supply.

He treaded water, making sure to keep a tight grip on the light. The sound of lapping water reverberated around in the upside-down cockpit. George shone the light into the cramped space over his head. The beam reflected blindingly off of the white fiberglass decking panels. He angled the light horizontally and played it around inside the air pocket, realizing now that he was floating aft of the center console, but saw nothing. There would be a corresponding air pocket forward of the console, and an air space to either side as well. George checked to port of the console, then swam around to the other side and moved through this narrow area toward the foredeck, shining the light ahead of him as he followed the air pocket forward.

The air pocket in the foredeck was about twice as big as the one aft of the console. Like their own boat, it had an enclosed head recessed into the console's forward bulkhead. There was also some space under the prow, but this area was submerged. Treading water, he played his flashlight around, but saw nothing. George could feel the strength ebbing from his arms and legs, which were growing numb and becoming resistant to his commands. It was time to go.

Then it occurred to him that he ought to check inside of the head, since there would probably be an air pocket in there as well. But the door was closed and latched. George reached down into the water and felt around for the door's levered handle, which he cranked into the open position. Since the door's lower portion stuck up about six inches into the air pocket, George had no problem opening it against the resistance of the water.

It was completely dark inside. George shone his light in. Suddenly he found himself face to face with Peter, who was floating in a life jacket, staring back at him with a big smile spread across his face. George's heart soared. Then he realized Peter's expression was a frozen one and his eyes were vacant. He was dead.

George was tired and cold, nearing if not at the end of his strength, and the sight of his dead friend made him feel even weaker. His mind raced. Why, he wondered, would Peter have gone into the head wearing his lifejacket? The life jacket indicated distress. Hardly consistent with the notion that he had been taking a bathroom break. Beyond that, if Peter were worried enough about the boat's seaworthiness to put on a vest, he would never have gone ahead and enclosed himself in a small space behind a latched door. The only reason for Peter to have climbed down into the head under duress would have been to get away from something, to hide, or cower, in there, which would explain the terrified expression that George had mistaken for a smile.

With his free hand George reached in and made a grab for Peter's sodden life jacket. George couldn't get his fingers to work properly, though. As George's clubbed hand brushed against Peter's life preserver, Peter's head started to tilt to one side. George tried to right him but knocked him the rest of the way over instead. Rather than bobbing back upright, however, Peter flipped over entirely, revealing that his torso had been severed, along with his lifejacket, just above the sternum. In the instant before he dropped the flashlight, George caught a grisly image of bone and nerve and sinew, all bloody and mangled.

In his panic, George tried to grab for the light but missed. He dove down after it just in time to watch its sickly yellow beam sink away from his reach in a slow spiral, twisting and turning as it disappeared into the silent, unknowable depths.

When George broke the surface of the open lake, the moon was visible through faint clouds and its beams were casting a silvery shimmer onto the waves that rose and fell around him. He could see the boat heaving lazily in the waters about 25 yards away, its colored navigational and white anchor lights glowing in the darkness of the night. He wondered if he could make it that far.

George willed his limbs into action and found he could use the waves to his advantage by paddling in the troughs and surfing down the peaks. He was beginning to feel better in the water now that he was moving once more, the sharp ache of the cold giving way to a tingling, numb sensation as his blood began to circulate again. The hard part was staying on a bearing toward the lights hovering over the water.

Even as he swam George knew he would not tell the others about the grotesque scene he had found underneath the capsized vessel. It was out of the question, actually. It would be sufficient, he told himself, to simply say that there was nobody down there, which was true, as far as it went.

The facts of their situation were abundantly clear to everyone without this piece of information, anyways. Besides, George did not need to relive the experience in the telling, for the sake of his own sanity if for no other reason. After all, he was in the same predicament as the others, fighting for his life against an unimaginable terror. If anything, the horror of his own ordeal had been magnified by what he had seen. He had been the one to expose himself to the risk of the dive, after all. Why should he be further punished for this willingness to sacrifice himself? He could have been the monster's next victim. And still might be.

As George neared the boat Jack and Danny quietly urged him on. When he finally managed pull himself alongside the hull, they were already reaching down for him.

It took considerable time and effort for them to wrestle George aboard since he wore no clothes for them to grab onto, but after a struggle they got him back into the boat. They wrapped him in blankets and sat him down.

"Anything?" Jack implored.

"Nothing," George replied, aiming a horizon stare at a random spot on the deck. "Not a damned thing."

The deck light poured down a pale cone of illumination upon the scene. George stayed huddled inside of his blankets for a long while, staring at his spot and shivering. He was cold and tired, but his mind was clear. His thoughts ran not to the danger in the waters below or the fact that one of his good friends was dead and two others were missing, but rather to the interrogation that he imagined would soon begin. However the questions never came. Nobody expected him to say anything more, apparently. He suspected he must have made a pretty pathetic figure.

George's teeth finally stopped chattering and soon afterwards his hands grew steady enough for him to hold a hot cup of coffee from the thermos. Danny brought his clothes over to him in a neat pile.

"When you're ready," he said quietly.

George cupped the mug of coffee in both hands and let the steam rise up to his face, trying to pull every possible bit of warmth back into his exhausted body. By degrees he regained his strength. As soon as he was dry he got dressed.

He suggested that they all put on their life jackets, which they did. Wearily, George took the helm, turned over the engine and brought the boat around. He pushed the throttle forward. Guided by the faint orange dot of their campfire, they headed back across the dark expanse of the lake toward their little lodge on the far shore.

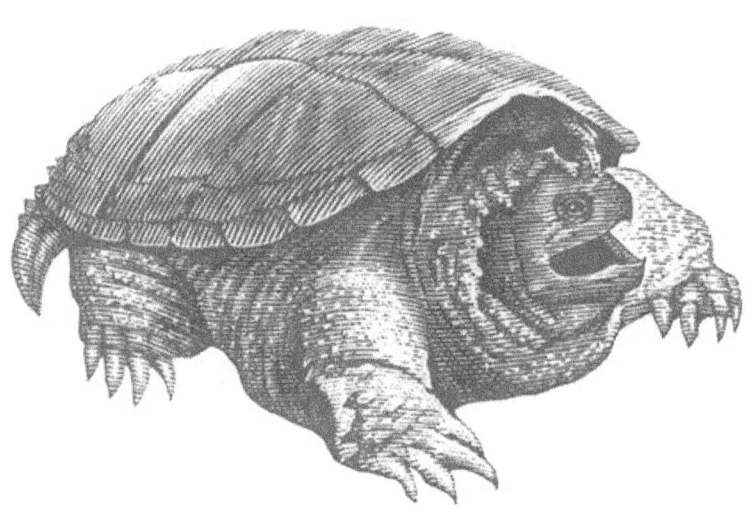

Chapter Sixteen

Webster's *New Collegiate Dictionary* defines "dread" as "great fear, especially in the presence of impending evil." To the modern Western mind, this is an alien emotional state. In a world of driveways and curbs, fire hydrants and traffic signals, light switches and thermostats, personal safety is taken for granted and predictability is the normal state of affairs. By definition dread is an aberration, an outlier on the extreme end of the spectrum of unpleasant human emotional experiences. It lurks somewhere between fear and terror, in a twilight zone of imagination, a space in the mind where horrific danger is apprehended as a probability but not yet experienced in reality.

Rarely does this involve the imminent likelihood of mutilation, dismemberment and sloppy death by way of the claw, beak, tooth or talon. Rampaging elephants, marauding chimpanzees, murderous attacks by big cats, bear maulings, shark attacks. No imaginable act of human depravity carries with it the primordial connotations associated with the predatory behaviors of a man-eating beast. We might beat our arms against fur-covered brawn, grope for eyes to gouge or snouts to pound, scream, shriek, squeal or beg - to no avail. When a beast of nature devours a living, breathing person it is an act of wanton indifference to the value of human life. Such a nihilistic fate represents the ultimate and absolute negation of what it means to be a person, a person with a name and a mind and a soul.

These were the dark pathways along which George's thoughts traveled as he sat in the lodge, staring into the fire, filled with dread. The ordeal on the lake that night had reduced him to a state of mental, physical and emotional exhaustion. Now, he could not stop replaying the night's events over and over in his mind. Peter's grinning face would appear in front of his eyes. Then he would flash on the sight of his wounds.

They had cursed themselves, sealed their fates, when they had killed and cooked and consumed that turtle. It was clear now to George that their prized catch on Day One had been the offspring of the monster that was now prowling around the lake in search of them with deadly intent, which was logical. After all, this group of men, by killing one of its young, had proven themselves to be a direct and tangible threat to the survival of its lineage. This meant that they had to be systematically eliminated.

George saw it all so clearly now. The turtle was in mortal conflict with their party. So far three of them had been systematically eradicated. But that was only so far. The killing was not finished as long as there were three more of them to go.

How, George wondered, had he come to deserve this exquisitely sinister fate? What invisible tendrils of destiny had led him like a puppet to this place, to the circumstance of eating the hatchling, to the state of unspoken enmity in which he now found himself relative to the two other survivors? Was it the lying? Was it his dealings with Laura? Was it the fact of his egotistical motivation for the trip in the first place? Was it even something personal at all? Maybe he was the sacrificial victim fated to die on behalf the whole human race and all of the mortal sins it had committed against nature throughout its generations.

As George sat staring into the hearth, the atmosphere in the cabin around him was pregnant with the tangible absence of the three missing men. There was no more convivial conversation, no one making drinks, or cooking, or dealing cards. There was just Jack and Danny, carefully puttering around the place, hardly speaking, as if, ironically, they were afraid to disturb George out of respect for his ordeal in the water.

If only they knew the guilt he carried in his conscience. Not only over his responsibility for the disappearances of their friends. Not only for their own dire situation. But also, and perhaps mostly, over the calculated deception he was at this very moment practicing at their expense.

There was grief in the air as well. Bill was gone. Nate was gone. And Peter, too, was gone. He had known them all since childhood. They had been his schoolmates, his companions over summer vacation, his confidants, his rivals, his wingmen. He had loved them, in his own gruff way, but truly. And now he would never see them again. George thought of their families. He pictured their wives, now widows, and thought the grief they would soon experience when he brought the news to them. Nate's wife, Elaine, would almost certainly slap him in the face. He could practically feel the sting of her open palm on his cheek. Sarah, Bill's wife, would react differently. George imagined her breaking down, sobbing and going limp in his arms. Alexis, Peter's girlfriend, would probably just go numb on him and turn away. He imagined the sadness the news would bring to their children, most of whom were still of tender years. Now they would all have to finish growing up without their fathers. Years of anguish and pain lay ahead of them all, George realized. When they got out of this place George's ordeal would only be beginning.

If they got out of this place.

He considered with fearful apprehension what horrors might still lay ahead. They might be picked off one by one or attacked collectively. They might be ambushed or frontally assaulted. It might happen at night or by day, on the water or along the shore. It might be imperceptibly swift and totally painless, or it might play out at a turtle's pace, with plenty of time for thinking and fearing as the beast lumbered inevitably nearer to some last cowering stand.

Aside from the marauding reptile, the sheer remoteness of their location was daunting. There was a so much wild, untraversable space in between them and any other human soul that leaving the lake for any reason was out of the question. They could not possibly survive in the wilderness for the many weeks that such a trek would require, let alone navigate their way back to civilization by dead reckoning. Their only hope was to stay put and wait for the float plane to show up again.

George imagined it up there in the big blue sky with its silvery pontoons hanging down, coming in for a landing, the drone of its engine sweet music to his ears. Air travel was the only way to overcome the physical isolation that enfolded them within this crucible of danger. But the float plane wasn't due for another 2 ½ days. That was a lot of time to kill, so to speak. It might as well have been an eternity under the circumstances.

Their best bet would be to hole up in camp for the duration, but that scenario was problematic, George knew. He felt claustrophobic at the mere idea. Jack and Danny both were visibly preoccupied, but George also read a brooding look in Danny's eyes that he didn't see in Jack's. It was a look he didn't particularly like. The air in the lodge was thick with tension. George sensed that his moment of reckoning was close at hand.

And at the very instant the thought crossed his mind, Danny spoke up.

"Well," he said, "I think I'm going to turn in."

It almost came off as a casual statement.

But something about Danny's tone was wrong.

He was forcing it.

George, sitting there, trying to warm up, with his hands folded across the musty plaid blanket that covered his legs, furrowed his brow.

"Okay, Danny," he said after a pause. "Are you . . . alright?"

"I'm fine."

George turned his head to look at him.

"Really, I'm fine," Danny repeated.

George exhaled. "Okay, Danny. I'll be over in a little while."

"Whenever you're ready, George." Danny got a flashlight and headed over toward the door. "Good night, Jack."

"See you in the morning," Jack said.

Danny slipped out the door, turned on his flashlight and headed up the path toward his and George's cabin.

Jack stood at the window, watching Danny's light bob and weave in the darkness as he navigated the winding, rooted path. Only when the lights went on inside the cabin did Jack turn around.

"He made it," Jack said.

George raised an eyebrow. Jack's comment had brought him to a realization that he hadn't squarely faced until that moment.

"Did you think he wouldn't?"

Jack walked over to the other chair, slouched deep down into it, and began rubbing the bridge of his nose with a thumb and forefinger.

"I don't know what to think, George."

"Neither do I."

"I mean, tell me the truth, George, do you think we're going to die here?"

It was a fair question. One for which George had no good answer.

"Not if we can do anything about it," George said. "We can fight, if we have to."

When we have to, he meant.

"I don't want to die here," Jack said. "I miss my kids. I miss my wife."

Jack was looking George in the eye now, pure desperation written across his drawn face. For a long, uncomfortable minute, they just stared at each other. The fire popped and crackled. Outside, a gust of wind rattled against a window pane.

"We have to be strong, for them," George ventured. "We need to stay grounded."

"I'm going to die here, aren't I George?"

"No, Jack. You're not going to die here."

Jack seemed completely unconvinced. Before George's eyes, the pallor drained from his face. It took on a grayish cast, like the skin of a cadaver. It was as if some switch had flipped inside of him and the will to live had been snuffed out. George had the impulse to slap him.

Only a sense of pity stayed his hand. He felt so sorry for Jack, sitting back in the shadows, believing he was at the end of his life, missing his family and speaking his own epitaph. Now tears were sliding down Jack's face. He sat forward and held himself. He began rocking back and forth.

George had to look away. He got up, walked over to the door, and stared through its window panes into the darkness outside. He tried desperately to think of the right thing to say.

He saw his own face reflecting back at him in the glass. He hardly recognized himself. His features seemed to have aged visibly all of a sudden. He looked like a version of himself that was ten years older than he last remembered. His cheekbones stood out more prominently and he seemed to have more wrinkles all of a sudden. He felt bone weary. He was ready for sleep.

Suddenly his reflection disappeared and the window in front of his face flashed brightly in a garish shade of orange. Outside, a hideous, distorted face leered in at him, ghoulishly lit up from below like a Jack O' Lantern silhouetted against the blackness of the night. George let out a loud yell and recoiled involuntarily away from the terrifying figure looming on their door step.

The door flew open and Danny stepped inside. He was holding his flashlight under his chin, joylessly playing the part of the grim prankster. He wore a smug look on his face as he strode into the room, taking obvious satisfaction over George's panicky reaction. In his hands, he clutched a sheaf of yellow papers. George recognized them immediately. They were his notes on *Le Lac Perdu*.

"Awfully jumpy, aren't you George?" Danny said.

"What the hell did you expect, Danny?" George retorted, shaking with excitement. "What kind of a prick does a thing like that?"

George's heart was skipping beats. He needed to breathe.

"I can't believe you," he said.

Then the adrenaline started wearing off and he felt himself go weak all over. "Seriously, Danny."

Danny just glared at him. "You'll never guess what I came across in the cabin, George," he finally said.

Jack looked up, apparently only now aware that Danny had even returned.

"Came across? You got them out of my briefcase. You were going through my things. Give them back."

"My apologies for snooping," Danny said. "Less than savory behavior for somebody who's supposed to be a friend. Of course, you're one to talk."

Sneering, he started leafing casually through the papers he was holding, running a spindly forefinger over the lines of handwriting and pointedly looking up from the pages every couple of seconds in order to fix George with a nasty look.

"Very interesting stuff, George. Your next book is going to be a real blockbuster. Especially now. I guess you found what you came here for. Your big scientific discovery. You'll probably be allowed to name the new species. What are you going to call it? *Georgeis aliar?*"
George wasn't so much intimidated as he was annoyed.

"That's a good one, Danny. How long did it take you to come up with that?"

"Um, screw you, George."

"What is going on here?" Jack wanted to know, looking around in his chair.

Danny turned to face him.

"Well, Jack, it seems as if you and I - and Nate, Bill and Peter, for that matter, God rest their souls - have been, shall we say, misled . . ."

"I don't know what you're talking about," Jack said. "Danny, what do you mean?"

"George, why don't you tell him," Danny said.

"We need to stay calm," was George's reply.

Danny shook his head with a smirk.

"Nice, George," he said. "Way to exercise those leadership skills. Keep everybody under control. For our own good, is that it? Saving us from ourselves, are you?"

"Danny," George said, "I know where you're going with this. It's not what you think."

"What do you think I think?" Danny asked. "No, don't guess, let me tell you. I think you're a scumbag."

"Go ahead, Danny. Lose control. Let's make this situation really complicated. You've always been good at that."

George reached out and snatched the papers from Danny's hands. This was more than Danny could stand. He took a swing and connected with the bridge of George's nose. Blood exploded from George's face and everything went white and then black and then white again. Mucous poured from his nostrils in clear stringy tendrils as his sinuses drained from the force of the blow.

Jack jumped up and ran over to Danny, grabbed him in a bear hug from behind and pulled him backwards away from George, who was reeling in blinding pain. He held onto Danny while George struggled with his messy wound. But Danny wasn't even trying to resist so Jack just let him go.

Danny just stood there, his anger slaked for now, watching the blood run through George's fingers as he cupped his hands to his face. Jack walked over and gave George his bandanna and then went into the kitchen to look around for some ice and a towel.

George's nose was certainly broken. The nerve endings in his face were on fire and stinging tears began to well from his eyes. His cheekbones ached and his eyes felt swollen. He could make out blurry shapes but only barely.

Danny, contrite now, tried to help him towards a chair but George shrugged him off defensively. Jack returned and took over. After several minutes, George was finally able to hold the ice pack against his aching face without any assistance from Jack. Immediately Jack turned around to confront Danny.

"What the hell was that about?" he asked him.

Danny's smugness was gone now, replaced with an expression of gloom. He didn't say anything.

"Danny?" Jack pressed.

"We have to talk, Jack," Danny told him. "We're in a lot of trouble. And I'm afraid it's George's fault."

"George's fault? How could this be George's fault?"

Danny went over the facts. Not only had George suggested the trip in the first place, he had picked the destination as well, knowing that *Le Lac Perdu* had a dark and troubled history arising from a reputation for extreme danger of a mysterious nature. This was actually why George had chosen this place, Danny told Jack. He was researching a new book about monsters and had wanted to do some field research.

But instead of telling them about all of this, he had kept it to himself, consciously choosing in fact to conceal this information from them not only before leaving on the trip but even after yesterday's sighting, and then all during their search of the lake that very night. And now three members of their party were missing and presumably dead.

"They would never have gone back out if they'd known," Danny told Jack.

"Known what, exactly?" Jack asked.

Danny gestured toward the yellow papers scattered around on the floor.

"It's all right there," he said. "They're notes that George made. Research. About this lake. And what's supposed to be living in it. The thing we saw. George was here to look for it. Go ahead, read them yourself if you don't want to take my word for it."

Jack bent over and picked up the nearest sheet of paper. He stared at the page, furrowing his brow. The expression in his eyes changed as he read the words in front of him. He looked over at George, who had his face buried in the blood-soaked compress, obviously incapable of participating in the conversation. Jack simply handed Danny the piece of paper and walked back over to his chair. He sat there in the shadows at the edge of the flickering firelight and just stared straight ahead.

"George, my cell phone doesn't work out here. Where's the radio?" Danny asked.

George didn't answer him.

"There isn't one, is there?"

George just shook his head, holding the compress with one hand now.

"I thought as much," Danny said.

George could see again, at last. But the pain was excruciating.

"Of course, you probably knew that, too, didn't you, George?" Danny was relentless.

"So," he continued, "these notes. That's what kept you up so late last night, wasn't it?"

"No!" George lied.

"So you made them *before* we left?"

George's mind was spinning. His face ached severely.

"No, I meant I did make them last night."

"Which is it George? Never mind." Danny paused and looked away. "You disgust me. Just tell me one thing. Why didn't you warn the others this morning?"

"I was going to," George lied again. "But they were gone before I got up . . ."

"Yeah," Danny said. "I see. Okay, I'm going to bed. Good night, Jack."

Snap

Jack looked up forlornly. "Good night, Danny," he said wearily.

Danny collected George's papers from the floor, got his light and left for the cabin. George, still pressing the compress against his throbbing nose, went into the kitchen, looking for something that might cut through the pain. In a cupboard, he found some Ibuprofen. He shook three of them out of the bottle and looked around for something to wash them down with. The bottle of Wild Turkey was handy. He popped the pills into his mouth and took a generous swig of bourbon, then another.

He carried the bottle with him back into the other room.

"What Danny was saying," he told Jack, "he's got it all wrong."

Jack fixed George with a vacant stare.

"I know, George. Don't take him too seriously. He's just . . . frightened."

George offered the bottle to Jack. Jack took a drink.

"We're all frightened, Jack."

"I just hope it's quick. When the turtle takes me. I want it to be quick."

"The turtle is not going to get you," George said. "I'm telling you."

Jack drank some more bourbon. He showed no sign of wanting to give the bottle back. The fire was dying down now and the room was mostly dark.

"Jack," George said softly. "It's going to be alright. Trust me."

"Just promise me it will be quick," Jack went on. "Quick and clean. Like the guillotine."

George understood the reference. The guillotine eliminated the factor of human error involved with execution by the axe, which frequently resulted in the need to deliver multiple wounding blows.

"I don't deserve to be tortured, George. I've lived a good life."

"I know you have, Jack."

It was true. Jack was a good citizen, a fine family man, a devout churchgoer, and a loyal friend. He didn't have a mean bone in his body. In the forty-plus years George had known Jack he had never once seem him hurt someone, even by accident. It would be important for Jack, at least, to make it out of this place alive. That much was all George could ask for by way of redemption. And failing that, he hoped that Jack would get his wish, and it would be quick.

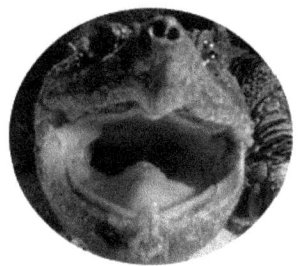

Chapter Seventeen

When George finally returned to the cabin, Danny was already asleep on his bed beside the window. He was laying on top of the covers, fully dressed, boots and all. Uninterested in further discussion, George took great pains not to wake him up as he crept across the room and climbed onto his own bed against the opposite wall. He settled himself down gingerly onto the pillow, his face throbbing.

The oil lamp was burning softly on the table beside the door and George was too tired and sore to get back up and douse the flame. Instead he lay there on his back, watching the lamplight flickering around in the rafters. His nose was crooked and swollen and he looked like a raccoon with his two black eyes.

As tired as he was George still couldn't find sleep. He thought about Nate, Peter and Bill and the discovery of the wreck out on the lake. What exactly had happened out there? George considered the few available facts and tried to piece together a reasonable scenario to explain them. Since Peter was wearing a life vest, it stood to reason that Nate and Bill had probably also been wearing theirs. The implications of this were arresting. First, it meant that they had probably been on notice of the danger for some time. Long enough, at the very least, to decide to get the life vests out of the forward gear compartment and put them on. George could only imagine the series of events that had led up to that grim moment. It must have been similar to the turtle's onslaught against George's boat the day before. The turtle would have staged a surprise attack, but this time, it had been able to destabilize the smaller boat more easily. They probably would not have had a chance to start their engine. Nate or Bill or maybe both of them might have been thrown overboard. That indicated the turtle had probably eaten them first. This was the second inconvenient inference to be drawn from the facts. If Nate and Bill had been floating on the surface in life jackets, they would have been easy prey.

George pictured the turtle circling them like a shark, closing in for one leisurely nibble after another. Somebody's leg. Screaming, and blood in the water. Someone else's arm. More screaming and more blood in the water. Eventually the turtle would have swallowed them whole, life jackets and all, which would explain why they hadn't seen corpses in the water when they had searched the area around the wreck earlier that night. This meant that Peter would have helplessly watched all of this from the boat. But he hadn't started the engine.

Which suggested he had instead tried to help the others back aboard even as they were being eaten alive. Then the turtle would have turned its attention back to Peter, who would have been alone now in the boat.

The fact that his head and shoulders had remained aboard would indicate that he had been dismembered while still in the vessel. Perhaps the turtle had belly flopped up onto the little craft and grabbed him, screaming, in its terrifying jaws, severing him at about nipple level, before falling back away into the water with the rest of his body clenched in its bloody maw. Then it would have bumped and battered the boat from below until it capsized, but not before Peter's upper body had been washed around on the foredeck, maybe for a couple of hours on end, until it finally slid into the head enclosure. With all of this heaving around the door would have swung back and forth until finally shutting itself, most likely as the boat heeled hard to port in the process of finally going over.

All of this while George had been killing time in the lodge with Danny, who hated him, and Jack, whose fondest hope at this point was for a quick death. Which got George thinking about what lay in store for them all. Without a doubt, they would need to stay off the lake until the float plane showed up in a couple of days.

A couple of days. Surely they ought to be able to manage that much, staying off of the lake, *Le Lac Perdue*, for the next 48 hours. Then they would finally be safe.

George imagined the view from the plane as it gained altitude, the lake receding beneath them and then disappearing forever behind the mountains as they soared away on homebound wings. Whatever might lay in store for him upon their return to civilization, it would be infinitely preferable to the horrible fate that had befallen the others. It was a grim solace, but it was solace nevertheless.

George closed his eyes and finally began to drift off. He was just about to sink into sleep when he became distantly aware of a noise outside of the cabin. His eyelids were heavy, making the temptation to ignore the sound almost irresistible, but he fought his way back to awareness. Stiffening on his bed, he listened some more. There it was again, a loud *snap* as something heavy stepped on a piece of deadfall lying on the carpet of leaves on the forest floor.

It occurred to George to try and sit up in his bed, but his head ached so profoundly. He resolved to stay awake and listen but soon began to slip back into sleep again despite himself. There came the snap of another branch and more rustling in the brush. Something was out there. He listened. Another snap. The rustling sounds were coming closer and closer. But he didn't know what to do. Danny was still fast asleep. George considered waking him up but the thought made his face hurt even worse. He might as well just go outside and investigate the situation for himself. Maybe it was only a bear. Quietly, he got up.

Just then he heard a distinct *thump* against the side of the cabin. George turned toward where the sound had come from, over by the window. The thing, whatever it was, was standing right under the eaves, on the other side of a thin wall constructed merely of half-inch pine planks nailed to a two-by-four frame. It was not, George realized, a very substantial barrier.

Time seemed to have come to a complete stop.

Then, without warning, the darkened window exploded into a thousand little shards of broken glass. The turtle's big, ugly beak pushed forward into the room, followed by its broad, square head, blowing out the window casing with a tremendous *crack*. Splinters of wood flew across the room as the surrounding wall gave way against the monster's suddenly advancing bulk.

Danny awoke with a start and tried to sit up in his bed, but he couldn't squirm away, and, to George's horror, the huge jaws gaped open and snatched him up. But instead of crushing him, the monster simply clasped Danny crosswise in its mouth, holding him fast, like a Flamenco dancer bites on the stem of a rose. Its eyes, George noticed, were two angry slits.

Danny started screaming. He kicked his legs and flailed his arms, desperately fighting to escape from the monster's unrelenting grasp. He craned his head around and fixed George with a frantic stare, pleading with his terrified eyes for him to do something to help.

But George couldn't bring himself to move. He just stood there, watching Danny writhe. George felt totally helpless. He tried to think of a way of helping poor Danny out of his dire predicament. Nothing came immediately to mind. The sight of the beast was enough to paralyze him with fear. It was so damned *big*. Completely out of the realm of the norm. A specimen of hitherto unheard of proportions.

This was when George's training took over. Springing into action, he reached over toward the nightstand for his camera and deftly manipulated its controls. When it was functional, he began snapping pictures. After a couple of dozen shots, he turned on the unit's video function. Fortunately, there was enough light being thrown off by the oil lamp to enable him to capture a stunning sequence of motion picture images. He could hardly believe his luck. George watched through the viewfinder as Danny's expression registered the realization that he was not going to come to his rescue. He started swearing at George, berating him for his cowardice.

"You bastard!" Danny screamed. "I hate you! God, how I *hate* you!"

The monster simply turned its head slowly from side to side, looking insouciantly around the room and taking in what it saw as if to satisfy a curiosity, or perhaps in order to gather intelligence about its enemy. George got it all on film.

"George!" Danny shrieked, as he rocked from side to side in the turtle's jaws. "You're a piece of shit! You are a stinking piece of *shit*!"

The turtle had seen enough. It withdrew from the cabin with Danny still in its mouth and retreated back into the darkness from which it had come.

When the turtle's head finally disappeared, George's paralysis wore off. He stopped filming, shoved the camera into his pocket and ran for the door. In his panic, he crashed into the table, sending the oil lamp tumbling onto the floor. The lamp shattered on impact and oil spread across the planks, immediately igniting when the burning wick landed in the middle of the slick. Flames leaped and danced around the room and in just a matter of seconds the wood-frame cabin, dried out with age, was fully engulfed.

On his way out of the cabin, George had stepped in the burning oil and now his leg was on fire. His clothes flaming, he ran screaming along the path in the direction of Jack's cabin.

The turtle was still lumbering around the camp with Danny in its mouth. Danny continued shrieking in pain and howling in fear, spewing vile and obscene insults about George, his awful screams reverberating in the night.

Just then Jack appeared on the path, approaching from the opposite direction. He ran over and jumped on George and wrestled him to the ground. They rolled around until George's burning clothes were extinguished.

They both stood up.

George looked around frantically, fearful that the turtle was coming their way.

"What's going on?" Jack shouted over the roar of the fire that was now voraciously devouring the cabin, throwing flames high up into the night. Then Jack's jaw dropped and his eyes went wide with amazement.

He pointed shakily toward the dock.

"Look!"

The whole camp was now brightly illuminated. By the glow of the conflagration George could see the enormous reptile, Danny still flailing and screaming in its great beak, down by the fire pit, plodding clumsily toward the beach on greenish dragon legs as thick as tree trunks with claws the size of railroad spikes.

George and Jack ran hollering down the path in wild pursuit. They caught up to the turtle, but when they approached it, it stopped and laboriously turned itself around to face them. This halted them in their tracks.

Danny, completely limp now, lay draped within the turtle's jaws like a rag doll. He no longer had enough strength to move his splaying arms and legs, so he was gravity's plaything. His head dangled backwards, swinging lazily in whatever direction the turtle's lethargic movements chose to send it. And with his eyes rolled back in their sockets, the whites obscenely revealed for all the world to see, he was still spewing his vicious blasphemies, in a voice hoarse and ragged, like a man possessed by an evil demon.

The turtle, now on its belly, began backing its way into the water in slow but jerky movements, craning its neck from side to side, dragging Danny's lolling head roughly to and fro across the pebbled beach like a hairy mop. The ground was strewn with some breadbox-sized boulders and as the turtle lurched to one side, Danny's head bounced off one, like a melon, with a sickening, hollow thud. Stunned by this brutal blow, Danny went silent. The turtle looked up, raising Danny's battered head a few feet off the ground, and as it dangled there wine-colored blood drained copiously from his ear holes and spilled onto the stones.

Jack and George advanced as close as they dared, but they could only watch in horror as the beast edged backwards into the water and then pushed itself away from the shore. Danny's head disappeared briefly under the water, only to resurface when the turtle reared around and began paddling toward the mouth of the cove.

When it reached the outer limits of the firelight's radius, it disappeared into the darkness. Suddenly Danny became reanimated. He gurgled and sputtered and gagged before resuming his torrent of abuse.

"Bastard!" Danny shrieked from somewhere out on the water. "You're a *bastard*, George Mapolis! A disgusting, *filthy* bastard!"

The turtle seemed to be circling around and around now, maybe a hundred feet from the shore, with Danny gripped in its mouth, ranting.

"I hate you, George Mapolis! I *hate* you!"

George just wanted it to end. He found himself rooting for the monster to finish Danny off then and there, not out of any desire that he be spared a lingering and gruesome death, but rather to simply shut him the hell up. Danny was no longer the innocent victim of George's duplicity but instead had become an embarrassing annoyance, making such an eternal fuss over his predicament, blaming and accusing and hurling vile insults, even in the throes of this horrible, drawn out demise of his.

But instead of putting a merciful end to all of the screaming and the name-calling, the turtle seemed to want to perpetuate it. It dawned on George that this was a deliberate act of psychological warfare by the reptile, sowing fear into the hearts of these warm-blooded mammals by forcing them to listen to the panicky squeals of one of their own.

Then George saw them, a gargantuan pair of reptilian eyes glowing carbuncular in the reflected firelight, bobbing together over the darkened waters. The turtle was floating out there now, facing back toward the land, coldly staring at them as they stood on the beach in the glow of the blazing cabin, filled with confusion and dread, transfixed by the bright red eyes and the terrible screaming in the night.

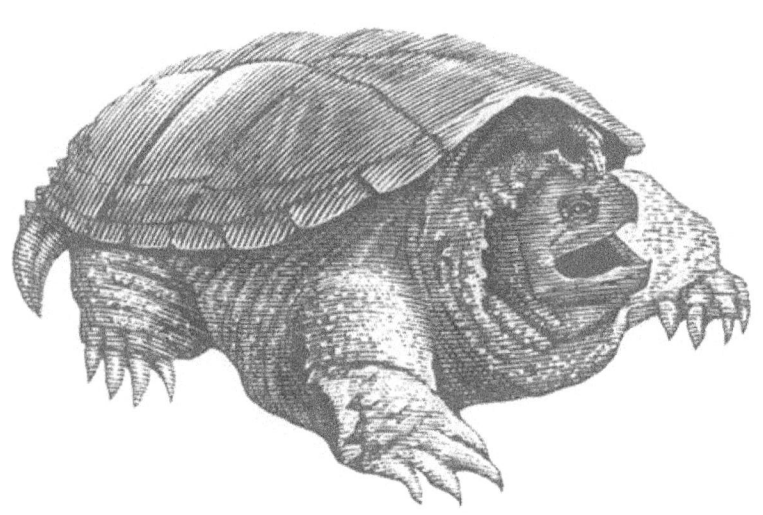

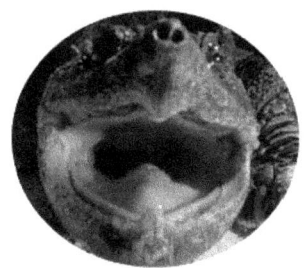

Chapter Eighteen

The awful screams and the crazy orange glow of the blazing cabin fire lent a surreal atmosphere to the scene as George and Jack stared at the eyeshine reflecting back at them from out in the middle of the darkened cove. George's elbows and knees were weak with fear. He stood frozen as competing impulses, the instinct to do something to help Danny and the abject terror that commanded him to turn and run away, clashed against each other like waves in a confused sea.

He heard Jack's voice, but only vaguely, like it was coming to him in a dream. George's mind drifted back to when he was inside the cabin, struggling to stay awake for the next noise, but sinking groggily, irresistibly, back into the easy, numb peacefulness of sleep.

"C'mon, George" Jack was saying. "C'mon!"

George still couldn't bring his mind around the situation. The words coming out of Jack's mouth were like the noises of a droning machine, incessant but meaningless. If he could only sleep for a few hours, and get back to Jack later, he thought, everything would be fine. None of this was happening, none of this *could* be happening. It was, George decided, just a bad dream, a nightmare from which he would awaken any second now. Any second now, he would wake up and find himself back in his bed inside the cabin with the lantern light flickering in the rafters, and he would realize that he had, what, a broken nose and a couple of black eyes, but it would be okay.

"GEORGE!!! C'MON!!!"

Snapping back to reality, George looked up and saw Jack on the dock beside the boat with a line in his hand, the fear in his eyes all too real. George pushed himself painfully to his feet and shambled across the beach and up onto the dock. The image of the wooden planks, wavering from side to side, appeared to George through tunnel vision as he staggered along toward the boat, which Jack had already untied. George flung himself over the gunwale and made his way unsteadily toward the helm as Jack cast them off and jumped aboard at the stern.

Operating on instinct, George fired the engine and turned his head around in time to see the eyes, those red eyes, looking back at him from the middle of the cove, just as they began to submerge. Although they were gone now, George had nowhere else to aim for so he gunned the engine toward the spot. A few seconds later he pulled the throttle back into neutral and the boat washed over the place in the water where the eyes had just been.

With the engine idling, George and Jack scanned the moonlit waters of the cove for signs of movement. They looked around but saw nothing. Jack made a throat slashing gesture and George cut the motor. They listened for any sound but the lake was quiet. It was lost on neither of them that Danny had gone finally silent. Then, unmistakably, there came a splash from somewhere further offshore. They shone a spotlight in the direction of the sound and saw a wake rippling over the black surface of the water at the mouth of the cove, where it opened up into the wider bay.

George started the motor and launched the boat once again toward the spot where the turtle had last shown itself. As he drew closer to the trailing wake it abruptly disappeared, leaving the gently undulating waters of the bay undisturbed once more, and so George throttled the boat back down. He turned on the spotlight and played it back and forth.

Five, maybe ten minutes dragged by. They floated there under the moon, scanning the darkened waters for any sign of the beast. Big gray clouds were moving in now, drifting lethargically across the sky, obscuring the moon and then revealing it again, bathing the lake in cool, silvery light one moment, abandoning it to darkness the next.

Then they saw it, a large brownish hump in the water, glistening in the fleeting moonlight out near the middle of the bay, making for the broad lake, perhaps a half mile off. They headed towards this ghostly shape at full speed, bounding over the swell of the open water with the wind and spray flying up into their faces. It took them several long minutes to catch up to the animal, which lumbered deliberately through the waves on a steady course toward the open water.

Drawing closer to the turtle George could make out the pointed spikes that jutted up on its shell like giant bark-colored thorns. These spiny protrusions, composed of triangular plates fitted together into pyramids of bony shell, lined up in jagged parallel rows along the enormous animal's massive, mounded back, giving its armored hull the contours of a Himalayan landscape. It was an ingenious conception in fractal geometry, taken to its extreme in this instance, but reiterated in many of nature's other primordial predators, like the shark, made up of three-sided teeth and fins and snouts, or the raptor, composed of beaks and talons and wingtips which are all similarly pointed.

The sight of this fearsomely arrayed monster in all of its incredible bulk was one thing but it was its gloomy green and brown coloration in these dark waters on this dark night that accounted for the exquisite spasm of fear George felt in his gut. But he held steady at the helm despite his jittery nerves, maintaining a tracking course as close to the giant turtle as he dared to take the boat.

Off in the distance there was the low rumbling of thunder. George looked in the direction of the sound and saw that the sky to the south had become ominous, with low-hanging black clouds beginning to gather in the funnel-shaped depression where the lake narrowed into its drainage basin. By what little moonlight there was, George could make out a purplish smudge over the water that indicated that rain was falling underneath the billowing thunderhead as it began moving up the lake.

Meanwhile, the turtle meandered along off their starboard bow, illuminated sporadically by their unsteady spotlight, leading them further and further out onto the open lake. The big jagged hump of shell planed through the water with surprising speed, propelled in serpentine fashion by the coordinated movements of four sinuously paddling webbed feet and a thick, rhythmically flexing tail that might easily have belonged to a large alligator.

They followed the animal for quite some time, circling it even, catching the occasional glimpse of Danny's dangling limbs still protruding at broken angles from the creature's ghastly black beak as it thrust forward through the water. They got a brief but clear look at Danny's bashed-in head, although they couldn't tell whether he was still breathing. At the same time it was impossible for them to declare him clearly dead. Even if he was, they needed to retrieve his body if at all possible. They were going to have to work fast because the wind was beginning to stiffen.

As the chase continued, George realized they had to devise some sort of a plan that went beyond merely following the animal as it dragged Danny further and further into unknown reaches of the lake. They needed to somehow get the turtle to let go of him. If it did and they could distract it they might be able to pick Danny up and get him into the boat. It occurred to him that a shot from the flare gun might stun the animal or even injure it, possibly forcing it to open its mouth. It seemed worth a try, at least. He told Jack what he had in mind, and Jack agreed that it was their only real option.

More thunder sounded off in the distance. The winds were starting to gust, and the swell was beginning to freshen now. George looked to the south in time to see a bolt of lightning drop down from the far-off storm cloud, illuminating the end of the lake briefly in a pulsating flash. Big drops of rain were now beginning to splatter on the deck and pock mark the waves around them as if someone were firing a few random bullets from somewhere high above.

Jack got out the flare gun and loaded a round. George positioned the boat for the best shot. He knew there would only be time for one attempt before the foul weather was upon them, which meant that he had to time his approach perfectly, no small challenge in the churning conditions. He wanted to give Jack an angle that would allow him to fire a flare directly at the turtle without running the risk of hitting Danny. This left an aiming point somewhere on the back side of the turtle's shell. He focused on maintaining a steady course in relation to the target area while keeping the boat angled on the quarter into the oncoming waves.

When the boat pulled into position, Jack, an expert marksman, knelt down on the deck, braced his elbows on the rail, and aimed the flare gun toward the turtle with two hands held straight out. The boat was now heaving in the swell, and the challenge was to anticipate the moment when the steadily held gun barrel would line up with the aiming point on the turtle's back as they pitched and rolled with the waves. Patiently, he waited for the right moment to pull the trigger. There was another pulsating flash in the sky as lightning touched down again off in the distance. More thunder rumbled in the moisture-laden air.

George looked back and forth between the turtle and the barrel of the gun, anxiously awaiting the attempt. Taking George by surprise, and yet timing it perfectly, Jack squeezed the trigger. The gun reported sharply and the flare shot from its barrel, a hissing orange contrail following in its wake as it flew briskly over the waves toward a spot on the upper left quadrant of the turtle's shell, where it impacted with a loud crack. The flare deflected off of the algae-slickened shell and caromed up into the air, sailing over the waves on a shallow trajectory for another couple of hundred feet before exploding in a ball of reddish light.

By this illumination they could see that the turtle, stunned, had stopped swimming and instinctively withdrawn into its shell. Sure enough, it had relinquished its grip on Danny, who was now floating nearby, face down in the water, his arms and legs spread out in the jumping jack position.

George gunned the boat over toward Danny, and then quickly threw the engine into reverse. A steady rain was now coming down and the boat was rising and falling on big waves. As the boat came alongside Danny's bobbing form Jack was ready with a rope, which he used to lasso him around the neck. Jack jerked the rope taut and began hauling on it as George gave the engine some throttle. But as the boat moved forward, Jack lost his grip on the rope against Danny's resistance in the water, forcing George to pull the throttle back to idle.

Giving up on the idea of simply towing Danny out of the turtle's range under power, George rushed forward to help Jack with the rope. Soaked now to the skin, they began hauling on the rope, bringing Danny's noosed body slowly closer toward them. Suddenly, the air around them flashed a bright bluish-white and there was an instantaneous booming clap of thunder that reported like a cannon shot. Tendrils of electricity darted erratically into the water around a spot about a hundred yards away, where a bolt of lightning had struck the lake from almost directly overhead.

Just then the turtle came back to life. Its blocky, scale-embroidered head emerged from within the leathery folds of dark-green skin lining its cavernous armor-plated collar. As it extended its neck, it opened its eyes and looked briefly around. It cocked its head toward the boat, fixing George in a cold-blooded gaze for a terrifying instant. Then the turtle's eyes aligned themselves on Danny, who was floating in the rain-spattered water at the end of the rope. The turtle's legs and tail emerged from within its shell and began to work the water in deliberate, powerful strokes.

George and Jack hauled madly on the rope, pulling Danny's heavy form toward them through the water like fishermen dragging in a baited line. As they worked, the turtle strove to gain traction in the water and overcome the inertia of its stationary bulk. In the pouring rain, they toiled strenuously, but the turtle was finally getting under way again and beginning to make progress towards Danny's limp form. They had another thirty or forty feet of rope left to go and the turtle was another thirty or forty feet back, but it was closing fast.

As Danny's limp body slipped through the water, the monster slithered up behind him, eyes glowing like oversized bicycle reflectors under the flare's illumination. George and Jack were horrified at the sight and even more disturbed when the turtle abruptly submerged, leaving only an empty expanse before them under the flare's dying light. A cruelly long moment dragged past as they pulled on the rope, frantically, and with all of their might. But in their hearts they knew it was a hopeless cause.

The rainfall was coming now in sheets as heavy gusts of wind began to sweep across the surface of the lake. Large waves were running northward in big sets, tossing the boat dizzyingly high into the air, then dropping it precipitously down into troughs so deep that they found themselves looking up at the swells from below. Pilotless, the vessel was beginning to yaw as it came around in the weather, and Danny on his rope was becoming unmanageable.

Just then the turtle struck. Cutting across the face of a big wave, it surfed right up to Danny and grabbed him in its mouth like a game fish striking a lure, then sank back into the moving wall of water with his body in its clutches. The rope started flying out of the boat as the turtle sounded, and George had no choice but to let go. Within seconds it was gone, and with it any trace of Danny, or the predatory beast that had made off with him once again.

George regained the helm and put the engine into service with an angry rumble. He brought the boat into the wind and concentrated on taking the waves head on. Now the wind was nearing gale force, and the raindrops were being blown directly into them. George and Jack huddled together in under the center console's hard top as beads of water ran straight up its Plexiglass windshield. Towering bolts of lightning struck here and there on the lake's broad expanse. Their searchlight threw a penetrating beam into the rainy waters off of their prow.

Once again they found themselves looking around for any sign of the turtle, but this time there was no need, since it reappeared within a few moments, breaking surface with incredible violence and rising high up into the storming sky, breaching, and crashing back down with a thunderous smacking splash. It sounded and breached repeatedly, and each time it became airborne George and Jack had to endure the grotesque sight of Danny's fractured, rubbery limbs flailing unnaturally around in wild, anatomically impossible gyrations as the turtle clenched his broken body in its great beak like an illicit prize.

George and Jack now knew with finality that Danny was dead, and that if they were to continue chasing the beast it would not be for the purpose of rescuing him but rather for the purpose of recovering his body, or, perhaps, of exacting some sort of revenge. And yet their need to persevere, or rather their aversion to the idea of breaking off the pursuit, was so deeply felt, whether for the sake of retrieving poor Danny or because the flare attack had whetted their appetites to do more violence to the monster, that neither of them felt the need to say anything about it.

They simply carried resolutely on, following the enraged beast around the lake as it sounded and breached over and over again. They covered mile after mile this way, trailing the animal's zig-zagging course despite the raging storm and the unruly seas. As the time dragged by, George sank deeper and deeper into a state of depression. The situation was completely out of control. Everything he did felt like a futile gesture in relation to a predetermined fate. A conspiracy of circumstances was drawing him steadily ahead toward his own doom. But tracking the turtle had by now become a mission, an obsession, a destiny, so he persevered, oblivious to any other thought.

The storm abated as suddenly as it had appeared. First the wind died down and then the waves dropped off and then the rain tapered into showers, and then it became a thin drizzle. As the night wore on, the precipitation waned until a hole appeared in the clouds over their heads and they could see the moon and a few stars under clear skies. They were in the eye of a big doughnut-shaped ring of clouds.

At about 3 a.m., moisture began to condense in the air, and soon a silvery mist was hovering over the water like cigarette smoke. As the hours passed, it thickened steadily until the hole of sky in the clouds was shrouded over. Eventually the boat became enveloped in a dense white fog that made it impossible to discern anything beyond its illuminated deck. Their spotlight was useless in this impenetrable gloom. George had no choice but to cut the engine. He turned on the sonar and stared at the luminous screen for any sign of a large shape passing beneath the craft.

They drifted along in the water, rising and falling on a gentle swell, quietly listening for any sound. The longer they heard only silence, the more nervous George became. He felt vulnerable in the fog. For all he knew the turtle could be floating right beside the boat. He had the uncanny feeling that it was, indeed, very close. George picked up the stick Danny had sharpened, and held it up defensively. Jack found the axe and stood ready to wield it. They prowled silently around the deck, staring out defensively over the rails, tingling in the anticipation of a sudden attack from out of the whiteness right in front of their faces.

When a small, round object flew down onto the deck and caromed off of it at a forty-five-degree angle, followed by another and then another, George thought someone was pelting them with white marble-sized pebbles. Then he realized that it was hail, falling on them from the back side of the storm cell. The hailstones suddenly began raining down, splashing audibly in the water and making popcorn sounds on the fiberglass decking. George covered his head, but not before taking a few stunning little shots on the top of his skull.

He darted under the canopy and waited for Jack to appear. The hailstones had grown bigger now, closer to the size of golf balls. They plopped into the water, throwing up large droplets in their backsplash until the surface of the lake began to froth. The fiberglass roof over George's head was now reverberating like a drum as the hail pounded against its surface, but still there was no sign of Jack. George went over to the other side of the console and saw Jack lying there, face down and senseless on the open deck.

Terrified at the thought of being left alone out on the lake with the monster at large, George knew he had to do something to save Jack. He looked around for anything to use as a shield against what was now a heavy fall of irregularly shaped chunks of ice, but found nothing. Impulsively, he rushed out and grabbed Jack by the scruff of his neck and pulled him back under the hard top.

George was bleeding from a cut on his head and he had received a hard blow to the side of his neck but he was otherwise intact. Jack was now mumbling, at least, and starting to move his arms and legs.

After a while, the hailstorm subsided and they were left to nurse their wounds, adrift in the fog-bound waters. Once in a while they would hear a noise near the boat, and wonder whether or not it was the turtle.

At last, the dawn broke. As the mists began to clear, they became aware that the turtle had, indeed, been there all along, floating just a couple of dozen feet off of their port side. It had been pacing them as they drifted along in the fog bank, lurking, unseen, right next to them the whole time. George felt a chill run down his spine at the thought.

He pulled out his camera and turned it on. He took a few pictures of the turtle floating in the thinning mists. But the memory was almost full. He reviewed the camera's contents and deleted some of the redundant, out-of-focus and red-eye shots he'd taken of Danny and the turtle inside the cabin. This would give him the ability to do some more filming if the monster hung around long enough for conditions to get better. He stashed the camera in the glove compartment underneath the console.

In the gathering light, they slowly realized that they were on an entirely unfamiliar portion of the lake. As the visibility improved, the turtle began to grow active once again, and soon, George had to start the engine in order to keep it close by. But as the boat got under way, the dark beast veered off, and the chase was back on. Soon the turtle was breaching and sounding again in the waters ahead of them, leading them ever further into these unknown waters under a chilly morning sky.

Satisfied now that the frightened men on the boat could clearly see what it was doing, the turtle began to fling Danny's rubbery corpse high up into the graying sky. Danny, the rope still wrapped around his neck, did wild cartwheels through the air, flipping head over heels like some boneless wonder performing a superhuman gymnastics routine. As impossibly high as he flew, Danny would tumble ingloriously back down toward the surface of the water with equally shocking force, sending up a resonating *smack* that would reverberate across the water when he impacted.

"My God," Jack said, watching this horrific display, "what sort of beast is this?"

"It's evil. Evil incarnate."

George remembered his camera, and took some video of the macabre spectacle.

He and Jack were so distracted by the sight of their dead friend cart-wheeling and belly flopping his way up and down the lake that they hardly noticed when the brownish-gray smudge of Black Island came into view off their starboard bow. As the island drew up, the turtle sounded once again. Expecting it to rear up again, George and Jack looked out over the water with a gathering sense of dread. But this time the turtle did not resurface.

George put the camera back in the glove compartment.

They motored along, looking for a sign as to its whereabouts. Eventually, their course took them directly into the enfolding curvature of the horseshoe-shaped island's sheltered little cove. George circled slowly around in the mouth of the cove for a few minutes, uncertain about what to do. It had been some time since the turtle had left them alone for this long. Having been terrorized by its insidious presence all these hours, the beast's prolonged absence was even more disturbing for George and Jack to ponder.

It was a big lake and the monster, filled with homicidal rage, intent on inflicting inconceivable terror upon them, could appear literally anywhere, in any manner. It might break the surface insidiously and simply stare at them, or it might rush up from the depths with maximal violence. This could happen a half-mile away, or right beside their boat. But it would certainly happen without warning. The lingering sense of anticipation was a form of torture in itself.

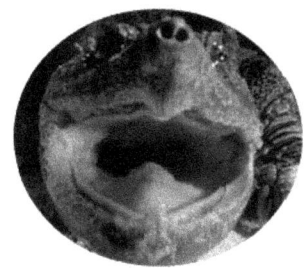

Chapter Nineteen

Sunrise over *Le Lac Perdu* was a time of peace and tranquility. The morning rays were muted, since the sun still had to clear the towering easterly ridgeline. But the flat, diffuse light that did manage to filter in brought out all of the subtle tones of silver and green that made up the colors in the pristine world around them—the dark waters of the lake, the towering, rocky faces of gray ledge that rose high up all around it, and the rugged, weather-beaten pines that clung to the landscape wherever there was enough sandy hardscrabble for them to put down roots. It was a cold light, but a transformative one, a light that baptized and anointed, a light that inspired.

The island itself was a study in brown. Water-stained beige boulders lay mounded at the feet of steep sandstone outcroppings that supported pine-grown promontories of exposed terra cotta soil. George registered the fact that it would be a nearly impossible climb from the water up the precarious bluffs to the floor of the forest that covered all but the uppermost reaches of the island's steeply sloping heights. The island was like a fortress, with its stands of tall trees towering like sentinels along meandering ramparts perched atop cliff walls. Piles of rocks at their bases formed a natural barrier against the breakers.

The island's only avenue of accessibility was by way of a sandy beach in the little crescent-shaped cove on its leeward side, where the terrain sloped more gently down to the shore. Near the center of this short stretch of beach, the land was only moderately pitched. But toward its edges, it rose more steeply upward to meet the high bluffs that closed in on either end. The woods were separated from the beach by an area of mixed growth, consisting mostly of saplings and some stands of scrubby brush along the tree line, with a strip of grassy meadow closer to the shore.

While there were no trees near the waterline, George thought he could see what looked like a log lying on the beach.

But something seemed odd about this log. It was white on one end, George noticed, and brown on the other. He craned himself up on his toes and squinted at it. He couldn't quite make it out. He decided to bring the boat in for a closer look.

He gave it some throttle and a bit of rudder, circled around, and headed across the cove toward the beach, his eyes focused on the thing lying on the shore.

Before he realized it, he was running the boat's hull up onto a sandy shoal, where it gently ran aground. George pulled back on the throttle and was about to set it in reverse when he realized that what he was looking at on the beach was actually no log. It was Danny's dismembered leg.

George shuddered at the sight, and as he did his hand jittered on the controls and this jerky tug on the throttle cable stalled the motor. Instead of trying to re-start the engine, however, George just stared at the severed limb lying on the shore. Jack, up on the foredeck, was also transfixed. Almost in a daze, he climbed out of the boat into water up to his knees, and waded across the sandbar onto the shore. George followed him over the side and together they walked over to Danny's leg, lying there, recognizable as a former part of his anatomy, but now just a piece of meat tossed randomly onto the gravel.

It was a repulsive sight, but one from which they couldn't seem to tear their eyes. The leg had been severed at mid-thigh, neatly cross-sectioned like a piece of meat at the butcher, the stump pinkish like the butt end of a bone-in ham, its knee slightly bent, well-muscled but all white and waxy, covered in matted hair. It was naked except for the beautifully crafted brown leather lumberjack's boot, which still looked almost new, along with the top of the sock inside of it. George remembered Danny, so proud, lovingly working the mink oil into that very boot just a couple of nights earlier. And now it had come to this.

"What do we do now?" Jack asked.

George slowly shook his head from side to side, completely unequipped to answer.

What do we do now? There they stood, Jack with his hands on his hips, George with his in his pockets, looking down at their friend's severed leg. This while being stalked by a giant man-eating turtle here on a huge, profoundly isolated lake of evil repute, with the three remaining members of their party missing and presumed dead. *What do we do now?*

It was a good question. But George couldn't even think. Nothing in his life's experience had prepared him for this. Horrific images from the last couple of days danced around in his head. The weight of his friends' deaths hung heavily in his heart. He hadn't eaten or slept in over 36 hours and his mind and body were dead weary. He was in a state of mortal dread over the relentless, terroristic onslaught of the beast, and oppressed by the pervasive atmosphere of doom that overshadowed him.

Meanwhile, his life, and Jack's, too, tipped in the balance. George doubted that he had the heart and nerve and sinew required to survive the ordeal which he grimly foresaw in the 24 hours that stood between him and the arrival of the float plane. George was no survivalist. He was a scientist. Cryptozoology was just a pet pursuit, a speculative escape, something fun to think and write about. While he was the farthest thing from a dogma-thumping academic, George was by no means a true believer, either. He was fond of describing himself as an open-minded skeptic when the topic came up at cocktail parties.

Still, his reputation as a serious scholar had been damaged by this foray into the world of myth, legend and folklore. The subject was considered taboo by most of his colleagues, who politely dismissed it as speculative or less politely condemned it as pseudoscience, a waste of resources better spent on studying the "real" world. In some circles George was seen as a heretic; in others, a crackpot. And now that he had accidentally discovered the monster hunter's Holy Grail, a real-life giant cryptid, there would be no hard-earned intellectual vindication - because it was probably going to eat him.

"Ironic," George muttered.

"What?"

"A cryptozoologist being eaten by a monster."

Jack laughed. A little shrilly, actually.

"That's funny, George. I like that."

Good old Jack, congenitally civil regardless of the circumstances.

"But can we be serious for a minute?"

George simply restated the big question.

"What *do* we do now?"

"I don't know, George," Jack answered. "But maybe this has all gone too far. It's getting way too crazy. I want to turn back. I want to go back to the lodge."

George thought about it. Then it occurred to him that there was something of more immediate concern that he was overlooking. He was perseverating over a few isolated facts because there was a much bigger, more important idea coalescing in his subconscious mind that needed to crystallize into a coherent thought: *This is a baited trap!*

With this realization, the hairs stood up on the back of his neck and an electric shiver traveled straight down his spine. He turned to look at Jack and just then there came a tremendous splashing sound from directly behind them. Instinctively, George recoiled in time to narrowly avoid the dark shape that sliced past him at waist height like a swinging scythe. It was the turtle's lower jaw, sweeping horizontally through the very spot where he had just been standing a second earlier.

The turtle must have been lying in wait below the surface of the water at the edge of the shore near Danny's leg, where there was apparently a sharp drop off. It had turned its head sideways in the process of lunging up, and now its jaws were closing like a giant pair of scissors where he had been standing next to Jack.

Except, Jack hadn't been quite so quick. When the turtle's gargantuan jaws had snapped shut, they sliced cleanly through Jack's body just below the belly button, and just above each ankle, in keeping with the radius of its bite. With equally incredible swiftness the turtle withdrew back into the water and disappeared beneath the surface with Jack's pants, and everything inside them, in its mouth. Only Jack's truncated upper body and his two dismembered feet remained behind, lying on the beach beside Danny's severed leg.

In a panic, George ran across the beach and scrambled up the sandy embankment onto the narrow strip of grassland behind it. He sprinted toward the tree line. Only when he reached the protection of the forest did he finally stop. Even though every fiber of his being commanded him to keep on running, he had to have a look. He hid behind a tree on the side of the hill overlooking the little cove, maybe 75 feet away from the carnage on the beach. Then he heard his name.

"George?"

He didn't move.

"George?" There was that voice again.

"George, where'd you go?"

George peeked out from behind the tree.

Below him, Jack was lying on his back in the sand, lifting his head up and looking around himself in confusion.

George could see Jack's face quite clearly.

He didn't seem to be in any pain.

He just looked . . . flustered.

And maybe a little ashen.

With dark circles under his eyes.

"I'm up here, Jack," George replied.

"Up where?"

"Up here, Jack, in the trees," George leaned a little further out from behind the protection of his tree trunk and gave a tentative little wave.

"Oh," said Jack, a talking head on a severed torso, "I see you! Say, what are you doing up there, George? Are you picking apples?"

"Yes, Jack," George said, "I'm picking apples. Crab apples."

"Don't eat too many of them, George," Jack said, "or you'll get a belly ache, like me. My belly is aching something fierce. I must have eaten too many of them myself. My mom is going to shoot me."

Jack's mother had died six years ago.

"She's going to kill me if I come home after dark again tonight, you know. I think we'd better get going. We're having fried chicken for dinner. I'm starving. Do you want to eat at my house?"

"Sure, Jack," George said. "You know I love your mom's fried chicken."

Jack smiled. "Well, then don't ruin your appetite on those silly old crab apples." He sighed.

"Too bad it's a school night or I'd invite you to sleep over."

"Well, there'll be other nights, Jack."

Jack was quiet for a moment.

Then he said, "George, I feel . . . funny."

"Yeah, Jack, um, I bet you . . . do . . ."

"George?"

"Yes, Jack?"

"What just happened?"

"Oh, nothing, really," George said soothingly. "You just ate a few too many crab apples."

"No, really." Jack's demeanor was suddenly somber. "What just happened?"

"You've been . . . bitten. By the turtle."

"Is it bad, George? Don't lie. Is it bad?"

"Yes, Jack. It's bad."

"Oh," Jack said. "I see."

Jack could still move his arms, and he began fishing around for something in his pockets. He found what he was looking for in the breast pocket of his shirt, a small picture of his wife, Beverly. He stared at it for a little while, then brought it to his lips and kissed it tenderly.

"I was looking at this last night. It's getting all bloody. It belongs in my wallet, actually."

Jack reached down to where his wallet should have been, in his hip pocket. But there was nothing there. Puzzled, he reached further down, feeling for his legs. Instead, his hands came into contact with the edges of his gaping abdominal cavity, opened wide like the mouth of a cornucopia from which spilled not fruit but lumpy entrails, steaming slightly in the coolness of the morning air. He strained to get a better look at himself from the waist down.

"George," Jack asked, his eyes wide with amazement, "where did my legs and stuff go?"

George couldn't lie.

Not now.

Not to his friend.

Not when he was in this condition.

Not when it was his fault.

"Well, most of you is inside the turtle, at this point," George said slowly.

"But," he added hopefully, "those are your feet, over there to your left."

Jack turned his head for a look. Then he did some more feeling around below the waist. He looked back and forth between his severed feet, rooted in the same spot where he'd been standing when the turtle had attacked, and the empty place in the sand where his lower body should have been.

"I'm flabbergasted, George," he finally said. "I'm absolutely flabbergasted."

Jack raised his left arm and used his right hand to pull up the cuff of his shirt sleeve so he could get a look at his watch.

"About how long have I been like this?"

"Oh, I don't know, Jack," George said. "Five minutes, maybe."

"Well, that's five minutes too long, as far as I'm concerned," Jack opined. Then he turned to look at George, cocking his head suspiciously to one side.

"Hey," he said, "is this some kind of practical joke?"

"No, Jack, it's no joke."

"Well, I'm flabbergasted," Jack said once again, "absolutely flabbergasted."

"I don't blame you, Jack. I mean, I hate that this happened to you."

"I know, George," Jack said. He was quiet for a minute. Then he sighed, and said, "This sucks."

George stepped out from behind his tree.

"Jack," he said, "This is all my fault."

"Nonsense, George," Jack replied. "I should have been more careful, gosh darn it. I'm such a klutz. I have nobody to blame but myself."

George took a few cautious steps closer to the edge of the tree line so that he could get a better look at Jack's face. Jack wore a bemused, slightly annoyed look, like a fussy geriatric, but there was no fear in his eyes. Instead, he was glancing shiftily around himself, taking in the beach, then the trees, then George, then Danny's leg to his right, then his own feet to the left, then the water beyond, then repeating this process.

"Well, I got us into this mess," George said. "The turtle did . . . *this* . . . to you, but I put you, and everybody else, in this position in the first place. I'm the one who set all of this in motion."

George gestured toward his two black eyes and misshapen nose. "That's why Danny did this to me."

"You're being too hard on yourself, George," Jack said. "You've got a good heart. A kind heart."

George shook his head sadly. "That's nice of you to say, Jack, and I wish it were true. But it isn't. I'm a . . . liar."

"I'm not going to listen to any more of this, George," Jack said. "I'm going to see if I can crawl. I'm so incredibly thirsty."

With surprising dexterity Jack flipped himself over so he was face down on the beach, then pushed himself partially upright onto the palms of his hands. He scuttled around a little bit, pulling himself along on his forearms and elbows, dragging his entrails and leaving a slimy trail of bodily fluids on the pebbled ground behind him. He wandered around the beach in an unsteady circle, then dragged himself awkwardly down to the edge of the water, lowered his head and began lapping at the lake's placid surface with his tongue.

Jack drank for a while.

"That's better," he said when he was finally finished.

Jack pushed himself away from the water and rested for a moment, then maneuvered himself around and pulled himself back up the beach toward Danny's leg. He got up close to it and examined it carefully, reaching out to stroke its clammy white skin gently with his trembling fingertips. He looked at it almost lovingly. It was a surreal sight, Jack, cut in half, contemplating a piece of Danny.

"Danny was such a good guy," Jack said. "I can't believe he died like this. It was so awful, having to listen to his screams. He died in fear, George.

"And Nate, and Peter, and Bill. God only knows what happened to them, what they must have gone through. Why did this have to happen to us?" Jack gestured toward his mangled torso.

"Why did *this* have to happen to me?"

George was at a loss for words.

"All I can say is I brought us here and then we ate the turtle soup and then everything went completely wrong. I'm sorry."

Jack crawled around a little bit.

"Sounds like survivor's guilt to me, George. I ate the turtle soup, too. We all ate the turtle soup. We ate the turtle soup and it turned out to have been the wrong thing to do."

"We ate the turtle soup . . . and I lied," George insisted. "And then everything went wrong."

"You're a believer in karma," Jack said.

"I'm a believer in equations that balance out," George replied. "I believe we set in motion our own destinies, that every day when we wake up, we inherit a world that we created ourselves, with the choices we made in all of the days and weeks and years that came before.

"And when we break the rules, we go into debt with fate. And some day, fate always shows up to collect on that debt. And stuff like this goes down."

"Then why did this happen to me?" Jack wanted to know. "What did I do to deserve this?

Look at me, George! I'm some sort of *freak!*"

A little bit of froth was forming now around Jack's lips. He struggled to regain his composure. A vein along the side of his forehead was throbbing.

"No, bad things happen to good people, George," he continued. "It's not so cut and dried. You don't pull your own puppet strings.

"You're living in God's world," he went on, "and sometimes we simply can't know the mind of God. We ask, how can a just God allow so much suffering? But then we overlook the miracles, like when a newborn baby is found safe in a treetop after a tornado. I'm not paying any debt to fate. This is *life* George."

George stared down at Jack, who was on the move again. He couldn't bear such a weird and pathetic sight, so he turned away.

"Maybe for every baby safe in a tree there needs to be a horrible death somewhere else, to balance out the equation," George said. "Maybe it's God's equation, but it's still an equation. It's been said that finding a unified field theory will enable us to know the mind of God."

"What dumbass came up with that?" Jack asked a little peevishly. "That sounds completely Victorian. Freud, Marx and Darwin thought they had it all figured out. And once they had the Universe sprawling on a pin, it turned out that the whole point of creation was to give us these very opportunities to manifest our supreme intelligence by deciphering it. Completely solipsistic thinking. And some of this stuff still passes for enlightenment today, not because it's any good, but because it makes us feel important. Einstein came up with engineerable theories but they became outmoded as our ability to observe became more refined, just like Newton's before him. Our theorizing doesn't teach us the mind of God; it teaches us the mind of us. That's only logical. Is that too much to ask of science? Besides, the next step is the mind becomes so self-inflated that it sees God as the competition, and feels the need to destroy Him. It's part of the dumbing down of science. Like deciding natural selection is evidence that God doesn't exist."

George just stood there, slowly shaking his head from side to side. "All I can say is it's starting to look pretty bad for God. Now it seems the law of gravity pre-existed the Universe. That means God is no longer necessary as the prime mover behind the big bang. Gravity has made God redundant. If God is unnecessary, he does not exist."

"Oh, that's even stupider," Jack said. "I'm calling bullshit. Seriously, is this what passes for trained thinking these days? Those, George, are the thoughts of a mind either insufficiently secure, or insufficiently capacious, to compass both a science and a faith. Obviously, if gravity makes God redundant then gravity must be tantamount to Godhead. Therefore Gravity is God. Ergo there is a God."

"That's not how you define God."

"What's the definition of God?"

"That which is omnipotent, omnipresent and omniscient," George answered.

"Then let me ask you this: What contains all power, is everywhere and can do any thing?"

"I don't know."

"Yes you do," Jack said. "The Universe itself. The Universe is omniscient, omnipresent and omnipotent. Since that is the definition of God, God exists in the form of the Universe. It's good news, George: There is a God."

"But gravity's made Him unnecessary."

"Why should Deistic necessity be prerequisite for God's existence? That's an invalid premise. In fact, isn't a 'necessary' God a contradiction in terms? If God is necessary, then that constitutes a limitation on Him. He'd have to be in certain places, doing certain things, at certain times, to keep it all running. That is inconsistent with the idea of his omnipotence, because by definition being omnipotent comprises the ability to do nothing. The real question is whether he could have been where the Universe began, when it began there. If so we can't rule Him out."

"But," George said, "that would mean God would also have to have the power to not be somewhere, but he's supposed to be omnipresent. His omnipresence limits his omnipotence by requiring that He exist in all places even if He doesn't want to."

"Which," replied Jack, "is why the universe is always either contracting or expanding. Because when God leaves a place, it cannot continue to exist, because his omnipresence requires that he be in it; Since he cannot be in that place which he has left by the exercise of his power of departure, that place must cease to be immediately as he leaves it. Meanwhile, God also must by virtue of his omnipotence have the ability to create new space, which he will instantaneously occupy in keeping with his omnipresence. Thus we have black holes and quasars. It's God simultaneously coming in and going out of different places at the same time, and the same place at different times, and vice-versa. They are the scientific proof that God does indeed exist, and, even though we don't need it, that he's 'necessary.'"

"Not so fast, Jack," George said, "What about the free-will/foreknowledge paradox?"

"The lop-sided idea that we can't have free will while God has foreknowledge is the product of clumsy intellectual workmanship," Jack said. "God simply knows the choices we're going to make before we make them. We're not that hard to figure out, and, since He's omniscient, God must know all of the possibilities. He sees them all play out, instant by instant, in their infinite iterations, and watches us do what we're going to do before we do it, all the way down each causal chain, in a flash of insight. With the passage of each temporal increment, vast numbers of these possibility chains evaporate, while the remaining ones coalesce into probability vectors that consolidate as choices are made. To the extent God cares to know about what any one person is going to do in reference to a given situation, he identifies the ultimate outcome of the decision maker's choices the instant he reflects upon the matter. "I might add," Jack said, looking with barely concealed disgust at George, the scientist, "it is through this form of contemplation that we may try to know the mind of God. We do no ennobling thing when we pretend to do so by presumptuously trying to deconstruct His creation. Truly evolved people are spiritual creatures who believe in a purpose and a power greater than themselves. There's more between heaven and earth than is dreamt of in your cosmology."

Suddenly something went whizzing past George's head, bounced of a nearby tree, and landed at his feet. He looked down and saw that it was Jack's severed left foot, still in its shoe. He looked up again in time to see Jack, down on the beach, picking up his other foot, which he hurled after the first. It landed harmlessly in the brush a few yards in front of George.

"Here," Jack yelled. "I guess I won't be needing these anymore!" Then he laughed that shrill laugh again. Then he sank down onto his chest. Then he cranked his head around in the sand so he could look up at George, and then he began to sing, slowly, in a languid, breathy voice:

> Mine eyes have seen the glory of the coming of the Lord;
> He is trampling out the vintage where the grapes of wrath are stored;
> He hath loosed the fateful lightning of His terrible swift sword;
> His truth is marching on. . .

He meandered around distractedly in the song, stumbling through the watch fires of a hundred or more circling camps, staggering near altars built in evening dews and damps, reading righteous sentences by dim and flaring lamps. He harkened to the trumpet that shall never call retreat, and followed a stony pathway toward the Father's judgment seat. He was dying to make men holy, he was dying to make them free. He was dying for no good reason at all, while the truth kept marching on.

When he was through, Jack lowered his head gently onto the sand. He lay there for a while in silence, his breathing now coming slow and labored.

"Stay with me, Jack," George said. "Stay with me. I'm right here."

"I feel cold," Jack said. "So . . . cold."

"Jack, don't go . . ."

"Who would have thought I would die out here like this, George, from eating too many crab apples?"

George waited for Jack to say something more, but there was only silence. Jack's jaw had gone slack. George could see his eyes glazing over, slowly hardening into a frozen stare. Then his face gradually turned an ashen shade of bluish gray. He laid there, his face craned sideways on the beach, gazing toward George, arms spread wide, half a man, not moving any more. He was dead.

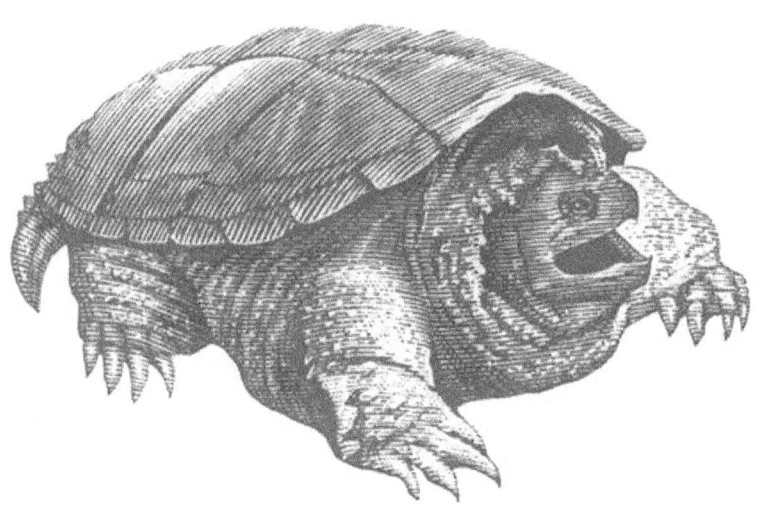

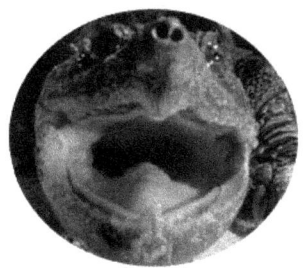

Chapter Twenty

George dropped to his knees. The effect of this final death was that he was now completely alone. The realization of this decisive and irrevocable change in the status of things hit him like a gut punch. All five of them were gone. And while he would grieve the loss of these lives in due time, it was the sheer loneliness that suddenly descended upon him as the sole surviving member of their doomed little party that accounted for the dreadful feeling in his belly. The despairing thought of his absolute and impenetrable solitude was enough, almost, to inspire him to panic. There was nobody else on the lake anymore, not another living soul, aside from George.

He cupped his broken face in his hands and began to sob. After a while, he felt the impulse to look up and when he did, he noticed that the turtle had reappeared on the beach. It had apparently been standing there for a while, just staring at him.

"Oh yeah," George said quietly, looking at the leathery old reptile. "You."

Wearily, George pushed himself back onto his feet. His joints ached and his muscles were tired and sore. He barely even had the will to continue. He wanted to retreat further into the protection of the tree trunks, but he was afraid that any movement might goad the turtle into action. Right now, it seemed lethargic under the hot midday sun, content for the time being to bask on the warming sand. Maybe it would fall asleep.

George realized that he had to get back to the boat. But unless the turtle dozed off, that would be out of the question. Even if it did, it would be nearly impossible for him to work his way down to the shore and sneak around it without waking it up. Then there was the issue of getting into the boat and backing it off of the shoal. Yet it was his only hope.

So George sat down again and settled in to wait. After a few minutes, he decided to lie down. Curled up in the fetal position, his face in the cool grass, he watched.

When George woke up, it was dark. Falling asleep had been a big mistake. It took an incredible amount of effort for him to pump the strength back into his weary limbs, and his mind resisted any effort at wakefulness. By degrees, though, he managed to gather himself.

He realized that he had lost not only the daylight, but also the opportunity to sneak past the turtle, in all likelihood. Sure enough, when he was finally able to get to his feet, he could see by the light of the moon that the turtle was gone. He looked around for any sign of it, either on land or in the water, but saw none. The boat was still there. But to run for it would have been suicidal. Certainly, the turtle was lying in wait, expecting him to do just that. Wherever it was, it would not be very far away. He knew by now that it was a creature of considerable cunning and determination, and that its preferred method of attack was by ambush. It was guarding the boat against an attack from the shore, he was certain.

George thought for a minute, trying to recall what he knew about the predatory habits of the snapping turtle. At night, it hunted mostly by its olfactory senses. It would be able to pinpoint his location even in the dark with its incredibly keen sense of smell. But George needed every possible advantage now, and stealth was chief among them. It occurred to him to take off his clothes and leave them there, on the little bluff above the cove, to keep the turtle's attention focused on that spot. He needed to move, but he could not afford to be detected.

The night was relatively temperate, and the air did not hold the chill that George had expected to feel once he had stripped off his clothes. On the contrary, he felt strangely liberated, animalistic even, like a naked primate, wary at the edge of a forest overlooking a moonlit cove on a prehistoric evening. He could hear the sounds of the night with incredible clarity, and when he sniffed the air he smelled the scent of pine along with the humidity of the lake. The floor of the forest felt familiar and comforting beneath his bare feet, and he could discern its subtlest textures and contours with his soles, like a blind man absorbing the contents of a page of Braille.

George's conscious mind began to recede, and as it did a preternatural sort of awareness replaced it, as if some primitive hominid deep inside of him had been awakened from its millennial sleep. George turned impulsively and withdrew into the blackness of the forest with a series of quick, stealthy steps. He crouched down and began to feel his way silently up the wooded hillside, maneuvering himself around tree trunks and underneath branches and over the thickly rooted, pine-needle-strewn ground with intelligently groping hands and forgiving, carefully placed bare feet. Even though everything around him was dark as pitch, George's nerve endings were alive and the hair follicles on his naked skin were like a thousand little antennae. Instinctively, he understood that to snap a fallen twig or rustle a low-hanging branch could hasten his death. His whole being was attuned to the subtle intricacies of the forest floor.

George climbed this way for what must have been an hour when he came upon a clearing, a patch of meadow several acres in size, about halfway up the island's sloping shoulder. He slipped into the waist-high grass and walked quietly across the field. He found a thorny patch of blackberries and stopped to gather and eat some.

When he was finished, he picked another couple of handfuls, made a paste of them and then smeared the juice on his face, arms, chest and legs, turning them a dark, inky purple. On the other side of the clearing, he reentered the woods and continued on up toward the height of the land.

Finally George emerged from the forest and stepped into the clear. He found himself on a craggy, treeless promontory of striated bedrock, the backbone of an exposed, twisting ridgeline at the island's summit. The opposite side of the ridge formed an escarpment that dropped off precipitously in a cascading series of cliffs and ledges perched high above the water. George stood at the edge of one of these cliffs and surveyed the broad expanse of lake spread out beneath him.

The moon cast a silvery light onto the calm surface of the water. In the distance he could barely discern the smudge of the opposite shore. The scene shimmered under a faintly pulsating light. It occurred to George that he might be seeing all of this for the last time but he didn't dwell on the thought. Instead he dropped onto his knees, turned around and edged his way backwards over the lip of the cliff, feeling around with his bare foot for a toehold in the rock.

He began the long climb down, clinging to the jagged rock wall over precipitously exposed drops, tracing a route down the cliff's face by trial and error, moving lower and lower through a series of descending ledges and outcroppings. When he finally reached the boulder field at the foot of the cliff, he sat down and rested. After a few minutes, George's cramping arms and legs started to loosen up again. He rose stiffly to his feet and began picking his way down toward the waterline at the base of the boulder field. Soon, he was standing at the shore.

The waves lapping against the algae-coated rocks were the color of root beer. George reached down and put his hand in the water. It was cool but not frigid. He climbed down into the lake, pushed off from the rocks and began swimming south along the island's windward coast, following its circumference, with the idea of finding the little cove on the other side and secretly slipping aboard the boat by way of the water.

George swam along the shoreline until he reached the island's southernmost tip, where he rounded the point and continued swimming on the leeward side. Now the towering bulk of the island blocked out the moon, and the darkness was profound. He stayed as close to the shore as he could, wading whenever possible, feeling his way among the submerged boulders, careful to avoid making any sort of noise in the water. He was beginning to tire, but he continued on, knowing that he was within a few dozen yards of his goal.

Once he reached that goal, however, he was not sure whether or not it would mean the end of his life. No more sunsets, no more hot dogs, no more kisses. Looking back on his life, he experienced a complicated admixture of both longing and regret. It was all bittersweet. So many of the good memories were tinged with melancholy, and most of the bad ones were redeemed by what had been amazing. His had been a wonderful but sad life, and it hit him that he was what people referred to when they talked about a lost soul.

He remembered simpler, more innocent times, when he was still a child in the bosom of his family. When he was two, his brother was born and he was given a bubble gum cigar. When he was three, he walked on his grandpa's feet. When he was four, he ran away from home, outfitted with a bandana made into a sack and tied on the end of a stick, given to him by his mother in support of his plan. He got as far as the woods behind the house, then got homesick. Now he was homesick for Laura in very much the same way. Did she ever think of him? Did she even want to remember anything about him? Had she kept any photographs of him? All he had were memories of her.

When he finally reached the little outcropping of land that marked the cove's southerly entrance, he quietly took cover alongside a partially submerged rock and covertly surveyed the scene before him. He could make out the crescent shape of the beach and the outline of the boat on the sandbar near the shore. There was no sign of the turtle.

George was separated from the boat now by a short swim directly across the cove. Assuming the turtle was expecting him to approach from the forest he might be able to sneak in undetected from the rear. If on the other hand it was guarding the mouth of the cove, George would probably be attacked in the water before reaching the boat.

Either way, George's decisive moment had arrived. He pushed off from the rock and began his silent swim across the little stretch of open water, unsure what might be lurking below. He made very slow progress, since his main concern was avoiding any noise. Naked and completely vulnerable in the dark water, it took every ounce of self control for George to maintain this deliberate pace, knowing he might be cut in half at any moment.

When George finally reached the swim platform at the boat's stern, he carefully opened the folding step ladder and lowered it gently into the water. He climbed slowly up onto the platform and lay down in the shadow of the transom. He didn't move at all, petrified about giving himself away.

He thought it through. He would carefully make his way over the transom, step into the cockpit and creep forward toward the helm. He would start the engine, put it in reverse and pull the prow off of the sand. Then he would bring the boat sharply around and gun it. The turtle would either give chase from the land, rise up attacking from the shallows, or appear ready to defend the mouth of the cove.

The only surprise was that in the actual event, he did all of these things, but there was no attack. No showing, even, of the turtle's presence. George had simply started the engine, backed off of the shoal and pulled out of the cove without incident.

Once he was in the clear, George steered a course directly away from Black Island at full speed. For a brief moment, he was exhilarated as the boat plowed through the water, leaving the island's craggy outline in its frothy wake. But then the engine began to sputter and cough, and then it stopped altogether. He had run out of gas.

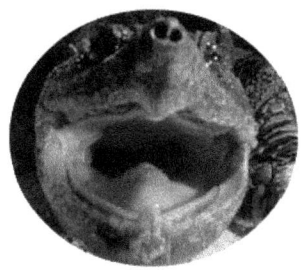

Chapter Twenty-One

In the darkness, George could make out the lurking silhouette of Black Island about half a mile off of his stern. He could see the outline of the lake's eastern coast perhaps a mile off of his port side, and the opposite shore of the lake lay about five miles off of starboard. He was drifting in a small chop, bobbing up and down, dead in the water.

No longer engaged in piloting the boat, George realized he was shivering in the cool night air. He looked around the vessel for some spare clothes. In one of the storage lockers, he found an old pair of nylon fishing pants, a spare windbreaker and a pair of sandals. There were also the blankets. He put on the clothes and wrapped a blanket around himself.

Then he checked on the fuel situation. They had switched over to the spare tank sometime last night, with the gauge reading empty. He switched the tank back but decided not to start the motor yet. It was possible if not likely that he would need power again before the night was over and he wanted to conserve whatever measly supply of gasoline remained for such an emergency.

At least he had gotten off of the island. George thought back on his harrowing escape, and it occurred to him that he might, after all, have the survival instincts to make it out of here alive. Now he had the hope that the float plane would spot him from the air when it arrived the next morning, if he could survive this one last night on the water. He even had a few flares left. All was not lost. As long as he could fend off the turtle for a little while longer, he would be okay, which raised, once again, the uncomfortable question: Where was it?

Bitter experience had taught him that this diabolical monster had not given up on killing him. He was the last victim on its list. His very existence was an insult, and it stood to reason that the turtle would be hell-bent on finishing what it had started. This led to the realization that the turtle knew exactly where he was, and had probably even engineered this whole situation. After all, it had had him pinned down. His escape could not have been an oversight. The beast was too methodical. And why would it not want to take the fight back onto the lake? It had taken three of them off of a boat, and the water was the environment in which its natural advantages operated to the greatest effect.

George turned on the deck lights. He grabbed the flare gun and sat on the seat in front of the helm, prepared to start the engine if need be. He settled in to wait out the night, one eye on the sonar screen, one eye looking over the gunwale, wrapped in his blanket, ready to respond to the coming attack. As the time passed, George began to think about his predicament. He was tired. He was undernourished. He was exposed. His inner primate had crawled back into its hole and he was now just a scientist again, in over his head.

That familiar old sense of pure dread began to rise up in his gut again. Beads of sweat broke out on his forehead. For the first time since Jack's death, he felt fear. George got up and pulled out the ax and the sharpened branch and some paddles and positioned them strategically around the boat. Against his better judgment he went to the rail and began peering over the side.

The overhead lights illuminated the water near the boat in a pale greenish glow, enabling him to see several feet into the water alongside the hull. But below that the waters were impenetrably dark. It made an arresting image, this bowl-shaped area of spectral fluorescence defined so sharply at the margins by a spherical rim of blackness. The water teemed with aquatic organisms, visible in the pulsating luminescence. It was a curious phenomenon, one with which he was unfamiliar. He decided to snap some pictures of the strange effect in the water, in the event that it might prove to be scientifically significant.

He went over to the glove compartment, pulled out his camera and turned it on. He was grateful that, for all of the suffering and death that had come of the trip, at least he still had this little piece of technology with all of the amazing images it contained. He leaned over the side and reached out with his left hand so that he could aim the lens straight down into the water. He clicked off a few stills, then switched on the video and extended the camera back over the rail to capture the shimmering effect.

Suddenly the phosphorescent patch of water he was filming began to boil before his eyes and an instant later the monster appeared, rearing upward from directly below with its huge jaws gaping. It climbed toward him with astonishing speed, breaking the surface before he even knew what was happening. Instinctively, George arched backwards as the turtle rose out of the water. A split second later its great bony beak snapped shut with a resounding *crack* within inches of his face. The monster hovered for one instant at the height of its climb then fell back into the water with a noisy splash, and quickly sank out of sight.

George reeled away from the rail in a state of shock, his mind a blur. He cowered in the middle of the foredeck, waiting for the next attack, but it never came. He had somehow survived once again. He had underestimated the danger, let his guard down, and the turtle had been there to seize the opportunity. But he was still alive. And suddenly, instead of being fearful, he felt defiant.

"Screw you!" he screamed into the night.

"Screw you!" he repeated.

To add emphasis, he raised both middle fingers toward the sky.

"SCREW YOU!!!"

Then George became aware of a warm liquid running down his left arm. He lowered his hands and saw, to his horror, that instead of two middle fingers, he only had one. His right hand was still making an obscene gesture, but his left hand had been neatly severed at the wrist, and was gone. The ends of his two arm bones were just visible, gleaming a dull bluish-white, and blood the color of Pinot Noir was spurting rhythmically from the amputated limb.

George dropped to his knees and held his bleeding stump out in front of him, trying to process what it was that was happening. Burgundy-colored blood continued to gush from the wound. A viscous, crimson puddle of it was expanding across the deck. Eventually, he realized that he was in the process of bleeding to death, and that he needed to do something about it, fast. Finding a length of cord and working with his good right hand, he wrapped it around his wounded arm. Then he tied it in a double half-hitch, which he tightened as best he could. Blood continued to dribble from his stump, but the worst of the gushing at least had been staunched by this improvised tourniquet.

He got up and staggered over to the helm. He turned off the deck lights but was overcome by dizziness before he could start the engine. He collapsed to the deck, rolled over on his back and lay there, staring up at the stars. Beside him was a canoe paddle. He reached for it with his good hand. He brought it up to his chest and clung to it. He tried to stay focused but his oxygen-starved brain refused to comply. He was starting to feel numb all over. The stars were whirling around and around in the sky over his head. He couldn't remember what it was he was supposed to be worrying about. Nothing made sense anymore. He knew he was blacking out, but there was nothing he could do about it.

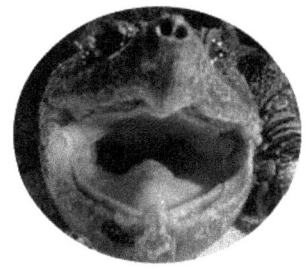

Chapter Twenty-Two

Lighter than helium, George rose up out of his body and floated above the boat, floated above the lake, floated above the mountains, kept going up into the night sky. The dark contours of the earth dropped away beneath his soles. He was enveloped in clouds until a hurricane's eye whirlpooled open and the heavens were revealed. George kept ascending. Finally the last ion-rich vapors of the upper atmosphere appeared, swirling against the firmament in iridescent curlicues. The craters on the cheeks of the moon had become more sharply defined. The constellations twinkled. All of the uncounted stars and galaxies of the universe were assembled. To the north, diaphanous tracings of light pulsated above the planet's curvature.

The Aurora Borealis rested upon the brow of the earth like a shimmering crown, its reds, greens and blues pastel and diffuse, the colors of rainbows, prisms, sundogs, crystals. Spectral shapes coalesced and dissolved within the aurora's undulating pleats. Where the sheets of tinted light overlapped, holographic figures were materializing and then fading out. The craters on the cheeks of the moon seemed more sharply defined. The occasional meteor flickered across the sky. The planet rotated and revolved.

George's attention circled back to the moon. It was nearly full, and glossy droplets of blood were beading up on it like sweat. The light it reflected had an amber cast. The lunar surface was buttery, while the beads of blood glistened darkly, a polka-dotted sphere dangling in the void. Eventually the blood began to ooze down the moon's face. As if through pores, new droplets began appearing to replace the ones that were creeping toward the moon's lower pole, where they were collecting in a little pool and then dribbling off, one by one. George was hovering on the boundary between two realms: Below him lay the world as he knew it, above lurked a moon that wept blood.

And then, slow but unrelenting, came the darkness. The aurora was shriveling and the heavens were growing dimmer. The bespattered moon lost its luster, and the blue-and-white belly of the illuminated earth shrank and shrank until the planet dwindled entirely into the black backdrop of space.

Eventually, even the most distant points of light blinked and then, one after another, disappeared, and George was abandoned into darkness as complete as if he'd had his eyes put out. From somewhere, the howling of mongrels.

Barrington, New Hampshire, was a sleepy little town in the early 1970s. It had one traffic light, at the intersection of State and Main Streets, where four blocks of three-storey granite buildings came together. The rest of the town, consisting of a mixture of granite, brick and wooden commercial buildings with storefronts along the sidewalks and various offices one or two flights up, was laid out around this central grid. It consisted of perhaps another eight or ten blocks arranged as permitted by the terrain, since the town sat at the bottom of a steep valley where two rivers joined. There were a couple of banks, a café, a general store, clothing shops for men and women, a shoe store, a record shop, one restaurant, a pizza parlor, a newspaper shop, a hotel, a movie theatre, a liquor store, a dive bar, City Hall, and the post office.

The townspeople's houses, mostly Victorians, were built along a few winding streets that radiated out of the valley in several different directions. Further up these hillsides, the housing became sparse and most of the land was wooded. On the outskirts of town were dairy farms. On the surrounding ridgelines, forests stretched for miles in every direction.

An old town, Barrington had four cemeteries. The newest one was on a hill overlooking the snake-like West Branch River and Route 9, which runs close to it, like its shadow. It rose in manmade terraces with gravel lanes winding through it. The gravestones were thick, and neatly arranged, and made of granite, reddish granite, whitish granite and bluish granite. These memorials had been quarried in the next town over, Barton. They were carved there, too, by immigrant Italian stone artisans who routinely managed to transcend their craftsmanship and produce art.

One marker of this sort was Black Agnes. Black Agnes, though, was a man, not a woman, and was made out of cast iron, not granite. Agnes sat there, wrapped in a flowing robe with the unmistakable look of death on his face. If you climbed onto his lap under a full moon, you were supposed to die within three months.

The older cemeteries in town, those that preceded the granite and its Italians, were still cared for after more than two centuries. Their markers were made of slate, and were weathered, weathered smooth, some of them, and were flaking. They were invariably gray, and protruded from the ground like rotting teeth. Here and there, a miniature American flag would wave over the grave of a veteran. One of these cemeteries was on Elm Street, which headed towards Worcester. It was not far from the center of town, situated among big old wooden Victorians with high, irregular roofing, sharp spires with weathervanes, odd gables, and peeling cupolas. This cemetery was surrounded by a rusty, wrought-iron fence. George himself used to crouch behind its stones to throw eggs at the cars which ran past in the night. It was there, on Halloween, that he saw his first ghost, a ruddy matron carrying a basket of carrots who was visible only from the knees up. The other boys didn't see it.

One of the other cemeteries in Barrington was equally suited for youthful mischief, if not more so, being set a few miles out of town, being surrounded by meadows of waist-high alfalfa and patches of forest, and being accessible only by dirt road. It was near an abandoned quarry, where rutted sand dunes provided only enough nourishment for a few gnarled bushes. This cemetery was enclosed by a white picket fence. In one of its corners stood an enormous maple tree. In George's day, teenagers used to couple there in cars with fogged windows under the night sky.

The last cemetery, where no one ever dared to go after dark, overlooked Barrington's small airport. Over this exposed heath, the occasional plane would drone winking and blinking in, guided by the sweeping searchlight that noiselessly measured the eternal stillness of the dead.

Barrington's living measured out their time as well. In trips past the golden-domed University Chapel they measured time. They measured time in well-regulated intervals of red and green, this way and that, at the town's central intersection. They saw time in the river, flowing in a white rush past the Grand Union supermarket. Time came over their radios and television sets, poured in yellow from the sun, fell in orange from the trees each autumn, rained down in clear drops to make mud in the spring, and in between time tumbled in white flakes from the cold clouds.

The winters in Barrington were long and hard. Temperatures of minus 39 were not unknown, and for at least six weeks a year the mercury never got above zero. The snow banks in town got so high in January and February that people drove around with strands of orange tape on the antennas of their cars. The rivers would ice over, causing troublesome jams in the spring. The Great Flood of 1927 killed a few dozen people, and the high-water level was commemorated on plaques in many of the older buildings. There were harrowing accounts of houses floating down the river with people still in them, standing on balconies, perched atop roofs or looking out of second-storey windows.

Barrington was above all else a college town, since it hosted the main campus of the State University. There was a heavy emphasis on agricultural sciences, forestry and biology, along with the liberal arts. The presence of the university gave the town a bit more vibrancy than its size would normally have warranted, but it remained a provincial culture at its core. There was one local radio station and an afternoon newspaper, and making a local call only meant dialing five digits. In those days, television was limited to one or two of the network affiliates broadcasting from upstate New York, Maine or Montreal. A movie would come to town and stay for months at a time, with two showings a night and matinees on Saturdays. Hockey and skiing were the dominant interests. Everybody in Barrington grew up on skis or skates. Jack, Nate, George and Bill were alpine skiers. They took a school bus to the resort every Saturday and Sunday morning all winter long and skied all day for five dollars. Tim and Danny were Nordic skiers. Nate also played hockey.

Classrooms were small. In grade school the teachers were usually older men and women with strong beliefs about standards of conduct and performance. The poor kids and the hippie children smelled of wood smoke in the mornings. Everybody learned French, since one of the state's borders was with Quebec. In English class they read Mark Twain. In science class they made volcanoes. In geography, they studied the Panama Canal. Each year they saw one film, and it was always the same one, an animated educational movie about the human circulatory system called *Hemo The Magnificent*.

Summers were spent playing baseball or football in the fields on the edge of town, exploring the woods, building forts, crawling inside of caves, and riding chopper bikes on winding dirt paths through the back country. They played kick the can and when they got a little older, camped out at night. Some of them took up hunting with their families in the fall. On Halloween they threw eggs at cars. There was a candlelight church service every Christmas Eve.

In high school they fanned out across the social landscape. George and Nate played football. Jack, Tim, Danny and Bill were on the ski team. All of them ran track. Bill did a lot of skateboarding. Nate was the first of them to get drunk, but Tim made it his mission to run with the partiers, a skill that he eventually parlayed into a lifestyle. Peter was his wing man. There was a lot of marijuana around town in the seventies, with names like Acapulco Gold and Maui Wowie. They had all had their girlfriends, although Tim never managed to make anything last for very long. In the spring of his sixteenth year, beside a stream, George copulated for the first time. It was both wonderful and horrible. It's really amazing what a dozen mosquitoes can do to a bare bottom in that length of time.

Senior year, George had been all set to run unopposed for the Presidency of the Barrington High School Class of 1978. And, yes, he had gotten a bit of a swelled head over it all, knowing, or rather thinking, that this would mean he was finally going to be someone, someone special, someone important, someone of distinction, instead of the shy under-achiever with a chip on his shoulder, which is what he was. He ran on a promise to bring better bands in for the high school dances. Like the one from downstate he had heard about, the one that was on the expensive side but really seemed to be going somewhere - and actually did, as it later turned out, under the name of *Aerosmith*.

But Danny had to decide getting elected Class President would go to George's head so he put the popular and seemingly happy-go-lucky Bobby Martin, who sang in the chorus, up to run against him at the last minute, even though running for Class President was the last thing on Bobby Martin's poor, troubled mind. And Bobby, no knock against the sad, crazy bastard, was woefully lacking in terms of temperament. To be Class President, that is. Anyways, Bobby ran. And with lots of behind-the-scenes help from Danny Farnsworth, he actually won - by one vote, no less. And so *Aerosmith* never came, and George never got to put "President, BHS Class of 1978" on his application to Dartmouth, and Jack Pelham, who'd had the good sense to run unopposed for Vice President, represented the school in the next year's freshman class there, and George ended up going to his "backup school". And the BHS Class of '78 never had any real reunions, like it would have had if George had been elected.

All of them had stayed in touch through their college years and they made it a point to get together when the holidays brought them back to town. They kept this up for years, with football games at Thanksgiving and ski outings around Christmastime. Most of them moved away but Danny stayed in Barrington. Peter came back in his late twenties after a few years spent teaching school in the Bronx. George returned in his mid-thirties to take a position on the faculty at the State University.

Snap

Out of the group, George remained the closest to Tim and Peter. The three of them had stayed in touch consistently over the years, arranging to spend a few days together several times a year even as George's academics and Tim's medical career led them to different cities around the country. Once George had joined Peter back in Barrington, it became easier for Tim to come and visit them. Most of these visits revolved around fly fishing.

Tim had been a troubled child. He had one sibling, a brother about 15 years older, which made him, in effect, an only child of an older couple. He spent a lot of time alone. He was brilliant but extremely volatile, prone to episodes of uncontrollable and violent rage, which became known among them as "the state". He experimented, sometimes disastrously, with chemistry sets, model rockets and homemade explosives. One afternoon he lobbed a Molotov cocktail into the town's tourist information booth, which launched an arson investigation.

Tim's dealings with women always ended in disaster. He would become obsessed with a girl, and whatever interest she might have had would inevitably evaporate once she realized what she was dealing with, and then he would hold her up in hatred, plotting and scheming to do her harm until the others talked him out of whatever it was he had in mind.

He became an infectious diseases specialist, which required a residency and then a fellowship after medical school. Most of this time was spent in Atlanta. He became something of a social maven, known for throwing lavish parties and, after a few years in private practice, for his priceless collection of exquisite wines. He married a television news woman who didn't know about his drug habit. He bought a townhouse on a cobblestone street and filled it with antiques. He bred championship Labrador Retrievers. After Tim's first suicide attempt the truth came out and she put him in rehab for the first of several tries. After their divorce, Tim's drug habit got even worse, and he lost his medical license. He became an antiques dealer.

One day, he called George from his cell phone while hauling a load of furniture back from an auction in Pennsylvania. He just wanted to say hi. He told George he loved him. Four days later, George was awakened in the middle of the night by a disturbance in his spare bedroom. He got up to check it out and found that the dresser had been knocked over. The next morning, he got a call from Tim's ex-wife, who gave George the news that Tim had shot himself during a standoff with the police in a woman's apartment the night before.

The news of Tim's death came just as George's marriage was falling apart. Ellen had simply left him, with nothing but a note of apology. George had been stoic about it, going through the routine of his daily business, keeping up with his responsibilities in the department and drinking himself to sleep at night all alone in an empty house. Then Laura had come along, and everything seemed okay, for a little while.

So when it became apparent that the 30th reunion of the Class of '78 wasn't going to happen, George had organized the fishing trip. The first forty-eight hours had been exactly what he had hoped for, long days of exciting fishing out on the lake and long nights of easy conviviality around their rustic little camp. There was a lot of reminiscing about the old days back in Barrington and a tearful conversation or two about Tim, but mostly it was time spent simply enjoying each others' companionship. After all of these years, their loyalty to one another still remained strong enough to bring them back together, and the comfort and warmth they felt when they were around each other, care-worn grown-ups though they might have been, made them feel like boys once more.

Back on Day One, when they were standing around the bonfire taking turns with Tim's picture, the conversation had been awkward. Tim's absence tore at their hearts, but they were having trouble understanding the wanton behavior he had displayed.

"It was suicide by cop," Nate had said.

"But he could have killed someone," Peter had replied.

"He *wanted* to kill someone," Bill said. "He went there with a gun looking for his girlfriend.

Thank God she wasn't there."

"Do you think she knew?" Jack asked.

"Knew what?" George asked.

"That he was on his way," Jack replied

"Oh," George said. "Probably she did. Now that you mention it."

During a lull in the conversation, they heard wolves off in the distance.

They were howling, the wolves.

Howling as the darkness of space yielded to the brightening of the Aurora, howling at the rising of the blood-shot moon, howling at the reappearance of the white-and-blue curvature of the earth.

They howled as the dark contours of the North American continent loomed up beneath him, and they howled as George, feeling heavier and heavier, descended back down through the shimmering ions, down through the wispy atmosphere, down toward the mountains, down toward the lake, down toward the boat.

The occasional meteor flickered across the sky.

The planet rotated and revolved.

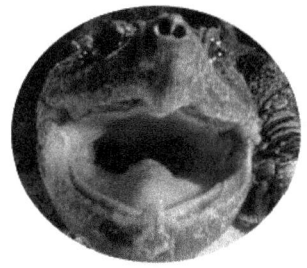

Chapter Twenty-Three

And now, George Mapolis was lying on his back, staring up into the pitch-black night sky, counting the seconds until dawn and praying to God he'd numbered the days correctly and that the float plane would actually be coming at first light, meanwhile clutching a canoe paddle like a newborn to his beating breast, shivering, and whimpering and waiting for the next sickening *bump* to come against the bottom of the boat.

Day Five had finally arrived, but these were the darkest hours before the dawn. The moon had gone down behind the mountains and the stars and the Northern Lights provided the only illumination now.

George fought to clear his mind. He had no idea how long his body had been shut down. But now that he was conscious again, it was pure misery. The stump of his amputated arm throbbed agonizingly. With every heartbeat the veins in his forearm would bulge against his tourniquet, sending sharp spikes of pain clear up to his armpits. His broken nose and swollen eye sockets were still sore and his head ached dully.

All he wanted was a drink of water, but he couldn't move. His body felt so heavy, as if he were made of lead.

He lay on the deck, awash in his own blood, drained of the will to carry on. He was ready to give up. He was starting to feel like it might be okay to die. But then he realized that would mean being beaten by the beast. The repulsion he felt at this idea was visceral. A fundamental unwillingness to accept such a result rose from somewhere inside of him, pushing its way up through all of the pain and resignation.

George's anger came back and began to boil in him.

Painfully, he rolled over and pushed himself unsteadily to his feet.

Holding his mangled left arm against his sternum and clutching the rail with his right hand, he worked his way to the cooler and pulled out a bottle of water. He drank it down in one long pull, swallowing over and over again until the bottle was empty. He threw it aside and opened another one and drank that too. George felt a tiny bit of his vigor returning and as it did his anger began to gel into a cool rage. Even if he was a lying sack of shit, a morally compromised waste of skin, he didn't deserve to die like this. None of them had.

Another *bump* came against the bottom of the boat, causing it to shudder beneath George's feet. The turtle was butting the hump of its shell into the hull, not attacking the vessel so much as making its presence felt. It was operating in between modes of predation, neither lying in ambush nor ramming home the attack. And while it seemed to be in no particular hurry to finish him off, George had been through way too much over the past few days to underestimate the animal's cunning, determination or cruelty. It had snatched Danny screaming from his own bed in the middle of the night. It had snipped Jack completely in half at the navel, leaving him with his entrails hanging out in a steaming pile from the bell of his gaping abdomen. It had essentially decapitated Peter. Two other people were missing, as was a piece of George's own body.

The light broke cold and gray over *Le Lac Perdu* on Day Five, as if the dawning of this morning marked the end of the brief Nunavut summer and the first of many ever shortening days that would grow colder and colder as the winter wore inexorably closer. It seemed like some flywheel in the movement of the celestial machinery had turned and the gears of its clockwork were now spinning of a different accord. A process had been set in motion and the cycle was working its way around to completion. The final, preordained configuration would soon manifest itself.

The morning light revealed a chaotic scene. The state of the boat reflected the hours of frantic activity it had witnessed and the tragedies that had been laid out before it, the gruesome deaths of Danny, and poor Jack. The boat was covered in blood. Reddish stains were spread across the deck and there were splatter marks, smears and bloody prints all over the seats and surfaces. Lockers and hatches were open and miscellaneous gear lay strewn around haphazardly. A line hung over the side. Some more tangled rope lay where it had been tossed in a corner.

The end of George's arm felt like it had been dipped in lava. It was an angry, unrelenting ache, an ache that gave way only to the hot flashes of agony he experienced as the blood pulsed against his tourniquet with each and every heartbeat. He could never have imagined anything could ever be so painful. It hurt so terribly he whimpered. It occurred to him that it would feel so good to just open the spigot and let his blood run out, ending the miserable throbbing once and for all. But to end the throbbing would be to end the life. And the pain was all that made the difference between being alive and being insentient, which made the decision a little simpler for George in this moment.

He'd take being alive.

He'd take being sentient.

This brought his attention back around to the turtle that was stalking the boat. Circling it, actually. And crisscrossing underneath it, submerged several feet below the water, cutting through it like a phosphorescent projectile. At one point it surfaced and came charging straight toward the craft, diving only at the last minute, directing its bow wave broadside against the hull with the deliberate intention of capsizing the vessel. But the boat withstood the onrushing wake, floating up onto and then precariously over the shoulder of the wave without ever tipping all of the way over.

Later, when the beast returned and roughly thrust its head up over the rail, the two of them spent a long moment looking directly into each others' eyes. The reptile blinked its leathery lids a couple of times. The shape of its beak traced a grin across its broad snout. Its nostrils were two shadowy holes. At first George was frozen in fear but then he managed to force himself to move, inch by inch, over toward the flare gun, all the while maintaining eye contact with the creature. Just as he reached the gun, the animal opened its cavernous mouth at him, as if to show him the fate that lay in store for him.

"Take this, you son of a bitch," George whispered.

George raised the gun and fired a flare right down the monster's throat, which sent it reeling backwards into the water with a great soaking splash. It floated belly up for a moment, then sank lifelessly away into the murky depths.

George's eyes were wide with disbelief as he stared into the water. He had done it. He had vanquished the beast. He was going to survive. Yet he didn't know how to feel. In fact, he felt nothing. He wasn't even glad to be alive, with his friends all dead. Nor was he able to appreciate the fact that the danger had finally passed. On the contrary, the sheer exhaustion was overwhelming and the pain of his wound was almost beyond endurance. There came no consolation with survival, just a continuing obligation to carry on.

George wanted to sit down and rest, but he decided it would be a good idea to use what fuel he had left to bring the boat back toward the lodge, where it would be easier for the float plane to find him. He grabbed another bottle of water from the cooler on his way over to the helm. He took a long, thirsty pull, then put it away and turned the key in the ignition. The engine sputtered and then came to life, and George gave the throttle a good push.

A few seconds after the hull began to plane, however, there came a tremendous crashing noise at the bow and the next thing George knew the entire craft was airborne. He sailed high up into the air along with it, then felt a trap door open under his feet as the boat began to fall away beneath him. He tried to hang onto the wheel but lost his grip and went flying. From above, he looked down on the boat as it hit the water, bounced, turned sideways and then flipped over.

George hit the surface face first and tumbled along until his flailing limbs bit into the water and dragged him to an abrupt stop. Sputtering, he fought to right himself in the water. The boat floated hull-up nearby. George looked around to see what in the world he had hit, then he noticed the big brown hump of shell towering above the water a few dozen feet away.

George immediately began swimming for the boat, crawling through the water as best he could with his one good arm. As he swam, it occurred to him that the turtle had probably been stunned by the impact. Possibly, it had even been dead when he had hit it in the first place. His best bet would be to see if he could climb on top of the overturned hull of his boat. When George reached the vessel, however, he found that he could not get any purchase on its smooth surface. He turned around and looked back at the turtle. To his horror, it was alive, alert and coming straight for him, staring down its snout at him with the glowering dark eyes of a charging bull.

Stunned, George reached out involuntarily for the nearest thing and latched onto a stout piece of wood. It was Danny's spear. Before he knew it the monster was upon him with its huge, sharply pointed beak open wide like a pair of dark pincers. Not knowing what else to do, George inserted the sharpened stick vertically into the turtle's mouth. When the turtle tried to close its jaws, the spear wedged itself into place, preventing the long cleaver-like blades of bone from scissoring shut. George pushed himself away from the bulky animal as it recoiled and dove underneath the waves, and that was the last that he ever saw of it because, just at that instant, the float plane appeared in the sky.

At first it was a distant, silent speck the size of a mosquito. As it grew larger, the faint drone of its engine became audible, growing louder and louder as it zeroed in on the lake. When it crested the ridgeline, the plane went into a steep descent, following the terrain as it fell away toward the water, leveling out just a few dozen feet above the surface.

The plane flew right over George's head, its engine an angry snarl. It continued on up the lake and then swung into a wide bank turn that circled it back around in the direction of the boat, with the wind now at its tail. The pilot brought the aircraft steadily lower until its tin-colored pontoons splashed down onto the choppy surface. The plane skimmed across the waves for maybe a hundred feet and then gradually settled down onto the water, slowing to idle speed a few hundred feet away from George's position. It taxied briskly over toward the boat, its engine blaring and backfiring.

George could see the pilot looking inscrutably down on him through the aircraft's windshield. Square-jawed, he wore a leather flight jacket, sunglasses, headphones and a red cap. His face seemed expressionless. He came up alongside the boat and cut the airplane's engine. He unbuckled himself, climbed out of the cockpit and headed aft into the cabin. A few seconds later, the cabin door opened and the pilot stepped out onto a strut where a ladder led down to the pontoon deck. He reached down to help George up out of the water.

"What's going on here?" the pilot asked.

"There's no time!" George replied. "We've got to get up in the air!"

"What happened to your hand?" the pilot wanted to know. "And where are the others?"

"They're all dead!" George said. "We've got to get out of here, now!"

George forced his way past the pilot and into the cabin. The pilot turned around to face him.

"What do you mean, dead?"

"Hurry up, get this thing up in the air," George said. "Now!"

"Not so fast. You've got to explain. Who's dead?

"Everybody else. All five of them. I'm telling you we need to get out of here before it comes back. I only wounded it!"

"Wounded *what?*"

"The turtle!"

The pilot just looked at him.

"It's *huge!*" George said. "We we ate the soup, and then it came after us. It bit Peter's head off and took Danny right out of his bed! It's swimming around *right nearby.* I'm telling you we need to get up in the air!"

"We're going back to the camp," the pilot decided. "We'll see about all of this. Strap yourself in. And try not to get so much blood everywhere."

A minute later they were taxiing through the water. The pilot brought the plane around and headed back into the wind. He hit the throttle and the plane sped up over the water and then rose swiftly into the air. After a short flight they reached the little cove on the other side of the lake where the encampment was located. The pilot circled over the area. It was deserted. The charred ruins of George's cabin still smoldered.

"There's no point," George said. "There's nobody here, I'm telling you. They're all dead. You can see body parts over on the beach at Black Island, for God's sake!"

The pilot turned to look at him. "Are you serious?"

George simply held up his stump.

"Let's go," the pilot said, putting the plane into a hard turn.

Several minutes later Black Island reared up below them, the boat a little white speck on the water a half mile off of its windward shore. The pilot circled the island and then brought the plane in low over the beach. Just as George had predicted, there was a dismembered torso and a severed leg lying on the sand, clearly visible to them as they overflew the scene. Jack lay on his back with his arms spread apart, gazing vacantly up at them. Danny's boot was discernible at the end of his amputated leg. Several large birds that had begun to mill around the carrion begrudgingly took wing as the aircraft buzzed the beach.

The pilot had seen enough. He pulled up and turned south, heading for the gap in the mountains from which he had appeared a little while earlier. The plane gained altitude and then leveled out, the engine settling into a steady hum. Beneath them, the broad expanse of the lake lay stretched out for miles in all directions. George stared down at *Le Lac Perdu*, shimmering in all of its pristine beauty, and contemplated the horrific events of the past week.

When, after a while, he looked up from the window he noticed the pilot was now flying the plane with one hand and pointing a revolver at him with the other. "We've got about a four-hour flight ahead of us," he told George. "And you're going to sit tight for the whole time. I'm warning you right now that if you so much as reach for your seatbelt I'm going to shoot you dead. There will be no hesitation."

"You have to believe me," George implored. "We were attacked."

"So you say. By a giant turtle." The pilot looked at George and waggled the barrel of his revolver a little. "No more talking."

They flew in silence for a couple of hours. The vastness of the Canadian tundra passed beneath them, mile after mile, with no sign of man to be seen in any direction. George resisted the impulse to argue his case with the pilot. Surely this was a misunderstanding that would be easily cleared up. This particular individual might not be reasonable but others would be called in to investigate and they would listen to his story. This was to be expected, really. Five fishermen had disappeared. Until the facts came out it would only be right for people to question what had happened to them. How could he not expect to be seen in a suspicious light, at least temporarily? It was no reflection on him personally. Let the pilot treat him like a criminal. The flight would have to end at some point.

His explanation would, ironically, have to be the simple truth, that a giant snapping turtle had killed the others because they had eaten the turtle soup. It struck him that this might sound incredible, especially coming from a cryptozoologist working on a new book. Who happened to be a murder suspect. The facts, on superficial review, were, indeed, concerning. George wondered where it would all lead. He would take a polygraph examination if it came down to that.

Eventually the pilot began trying to raise a signal on the radio. "Whale Cove Base this is

Bravo Tango One One Two. Do you read? Over."

He repeated this call every couple of minutes for perhaps a half an hour before finally receiving a faint reply.

"Whale Cove Base to Bravo Tango, we read you. Over."

"Whale Cove Base, we have a situation on board," the pilot said. "Requesting assistance. Over"

"Go ahead, Bravo Tango. Over."

"We'll need Jim Fisher to meet us when we land. I have my weapon drawn. We'll also be needing the ambulance. Over."

There was a moment of hesitation. "Roger. What is your E.T.A.? Over."

"About 18:30. Out."

The pilot turned to George. "Jim Fisher's the RCMP constable. You can tell your story to him."

When the outpost finally appeared, the pilot circled the little airport a couple of times and then approached the runway. George could see a police cruiser and an ambulance parked on the tarmac below, in front of a corrugated steel hangar. A small group of people were huddling around watching as the plane, equipped with amphibious landing gear, touched down and then taxied toward the hangar. The pilot pulled up alongside the building and cut the engine. Under gunpoint, George unbuckled himself, stood up, opened the door with his good hand and maneuvered himself out of the plane and down the ladder. At least now he would be considered innocent until proven guilty. And any reasonable investigation would exonerate him of murder. He was certain of it. At the very least he could expect to be accorded the treatment due someone who had been rescued from an ordeal in the wilderness, someone who had a broken face and a bloody stump instead of a hand.

The RCMP constable, a tall, strapping young man wearing a fur-lined hat and a dark blue parka, stood on the tarmac looking George up and down. The pilot was standing next to him, saying something in his ear. George could only think to keep on walking over toward the ambulance. He shuffled along hoping not to draw any attention to himself. But the constable accosted him.

"Excuse me, sir," he said, clearing his throat, "but I was wondering if I might have a word."

"Yes," George said, "Of course officer."

"You're George Mapolis?"

"Yes, sir."

"You've just returned from the Lost Lake?"

"Yes, sir."

"Where are your friends?"

George just looked at him. He thought of Peter under the boat and Danny sailing through the air and Jack on the beach. An image of the turtle's black maw reared up at him. He recollected his atavistic night on Black Island. In his mind's eye he saw the cabin burning in the woods. He felt the pain of his burned leg and his broken nose and his two black eyes and his missing hand. He just wanted to go to sleep, and would have done or said nearly anything on the promise of a place to lie down.

The constable pulled out a pair of handcuffs. "Hold out your hands, please," he said. George impulsively complied. When the constable saw George's bloody stump, he flinched his head a bit, but the flinty look in his eye remained. "Medic!" he bellowed, more in the tone of a military commander giving an order than of someone calling for help. The people standing uncertainly over near the ambulance picked up their gear and ran over.

"You're their patient," the constable told George, "but you're also my prisoner." He turned toward the medics. "Gentlemen, make sure this fellow doesn't go anywhere. He's in the custody of the Crown now."

When George realized what was happening, he panicked.

"No!" he yelled, and made a run for it.

But the constable was too quick for him, and before George knew it he was tackled roughly and pinned face down onto the tarmac. A hot lance of pain shot through his right shoulder as the constable twisted his elbow toward the small of his back. It hurt so bad George could only scream, so he never heard what the constable was saying, which turned out to be the reading of his rights.

Logos

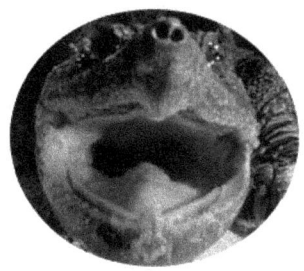

Chapter Twenty-Four

Two days later George woke up in a hospital bed. At first he had no idea where he was or how he had gotten there, but then it all came crashing in upon him. The fishing trip, the ordeal on the lake, the flight back, the awful episode on the tarmac, an ambulance ride. From there on his recollection consisted only of a series of hazy images involving doctors and nurses looking down on him under bright lights. He had no idea how much time had passed, and he noticed with some surprise that he was wearing a pastel green Johnny. His left hand was heavily bandaged, and blood was leaking through the white gauze around his stump. When he tried to raise his other arm, it turned out to be handcuffed to the bed rail.

Before George could collect his thoughts the door opened and a pretty nurse came in. When she saw that George was awake, her eyes widened and she gasped. Then she dropped the tray she was carrying, with a clatter, and ran out of the room again. He heard voices out in the hallway. A few seconds later the door burst back open and two RCMP men strode briskly into the room and officially introduced themselves.

The police had drawn all the wrong conclusions, as it turned out. Certainly the facts pointed in an inconvenient direction. After all, George had known all five of the victims prior to the trip. There was a paper trail showing he had been the one to bring them together at the lake. He, alone, had come back alive. He was under duress in his personal life. By his own admission, he was a chronic, if not a compulsive, liar. And his continued insistence on the turtle story they found infuriating.

By the time an expedition of crime scene investigators had managed to reach the lake, the body parts had disappeared from the beach, most likely the work of scavengers, so there was no way to perform a forensic analysis of their wounds. Peter's torso was never found. Nor were the bodies of any of the others. George's stump offered nothing of any evidentiary value. It didn't rule a turtle out, but it didn't rule one in, either.

The Mounties spent a week at the site conducting a meticulous forensic examination, but they found nothing to corroborate George's tale, or give them any reason to question their own theory of the case. George's notes and the journal of Jacques Fortin had been consumed in the cabin fire and his camera had been lost along with his left hand, so there was no evidence to support any of the most important details of his story. Nor even to back up his claim of the very existence of the monster in the first place.

The cabin itself had burned completely, leaving no basis to credit George's account of how Danny had been attacked through the bedroom window. A heavy rain had obliterated the tracks left by the turtle around the camp and also at the beach in the cove on Black Island. One of the boats was recovered, but it bore no conclusive sign of anything at all consistent with the attacks George had described. Divers and a submersible had been brought in but the waters were too deep and murky for them to find anything.

After relating all of this, the Mounties, one standing on either side of George's bed, read him his rights once more. Then they asked their first trick question, which was whether he had anything to say. One of them, he noticed, was holding a tape recorder.

"Not yet," he answered.

"So be it," came the reply.

The next day, George was discharged from Qikiqtani General Hospital and transported to the RCMP detachment in Iqaluit, where he was lodged in a drab concrete holding cell. There he was interrogated on videotape. He told the police he was scared of what they might do to him. The sergeant, who had the face of Babe Ruth and fingers like Italian sausages, assured him he was safe, but encouraged him to tell the truth. George stuck to his story about the turtle. A detective handed him a pen and paper and asked George to write a letter of apology to the victims' families. In his blocky hand, George wrote that he was sorry for what had happened and that he wished he could bring back their lost loved ones.

The Canadian Crown assumed George's prosecution, filing an information alleging five counts of first-degree murder in the Court of Justice in Iqaluit. Each charge carried a sentence of life in prison, and the sentences could be meted out consecutively. Pending indictment and trial, George was held without bail under maximum security in an 8-foot-square cell with a bunk, a sink and a toilet. He was under suicide watch, so he was deprived of his belt and shoelaces, and subject to welfare checks every fifteen minutes, around the clock.

George's court-appointed lawyer was a prim, bookish man in his late thirties, thin and pale, who wore wire-rimmed spectacles and a maroon bow tie. The obvious product of an upper-crust education, he spoke with a crisp, quasi-British accent inflected with a Canadian lilt. He said "oot" instead of "out" and "aboot" instead of "about." He explained the gravity of the charges and the weaknesses of George's defense. Circumstantial evidence, he explained, was admissible in a court of law under the Anglo-American tradition of jurisprudence. And the circumstantial evidence in George's case was damning. He had a right against self-incrimination but his written statement and the videotape of his interrogation were probably admissible.

"Your story about the turtle is concerning to me," the lawyer said. "It leaves me very little to work with, except perhaps an insanity defense."

George bristled at the suggestion. "I'm not crazy," he snapped. "And I didn't kill anybody."

"Do you believe, I mean really *believe*, this?" the lawyer asked him.

"It's not a matter of belief," George replied. "It's the truth."

"Then I'm going to have you evaluated," the lawyer said.

"Evaluated?"

"By a psychologist."

"He'll tell you I'm not lying."

"Then there may be some hope for you yet."

At the conclusion of their meeting, two guards came in and put George in arm and leg shackles. They each took an elbow and directed him in halting steps toward the door. He hesitated for one moment on the way out, turning back to look his lawyer in the eye.

"I'm innocent," he said. "You have to believe me."

The lawyer didn't reply.

The psychologist, who turned out to be an elegantly attractive woman of mature but indeterminate age, betrayed no apparent sign of any opinion one way or the other about the story George told her. She simply accepted the information as it was relayed, carefully noting the details, occasionally asking questions, probing for clarification or requesting further elaboration at various points in George's bizarre narrative. She was particularly interested in George's subjective experience of each event, and in documenting his emotional responses. She delved into his relationships with each of the other members of the party, their significance in his life, and his own feelings about their individual deaths. He admitted that he concealed from his friends his prior knowledge of the lake's dark past, the discovery of the footprint, the results of his research and the existence of Jacques Fortin's diary, all while allowing them to expose themselves unwittingly to danger, going so far as to distract them from it, even.

She probed his relationship with Danny, forcing him to reveal the dirty thing that Danny's Mom had done to him on a summer's day when he was twelve, and how, when everything came out, it had ruined Danny's parents' marriage. George admitted to his rage about the incident, but the lesson he took from all of this was that certain truths could cause pain and even destroy lives. She asked him if he felt in any way responsible for Tim's death, and George admitted he had never stopped treating him as a rival, although he kept quiet about seeing and speaking with Tim's ghost.

"And your girlfriend," the psychologist asked him frankly, "what do we do with her?"

"Her name was Laura."

"And she was beautiful."

"Yes."

"And you hurt her very badly."

"I did."

"What is your biggest regret?"

"That I didn't run after her in the rain."

"Not that you were her professor?"

"No."

"Not that you deceived her?"

"No."

"What good do you think it would have done, George?"

"That's the problem," he replied, slowly shaking his head, "I'll never know. But what was I supposed to do, run up to her and blurt out, 'Guess what? I still love you. I'm a lying scumbag but I love you! There's only one small problem, I don't know how to be any different.' No, she had just gotten used to the idea that I was dead. I wasn't going to let her mourn me twice."

But it was George's involvement with cryptozoology that seemed to truly fascinate the psychologist. She questioned him about the subject at length, wrestling with the mystery of its significance in the framework of his psyche and its presumptive relationship to his pathology. From gigantic turtles it is only a small step to the concept of monsters in general, and a subset of monsters were humanoid ones, such as Bigfoot, and from there it was another small step to the legend of the Wild Man, the costumed character present during Medieval European fairs and festivals and who still appears in the Tarot deck. The degree to which George had anthropomorphised his turtle suggested that it was a surrogate for the Wild Man, which itself was a surrogate for the bestial impulses inside of him. This in turn resulted from the rage he felt over his childhood trauma at the hands of a predator disguised as a caregiver.

The archetype of the beast as a surrogate for the Wild Man represented not so much a foreign threat as it did the projection of the feral side of man himself. In George's case, the unknowable beast was the externalized embodiment of the predator within. Clearly, George's interest in cryptozoology derived from an abnormal need to banish these impulses by projecting them onto the larger world, and the question became whether his monstrosity bred his interest in the subject, or whether his interest in the subject gave form to and then unleashed his own inner monster.

It was indeed a strange subject, cryptozoology, a form of intellectual tail-chasing. Once found, a cryptid loses its status as a mystery animal and enters the province of mainstream science. Specimens of previously unknown animals are catalogued, dissected, sampled, genetically mapped and discussed by others, while the cryptozoologist must move on to hunt for a new quarry. In the end, mystery is the subject's steady state. Cryptozoology keeps the researcher in a constant relationship with the unknown itself, rather than with any particular creature.

The fact of George's obsession with the subject led the psychologist to inquire about his perception of the lake prior to their trip. Its size, its depth and its remote location made it an ideal context in which the beast might exist. For generations, The Lost Lake had been seen in this very light by explorers as well as the indigenous people. These facts needed to be viewed within the context of a belief system that accommodated, even focused on, the existence of the beast. Perhaps he had gone there primed to encounter his anger and fear in the form of a monster, and then created one, or rather became one, when none was found.

Her report would eventually reflect the conclusion that the mythical beasts with which George was obsessed represented archetypes onto which he projected subconscious impulses and desires that could not be consciously integrated into his self-concept. George had in essence fragmented his personality. Incapable of confronting his own violent impulses, he instead externalized them in the form of an imaginary monster, one which posed a perceived threat not only to the surrogate targets of his psychopathic rage but also to himself. He would have had no awareness of his own actions even as he'd carried out his atrocities. On the contrary, George would have believed he was helplessly watching the killings in mortal fear for his own life. In other words, he was a mass murderer, but one who was not guilty by reason of insanity.

The distinction, unfortunately, was purely semantic. Whether he was convicted of murder or found to be criminally insane, George would undoubtedly be confined in maximum security for the rest of his life. His only hope was to be believed, or proven right. He pleaded with the psychologist to accept his account of the events on the lake.

She leaned forward in her chair and took George's hand.

"I believe you are telling the truth, George," she said, "as you see it."

"No!" George implored. "As it really happened. I'm telling you, the turtle, it was real! I am *not* insane!"

"Stop it!" she exclaimed, raising her voice for the first time.

A guard stuck his head into the room.

The psychologist held up her hand.

"It's alright," she said.

The guard seemed uncertain.

"We're fine. Really. I'm just finishing up."

When they were alone once again, she fixed him with an earnest gaze and said, "George, what you believe you saw was not real. You need to confront whatever it is that you have done. As long as you believe you are telling the objective truth about the turtle, you are by definition a very sick man. You *must* try to understand this. Otherwise you will be beyond all help."

George became overwhelmed with a sense of despair and, for the first time since leaving the lake, dread. He felt suddenly claustrophobic within the grim confines of the prison. But even more oppressive than his physical confinement was the psychological alienation that came with being universally disbelieved. Being trapped in this foreign penal system with the weight of everyone's doubt pressing down on him, he felt buried alive. He was almost breathless with panic, and utterly speechless.

It was the psychologist who finally broke the silence.

"I'm sorry, George," she said. "I'm very sorry."

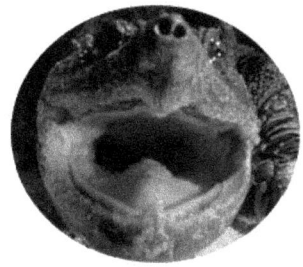

Chapter Twenty-Five

Left in solitary confinement to await his trial, George spent many long hours considering whether the turtle was real or not, and questioning his own sanity. If the psychologist was correct, he was by definition insane, which meant that he could not trust his own thoughts or perceptions. If this were true, perhaps he really had killed his friends. He began to realize that even he could never know for certain.

He believed in the turtle's objective reality. But he had also seen a ghost, even carried on a conversation with it inside of his head. Years earlier, he had confronted a large, hairy man-like creature in the woods, which disappeared with absolutely no trace. No one else besides George had seen that being, either. Perhaps his sensitivities were heightened, enabling him to see things that other people were not calibrated to perceive. This would make sense if the inter-dimensional theory was correct. But he also had to admit there was a possibility these were apparitions manufactured by his own psyche.

If he weren't hallucinating or seeing through second sight, that left only two remaining possibilities. Either the turtle was real, or he was so hopelessly tangled up in a web of lies that, while sane, he had lost the ability to know, let alone tell, the truth. He had, in fact, been guilty of passing off so many deceptions, some small, some not so small, that even he himself could not keep track of them all. He had lied to his dead friends. He had lived a lie with Laura. If he murdered the missing men, what was there to stop him from lying to himself about it?

How would he have pulled it off? Would he have drugged their drinks, or hacked them to pieces with an axe? Strangled them one at a time in their sleep? How would he have disposed of their bodies? Weighted them down and thrown them into the lake? Poisoning or strangulation might account for the lack of forensic evidence of a violent crime, but what about the body parts on Black Island? How would he have carved them up without leaving a trace? And how had they gotten there, when there was no evidence of anyone else's blood in the boat besides George's own? And what about his hand? Had he chopped it off himself in order to support his turtle alibi?

Maybe there had been a confrontation between himself and Danny in the cabin late at night.

Perhaps they had come to blows. This would explain George's broken nose. Maybe Danny fell and hit his head. Maybe George jumped on him and, finally overcome by his smoldering rage, wrung the life out of him with his bare hands. His next move would have been to take care of the others, maybe by slipping into their cabins, creeping up to them as they slept in their beds and garroting them, one by one, perhaps with a length of steel fishing leader, probably while wearing gloves.

His next task would have been to eliminate the corpses. He could have moved them onto blankets and dragged them down to the dock, laying them side by side there like so many caught fish all in a row. He could have lugged their bodies onto the bigger boat, piling them in a heap on the foredeck. Then he might have left the cove, pulling the smaller boat in tow.

He could have found a low-lying rock along the shore at some spot far removed from the lodge, where he could have dismembered Danny and Jack using, say, a filet knife. Afterwards, he could have scrubbed the stone, and then himself, clean. Then he could have towed their body parts over to Black Island on a line behind the boat, and then he could have dragged them up on the beach without ever directly handling them.

Come to think of it, what had happened to the other boat, the one with Peter's head still in it, last seen floating upside down in the lake? The Mounties never found it, or so they said. Had he in fact scuttled it, sent it to the bottom along with the bodies and the steel leader and his gloves? Maybe the case against him made sense after all. Maybe there was no camera, maybe there was never any footprint, maybe there were no notes, maybe there was no journal left by Jacques Fortin, and maybe there wasn't a turtle.

For days on end George sat in his cell, trying to figure out which of these nightmarish scenarios, that of the turtle or that of the murders, was the real one, and which was the fantasy. Each would have been deeply traumatic, just the sort of thing to trigger a psychotic break in an inherently unstable personality that was in addition under generalized emotional, if not psychological, duress. If he were really fragmented into two separate personalities who never coexisted at the same time in his conscious mind, he might never know about the existence of one of them while he was living as the other. In fact it might have been necessary for him to completely compartmentalize the part of himself that had been present to experience such traumatic circumstances.

But in the end, it did come down to a question of belief. And George simply did not believe that he was insane, that he had murdered the others, that he was his own evil doppelganger. No, there had been a turtle. It was, he believed, the truth. He was, he believed, innocent.

And so George's trial was an odd affair. He testified to the details of his story, stoically maintaining a matter-of-fact demeanor under a tense cross examination that lasted for several days. The Crown was trying to expose inconsistencies in George's account by probing around the edges of his version of events. Lines of trick questioning were carefully developed in the belief that George would eventually have to improvise explanations and fabricate the supporting details, giving them the opportunity to expose and exploit any resulting inconsistencies. George's alibi would then crumble.

But George's ability to answer the prosecution's questions with an internally consistent logic was disconcerting. He did this by sticking scrupulously to the facts as he believed them to be. If he hadn't observed something or couldn't remember it, he simply said so. He resisted the temptation to make anything up. He told the Court what he believed he had seen and what he thought he knew. George, the compulsive liar, fighting for his life with the truth, the whole truth and nothing but the truth. And so his story, implausible though it might have been, hung together quite resiliently. It made for some frustrating moments for the Crown, which had actually undertaken a risky strategy. By implication, the government must have believed that since George was lying, he would eventually impeach his own story if it were explored in sufficient detail. Yet this he never did.

Ironically, George's legal defense was that he was in fact a liar, but a liar who believed in his own lies. While his lawyer dutifully established the exculpatory evidence—the lack of any bodies, the absence of physical evidence connecting him to any specific act of violence, the loss of his own hand—it focused most of its efforts on establishing George's insanity. In this sense his defense was in conflict with itself. George begged to be believed. His defense lawyer argued that his own client's story was impossible.

Police officers called by the Crown were nevertheless cross-examined at length about the numerous aspects of their murder theory that relied on pure speculation.

How had the victims been killed?

They didn't know.

How had their bodies been disposed of?

They didn't know.

How had one man accomplished all of this, covering every trace of his actions?

They didn't know.

What was his motive?

They didn't know.

But they did have one crucial element in their favor: The victims were missing and George himself had testified that five violent deaths had in fact occurred. The mere fact of these five killings, in the absence of a plausible explanation, was presumptive evidence of guilt, and an insurmountable obstacle to the defense. This meant proving that George was not a deliberate murderer but a psychopath operating in a delusional dream world where he was detached from any responsibility for, or even knowledge of, whatever it was that he must have done to the missing men.

This brought into evidence the testimony of the psychologist and the conclusions she had reached on behalf of the defense's insanity theory. The Crown, in turn, put on a rebuttal expert who had reviewed her work and arrived at a very different forensic opinion.

"Borderline personality disorder involves intense feelings of resentment over perceived slights," Dr. Munford Robertson told the Court.

"It may be characterized by dissociation, paranoid schizophrenic ideation, and delusions, even. But it is really an identity disturbance most prominently characterized by paranoid and manipulative behavior aggravated by extreme emotional instability. And yes, this can be a prescription for murder."

"And by murder, you mean . . ."

"The intentional killing of another human being under circumstances in which the perpetrator understands the difference between right and wrong, and proceeds nevertheless," was the doctor's answer.

"Can someone with Borderline Personality Disorder make such a distinction?"

"Absolutely."

"And the explanation provided by the Defendant?"

"The story of a giant turtle?" the doctor asked, with a polite smile. "Why that's simply a lie. A complex and detailed lie, but a lie nevertheless."

"When you use the word 'lie', you mean what, exactly?"

"I mean a conscious falsehood deliberately fabricated and maintained in furtherance of a self-serving purpose."

"What do you think happened?"

"I think he just snapped."

And with that the Crown rested its case.

Closing arguments began at nine o'clock the next morning. The Crown's prosecutor was a tall, thin man with piercing bird-like eyes deeply set beneath bushy, upturned salt-and-pepper moustaches where there should have been eyebrows. Silver-maned and trim in his tailored navy suit, he rose slowly from his chair and ambled somewhat stiffly up to a podium that had been set in front of the jury box. The jurors observed him attentively. He gave them a polite nod.

"This is a tragic case, ladies and gentlemen," he began, his voice low, his cadence measured. "Five men are dead. One man stands accused. The twelve of you must make a difficult decision. I'm here to speak with you about that decision." He reviewed the facts of the case, then itemized the inferences reasonably to be drawn from the evidence, both direct and circumstantial. He recited the names of the dead men, and then spoke a few words about each one. Then he gestured toward their families, who were packing the courtroom. "And what does the accused offer these people by way of an explanation? He talks about a giant snapping turtle.

"His own lawyer doesn't even buy it. Instead, he comes up with a convoluted excuse built on an insanity defense that's nearly as implausible. In either case, you're now being asked to accept, no to *believe*, a tall story from an admitted liar with every motive in the world to deny the truth.

"The evidence of guilt is great. Clearly, it rises to a preponderance. The Crown has met its burden. You must convict. That's all I have."

George's lawyer waited for the prosecutor to make his way stiffly back to his chair, then rose to his feet. As he walked to the podium, the jurors, who had been sitting still for nearly two hours, took advantage of the opportunity to move around a little in their seats.

"My job is not an enviable one, ladies and gentlemen," he said, when they had settled down.

"I am here to defend a man accused of committing a heinous crime. I make no apologies. The crime must be abhorred. It is only natural, only human, to feel that way. But now I must ask you, on behalf not only of Professor Mapolis, but also on behalf of our society, to place those feelings to one side. In short, I must ask you to do your sworn duty here today.

"You will be instructed by the Court as to the elements of the offenses the Crown has brought against my client," he went on. "You will also be instructed as to the requisite level of intent, and the elements of the defense of insanity. There is no room for emotion, no room for sympathy, for or against, in this process. I proceed in the belief that we agree on at least this much, and for that I thank you.

"There are five missing men. I do not ask you to believe they are still alive. I do not ask you to believe in a giant turtle. I ask, instead, whether you believe my client is criminally responsible for murder.

"Ladies and gentlemen, my client is unwell. He is suffering. He has an illness." He pointed to the witness stand. "I think you saw that, while he was up there testifying. Clearly, he believed he was telling us the truth. You saw not a monster, but a man who sees monsters. And he sees monsters because he can't accept the truth. The truth about what happened to him as a boy, and what it did to him inside. He had no awareness of what he was doing. Those men were his friends, and he loved them."

The lawyer paused for a moment.

"George Mapolis may be a killer," he finally said, "but he is not a murderer. We ask that you acquit."

After two days of deliberations, the jury returned to announce that they had rejected both the insanity defense and the turtle story. Instead, they found George guilty of five counts of first-degree murder in the deaths of Danny Farnsworth, Jack Pelham, Bill Isley, Nate Peterman and Peter Gordon. The courtroom broke out into an uproar as the people sitting in the benches reacted to the verdict with applause, loud yells and wailing sobs.

In arguing for the maximum sentence, the Crown's prosecutor told the Court that George's depravity required that he be permanently removed from society for reasons of protection, punishment and deterrence. George's own lawyer simply noted that George had shown remarkably little self-pity, and practically no interest in participating meaningfully in his own defense. "He will be forever remorseful for his unspeakable actions," he said.

When it came time for the Presiding Justice to deliver his sentence, he made a point of addressing George face to face, eye to eye. "The human destruction caused by your heinous atrocities is beyond calculation," he began. "Each of us has a monster lurking within, but it is essential to our humanity that this inner beast remains shackled. You have allowed yours to escape, and to run rampant.

"Now, there is a stain on your conscience, a stain etched in the tears of the wives and children of your victims. For your crimes, the law requires that you be sentenced to a living death. This sentence marks the end of life for you and the beginning of your struggle for survival. And so, I wish you to understand, and to bear in mind as you sit in your prison cell over the coming years, that you have caused fear, pain and grief. And this knowledge represents a life sentence as well, one from which there can be no escape, nor any parole.

"You, sir, are a monster. For this you will now pay a most terrible price. I hereby remand you over to the custody of the Correctional Service of Canada."

Without further delay, two security officers approached George from either side and placed their hands underneath his elbows, pulling him from his chair before he even had the chance to rise under his own power. The courtroom erupted as George was hustled out a side door. After a short wait in a conference room, he was led down a corridor, taken on an elevator ride to the basement, trundled into a prison van and whisked away from the building toward the airport, and his final destination.

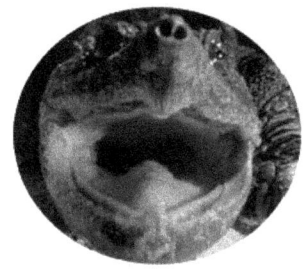

Chapter Twenty-Six

As a convicted mass murderer, George was automatically designated a dangerous offender. He was assigned to the Kingston Penitentiary in Ontario, Canada's oldest federal prison. A maximum-security facility, it was surrounded by 10-meter-high stone walls topped with razor wire, with turreted guard towers manned by armed corrections officers who stood watch twenty-four hours a day. He was held in solitary confinement in a cell about nine feet long and four feet wide. There was room enough for a desk with a bunk overhead, plus a sink and a toilet. A small barred window high on one wall allowed some direct sunlight into the cell and gave him a view of the yard, the gray perimeter fence and, beyond it, a glimpse of Lake Ontario.

Because of the infamous nature of his crimes, the other inmates held George in fear. He had been convicted of killing five men whose bodies were never discovered, and there was talk of cannibalism. It was even rumored that he had cut off and eaten his own missing hand. He was considered a homicidal psychopath. The prison guards were required to attend to George in groups of three, and he was never allowed out of his cell without shackles. He was continuously confined except for a half hour, in the darkness, early each morning and late each evening, when he was escorted into the deserted prison yard and allowed to walk around by himself.

For the first few years of his incarceration, George was haunted not by nightmares about the turtle, but by visions of the benches in the courtroom, full of the surviving family members of the dead men. Whenever he closed his eyes, he saw them, and felt the blistering heat of their reproachful looks. Whatever sympathy he might have had for them was ultimately replaced by a smoldering resentment over their misguided complicity in the process of organizing the miscarriage of justice that had condemned him, ruined and despised, to a life behind bars.

Some nights, George would lay awake thinking about what had happened all of those years ago on the Lost Lake. Other times, his fantasies would carry him off to freedom. A white winged horse like the ones he read about in his childhood comic books might come and land in the recreation yard, snorting and pawing at the red earth, and only George would be able to mount him and it would carry him up and away, away over the prison's high stone walls with the broken glass and razor wire on top, over the two perimeter fences and past the towers where the sharpshooters kept their steady watch, beyond into the outside world, the world George had left behind, the world he looked at every day dimly through the porthole of his television set, but which he could only vaguely remember in terms of any real experience.

Maybe Laura would be there with him, her arms wrapped around his waist as the stallion, running on thin air, bore them higher and higher into the sky, its mane teased back in the sweet wind of the free world. He could see the other inmates, arms dangling by their sides, looking up at them with their mouths open, falling away dizzyingly below him with the prison and the fields around it. They would fly away, away to a place where they could start all over again.

Certainly George could not have foreseen, let alone intended, the ultimate outcome of the trip he had organized, even though he understood why he was being punished for it. And this he needed to believe. Otherwise, how could he live with the guilt? Then again, living with the guilt was precisely the point of a sentence of life in prison. And in retrospect, he was indeed guilty—guilty of lying, guilty of helping to bring about the deaths of five men, guilty of breaking the hearts of two good women, and guilty of making a thousand selfish little decisions in life that put truth and honor at the disposal of selfish expedience. It was only fitting, then, that ultimately expedience would dispose of the truth. Jack had been wrong. It wasn't about tribulation dispensed at random, unjustly, by a God who allowed the innocent to find redemption for their original sin through undeserved suffering. It was indeed about the balancing out of an equation.

By speaking the truth, finally, in court, while everyone listened, albeit in total disbelief and even disgust, George gained for himself a small measure of redemption. The direct victims of his lies never did get to hear the truth, but the rest of the world did. And if his dead buddies had been up there looking down on him in that courtroom, they could not have faulted his testimony in any way. He had told their story, honestly exposing his own moral failings and weaknesses of character in the process.

Indeed, while they might have been spared had George made different decisions, they were dead not *because* of him. They were dead because of the turtle. They were dead because they had eaten the soup. They were dead because they had chosen to insert themselves into the wilderness, where the rules of engagement were deterministic. George could not bring them back any more than he could have saved them, once the forces of destiny had been set in motion by his relatively venal transgressions. Imperfect and uneasy as it was, he had made his peace with the departed.

He also made an imperfect and uneasy peace with *Le Lac Perdu*. Whatever dark forces were at work in its unknowable waters, however cursed and forsaken by man, it was nevertheless a place of stunning natural beauty, pure and unspoiled, with its own rules of survival and death. He had willingly entered that forbidden world, and in so doing had voluntarily submitted himself to its cruel exigencies. The lake knew no mercy, but it bore no malice either. It was what it was. And all of these years later, George, sitting in his small, stark prison cell, still contemplated its magnificence. It lay out there, somewhere beyond his little barred window, those many hundreds of miles away, nestled in its mountainous cradle, teeming with life, sparkling in the sun, a place of wondrous beauty—and unimaginable danger.

Cryptozoology still held its fascinating sway upon George. He immersed himself in the literature, passing endless hours devouring books about fantastic monsters and legendary beasts and assimilating the thinking of the researchers who hunted them. He traveled in his imagination to dark Amazonian jungles where giant snakes were supposed to be lurking; to the rain forests of the Pacific Northwest where Bigfoot was said to roam; to the woods of Michigan's Upper Peninsula where dog men were believed to be prowling; and to the Pine Barrens where the Jersey Devil was reportedly on the wing. His insatiable desire for information about these mysteries was fueled by the personal belief that there was indeed a basis in reality for at least some of them.

A rigorous inquiry into the meaning of these experiences held for George the irresistible promise of some insight into the esoteric secrets of the metaphysical. He spent many long hours pondering the significance of the surreal encounters and other-worldly manifestations that had been documented over the many centuries by witnesses scattered all around the globe. Even if the reports and sightings reflected an epiphenomenon of human perception - a prehensile artifact, perhaps, of the collective unconscious—the implications were still truly compelling. Be they real or imagined, the beasts of myth, legend and lore were important to consider.

Although forbidden to publish from prison, George embarked upon a scholarly volume of ambitious scope over which he toiled for several decades on end. Seeking to assimilate all of the correlations and insights he had divined through his studies and contemplations into a comprehensive treatise on the preternatural kingdom, he explored not only the biological but also the existential and metaphysical dimensions of the subject. This esoteric manuscript accumulated in a pile, wedged against one corner of his cell, which eventually grew to more than three feet high. He held out the shaky hope that his prodigious *Bestiarum vocabulum* might at least be released posthumously, but had a gut feeling that it would ultimately wind up in the prison incinerator.

George's turtle, of course, fell all too painfully into the realm of objective reality. It had, after all, taken his hand - which, by virtue of its endlessly inconvenient absence and the more-than-occasional episode of phantom pain, served as an ongoing reminder of the monster's actual existence. The oldest reptile on earth, the turtle appeared more than 200 million years ago, and has hardly evolved ever since. It has been regarded as sacred by many civilizations, including the Chinese, the Greeks, the Mayans, and all Native American nations, held to be a guardian and helper in mankind's pursuit of truth and wisdom. It had played this role beautifully so long ago on the Lost Lake.

Just like the lake, *Le Lac Perdu*, it was, he was certain, still there. It had been wounded by the flare, of course, but had probably suffered nothing more than a bad case of indigestion over the incident, and its spear wound was probably painful but not serious. It was alive, and so were its offspring, and as long as the ominous legend of the Lost Lake was accorded the proper respect, it would continue to live on forever, occupying its rightful place as the unchallenged ruler of the waters. And so, George finally made his imperfect and uneasy peace with the turtle, too.

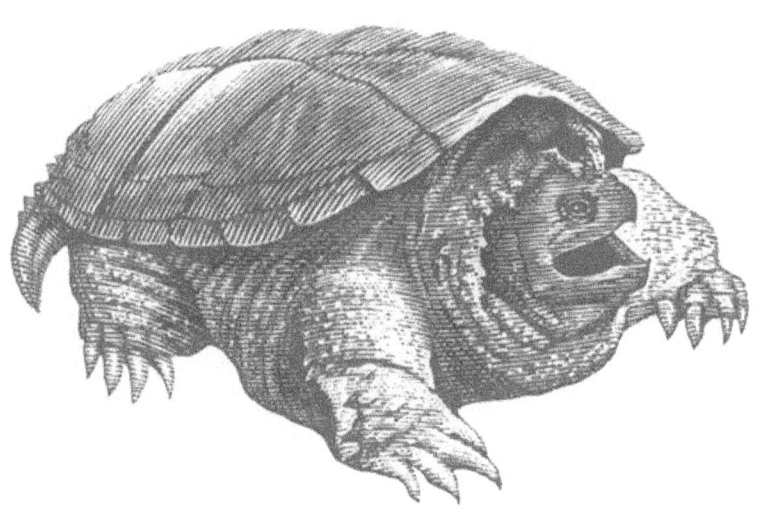

Epilogue

It was a feature of Canada as a civilized nation that it abhorred the death penalty. Which was, to George, a curse instead of a blessing. Execution was inherently horrible to contemplate, but year upon year, decade after decade, confined in maximum security was ultimately a punishment of far greater cruelty. There was no sweet release, just the measured ticking of the clock.

It was indeed a living death.

It was the year 2059, and George was still in the same old cell. In prison, he had outlived all of the principal actors in his drama - his lawyer, the prosecutor, the judge, the police, the psychologists and the widows of his victims. He had seen generations of prison guards come and go, and watched the population of regular inmates turn over too many times to number.

He himself had also changed, growing smaller, and thinner, and grayer, and less acute. His connection to the life he had led before coming to prison became progressively more tenuous, especially once he passed the point where the balance of his days had been spent behind bars rather than outside of them, until he no longer viewed himself as a free man in captivity, but as a captive man who had once been free.

What George still remembered of the events at *Le Lac Perdu* in his ninety-ninth year of life, a half-century removed in time, was a series of dim images, an ever-dwindling number of factual details and a few related mental impressions. He recalled the names of the men who had been with him, the fact of the trip, some of the fishing they had done, and the beast that had terrorized and finally decimated the party. He remembered some of the details of his trial, and the early years of his sentence, when he still had some interest in rehashing the events that had led to his incarceration. When he thought about Laura, he could recall only a few vague details.

These days, he mostly spent his time with Tim, who was very good about visiting him. The one person from the outside world who still remembered and cared about him, Tim showed up every morning with a checker board or a deck of cards, and they would pass the day quietly playing games or simply talking. Of a scientific bent with a healthy sense of curiosity, Tim had a natural interest in cryptozoology, which became a favorite topic of conversation, and of debate, when they weren't discoursing about less consequential matters. George had always meant to grow old with Tim, so he was highly appreciative of Tim's willingness to stop by every day and sit with him.

Only once, in all of his years in prison, did George ever get a visit from anyone besides Tim. It came out of the blue, the day after his ninety-fifth birthday, when a puffy man in a tweed jacket appeared at the door of his cell carrying an attaché case. He introduced himself as Dr. Robertson Abercrombie of the Canadian Office of Wildlife Resources. Dr. Abercrombie was interested in George's story about the turtle. He wanted to know all about what had happened up there on *Le Lac Perdu*, so many years earlier. He listened to George intently, and pressed him for every detail he could possibly remember.

How big had the turtle been?

What color was it?

How was its shell configured?

How did it move in the water?

How did it move on land?

Could he sketch it?

The man was there for perhaps an hour. When he had finally exhausted George's recollection, he asked for one more moment of George's time. "Here," he said, pulling some papers from his bag. "Have a look at these."

He handed George a pair of news clippings. One of them was quite old. Dated November 17, 1759, it told the story of a fur trader who returned alone from a trip to *Le Lac Perdu* blaming the loss of the rest of the members of his expedition on the predations of a giant snapping turtle. He was convicted of their murders and hanged. The second was a contemporary article about a man from Chicago who was being charged with murdering four members of his family after their disappearances during a fishing excursion to the lake. He seemed to have gone completely insane. There was no reference, in this last story, either to George's case or to the case of the fur trapper.

George gave the clippings back to Dr. Abercrombie without saying anything.

"Well," the doctor said as he packed up his things, "I'm going to leave you now. It's been a most enjoyable chat. One thing, though. We aren't going public with any of this, you see. It would be bad for the tourism.

"However," he said, "I *am* going to work through channels for your release."

"Don't hurt it."

"Excuse me?"

"Don't hurt it," George repeated. "The turtle. For the sake of tourism."

"I'm certain that we . . . won't," Dr. Abercrombie replied quietly.

Nearly five years passed without further word from the mysterious doctor. George was neither surprised nor disappointed. Tim had warned him not to get his hopes up. Governments hated to admit their mistakes. Dr. Abercrombie had just been humoring him. Or he had forgotten about him. Or they had gotten to him. Perhaps he was dead.

Besides, there was no reason for George to even want to leave prison at this point. What did he have left to return to? Alone and forgotten, he had outlived practically anyone who ever had a reason to know his name, let alone the painful story of his wanderings over the earth, a lost and wounded man with neither a country nor a soul, damned by his lies, condemned for finally speaking the truth, guilty of moral failing but innocent of the criminal wrongdoing for which he had been ostracized. In truth, he was imprisoned not by the steel and concrete cage confining his body, but rather by the invisible bars of his own conscience. Any day now, his body would give out and then he would, at last, be truly free.

"Come on," Tim said, "we'll have a hand of cribbage. It will take your mind off of things."

"I suppose I could take you on," George replied with a modest grin.

"That's the spirit," Tim said. "Only promise me, this time no cheating."

"Tim, I give you my word." George brought his good hand up to his breast and gave his friend a slight bow. With that, they sat down, feeble in their aged and withered bodies, and played out their last game.

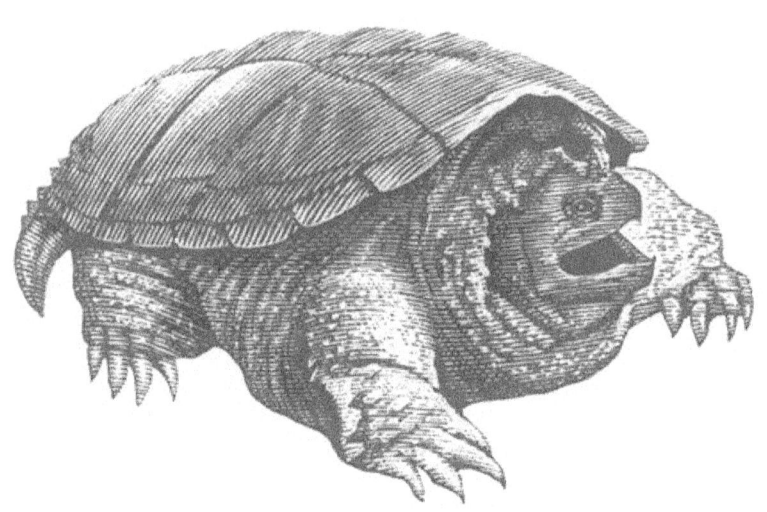

STILL ON THE TRACK OF UNKNOWN ANIMALS

The Centre for Fortean Zoology, or CFZ, is a non profit-making organisation founded in 1992 with the aim of being a clearing house for information, and coordinating research into mystery animals around the world.

We also study out of place animals, rare and aberrant animal behaviour, and Zooform Phenomena; little-understood "things" that appear to be animals, but which are in fact nothing of the sort, and not even alive (at least in the way we understand the term).

Not only are we the biggest organisation of our type in the world, but - or so we like to think - we are the best. We are certainly the only truly global cryptozoological research organisation, and we carry out our investigations using a strictly scientific set of guidelines. We are expanding all the time and looking to recruit new members to help us in our research into mysterious animals and strange creatures across the globe.

Why should you join us? Because, if you are genuinely interested in trying to solve the last great mysteries of Mother Nature, there is nobody better than us with whom to do it.

Members get a four-issue subscription to our journal *Animals & Men*. Each issue contains nearly 100 pages packed with news, articles, letters, research papers, field reports, and even a gossip column! The magazine is Royal Octavo in format with a full colour cover. You also have access to one of the world's largest collections of resource material dealing with cryptozoology and allied disciplines, and people from the CFZ membership regularly take part in fieldwork and expeditions around the world.

The CFZ is managed by a three-man board of trustees, with a non-profit making trust registered with HM Government Stamp Office. The board of trustees is supported by a Permanent Directorate of full and part-time staff, and advised by a Consultancy Board of specialists - many of whom are world-renowned experts in their particular field. We have regional representatives across the UK, the USA, and many other parts of the world, and are affiliated with other organisations whose aims and protocols mirror our own.

You'll find that the people at the CFZ are friendly and approachable. We have a thriving forum on the website which is the hub of an ever-growing electronic community. You will soon find your feet. Many members of the CFZ Permanent Directorate started off as ordinary members, and now work full-time chasing monsters around the world.

Write to us, e-mail us, or telephone us. The list of future projects on the website is not exhaustive. If you have a good idea for an investigation, please tell us. We may well be able to help.

We are always looking for volunteers to join us. If you see a project that interests you, do not hesitate to get in touch with us. Under certain circumstances we can help provide funding for your trip. If you look on the future projects section of the website, you can see some of the projects that we have pencilled in for the next few years.

In 2003 and 2004 we sent three-man expeditions to Sumatra looking for Orang-Pendek - a semi-legendary bipedal ape. The same three went to Mongolia in 2005. All three members started off merely subscribers to the CFZ magazine. Next time it could be you!

We have no magic sources of income. All our funds come from donations, membership fees, and sales of our publications and merchandise. We are always looking for corporate sponsorship, and other sources of revenue. If you have any ideas for fund-raising please let us know.

However, unlike other cryptozoological organisations in the past, we do not live in an intellectual ivory tower. We are not afraid to get our hands dirty, and furthermore we are not one of those organisations where the membership have to raise money so that a privileged few can go on expensive foreign trips. Our research teams, both in the UK and abroad, consist of a mixture of experienced and inexperienced personnel. We are truly a community, and work on the premise that the benefits of CFZ membership are open to all.

Reports of our investigations are published on our website as soon as they are available. Preliminary reports are posted within days of the project finishing.

Each year we publish a 200 page yearbook containing research papers and expedition reports too long to be printed in the journal. We freely circulate our information to anybody who asks for it.

We have a thriving YouTube channel, CFZtv, which has well over two hundred self-made documentaries, lecture appearances, and episodes of our monthly webTV show. We have a daily online magazine, which has over a million hits each year.

Each year since 2000 we have held our annual convention - the Weird Weekend. It is three days of lectures, workshops, and excursions. But most importantly it is a chance for members of the CFZ to meet each other, and to talk with the members of the permanent directorate in a relaxed and informal setting and preferably with a pint of beer in one hand. Since 2006 - the Weird Weekend has been bigger and better and held on the third weekend in August in the idyllic rural location of Woolsery in North Devon.

Since relocating to North Devon in 2005 we have become ever more closely involved with other community organisations, and we hope that this trend will continue. We have also worked closely with Police Forces across the UK as consultants for animal mutilation cases, and we intend to forge closer links with the coastguard and other community services. We want to work closely with those who regularly travel into the Bristol Channel, so that if the recent trend of exotic animal visitors to our coastal waters continues, we can be out there as soon as possible.

Apart from having been the only Fortean Zoological organisation in the world to have consistently published material on all aspects of the subject for over a decade, we have achieved the following concrete results:

• Disproved the myth relating to the headless so-called sea-serpent carcass of Durgan beach in Cornwall 1975
• Disproved the story of the 1988 puma skull of

Lustleigh Cleave
- Carried out the only in-depth research ever into the mythos of the Cornish Owlman.
- Made the first records of a tropical species of lamprey
- Made the first records of a luminous cave gnat larva in Thailand
- Discovered a possible new species of British mammal - the beech marten
- In 1994-6 carried out the first archival fortean zoological survey of Hong Kong
- In the year 2000, CFZ theories were confirmed when a new species of lizard was added to the British List
- Identified the monster of Martin Mere in Lancashire as a giant wels catfish
- Expanded the known range of Armitage's skink in the Gambia by 80%
- Obtained photographic evidence of the remains of Europe's largest known pike
- Carried out the first ever in-depth study of the ninki-nanka
- Carried out the first attempt to breed Puerto Rican cave snails in captivity
- Were the first European explorers to visit the `lost valley` in Sumatra
- Published the first ever evidence for a new tribe of pygmies in Guyana
- Published the first evidence for a new species of caiman in Guyana
- Filmed unknown creatures

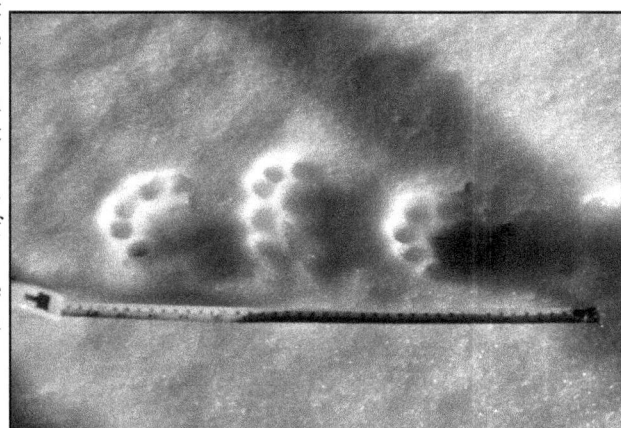

on a monster-haunted lake in Ireland for the first time
- Had a sighting of orang pendek in Sumatra in 2009
- Found leopard hair, subsequently identified by DNA analysis, from rural North Devon in 2010
- Brought back hairs which appear to be from an unknown primate in Sumatra
- Published some of the best evidence ever for the almasty in southern Russia

CFZ Expeditions and Investigations include:

- 1998 Puerto Rico, Florida, Mexico (Chupacabras)
- 1999 Nevada (Bigfoot)
- 2000 Thailand (Naga)
- 2002 Martin Mere (Giant catfish)
- 2002 Cleveland (Wallaby mutilation)

- 2003 Bolam Lake (BHM Reports)
- 2003 Sumatra (Orang Pendek)
- 2003 Texas (Bigfoot; giant snapping turtles)
- 2004 Sumatra (Orang Pendek; cigau, a sabre-toothed cat)
- 2004 Illinois (Black panthers; cicada swarm)
- 2004 Texas (Mystery blue dog)
- Loch Morar (Monster)
- 2004 Puerto Rico (Chupacabras; carnivorous cave snails)
- 2005 Belize (Affiliate expedition for hairy dwarfs)
- 2005 Loch Ness (Monster)
- 2005 Mongolia (Allghoi Khorkhoi aka Mongolian death worm)

- 2006 Gambia (Gambo - Gambian sea monster , Ninki Nanka and Armitage's skink
- 2006 Llangorse Lake (Giant pike, giant eels)
- 2006 Windermere (Giant eels)
- 2007 Coniston Water (Giant eels)
- 2007 Guyana (Giant anaconda, didi, water tiger)
- 2008 Russia (Almasty)
- 2009 Sumatra (Orang pendek)
- 2009 Republic of Ireland (Lake Monster)
- 2010 Texas (Blue Dogs)
- 2010 India (Mande Burung)
- 2011 Sumatra (Orang-pendek)

For details of current membership fees, current expeditions and investigations, and voluntary posts within the CFZ that need your help, please do not hesitate to contact us.

The Centre for Fortean Zoology,
Myrtle Cottage,
Woolfardisworthy,
Bideford, North Devon
EX39 5QR

Telephone 01237 431413
Fax+44 (0)7006-074-925
eMail info@cfz.org.uk

Websites:

www.cfz.org.uk
www.weirdweekend.org

THE WORLD'S WEIRDEST PUBLISHING COMPANY

HOW TO START A PUBLISHING EMPIRE

Unlike most mainstream publishers, we have a non-commercial remit, and our mission statement claims that "we publish books because they deserve to be published, not because we think that we can make money out of them". Our motto is the Latin Tag *Pro bona causa facimus* (we do it for good reason), a slogan taken from a children's book *The Case of the Silver Egg* by the late Desmond Skirrow.

WIKIPEDIA: "The first book published was in 1988. *Take this Brother may it Serve you Well* was a guide to Beatles bootlegs by Jonathan Downes. It sold quite well, but was hampered by very poor production values, being photocopied, and held together by a plastic clip binder. In 1988 A5 clip binders were hard to get hold of, so the publishers took A4 binders and cut them in half with a hacksaw. It now reaches surprisingly high prices second hand.

The production quality improved slightly over the years, and after 1999 all the books produced were ringbound with laminated colour covers. In 2004, however, they signed an agreement with Lightning Source, and all books are now produced perfect bound, with full colour covers."

Until 2010 all our books, the majority of which are/were on the subject of mystery animals and allied disciplines, were published by `CFZ Press`, the publishing arm of the Centre for Fortean Zoology (CFZ), and we urged our readers and followers to draw a discreet veil over the books that we published that were completely off topic to the CFZ.

However, in 2010 we decided that enough was enough and launched a second imprint, `Fortean Words` which aims to cover a wide range of non animal-related esoteric subjects. Other imprints will be launched as and when we feel like it, however the basic ethos of the company remains the same: Our job is to publish books and magazines that we feel are worth publishing, whether or not they are going to sell. Money is, after all - as my dear old Mama once told me - a rather vulgar subject, and she would be rolling in her grave if she thought that her eldest son was somehow in `trade`.

Luckily, so far our tastes have turned out not to be that rarified after all, and we have sold far more books than anyone ever thought that we would, so there is a moral in there somewhere…

Jon Downes,
Woolsery, North Devon
July 2010

Other Books in Print

ORANG PENDEK: Sumatra's Forgotten Ape by Richard Freeman
THE MYSTERY ANIMALS OF THE BRITISH ISLES: London by Neil Arnold
CFZ EXPEDITION REPORT: India 2010 by Richard Freeman *et al*
The Cryptid Creatures of Florida by Scott Marlow
Dead of Night by Lee Walker
The Mystery Animals of the British Isles: The Northern Isles by Glen Vaudrey
THE MYSTERY ANIMALS OF THE BRTISH ISLES: Gloucestershire and Worcestershire by Paul Williams
When Bigfoot Attacks by Michael Newton
Weird Waters – The Mystery Animals of Scandinavia: Lake and Sea Monsters by Lars Thomas
The Inhumanoids by Barton Nunnelly
Monstrum! A Wizard's Tale by Tony "Doc" Shiels
CFZ Yearbook 2011 edited by Jonathan Downes
Karl Shuker's Alien Zoo by Shuker, Dr Karl P.N
Tetrapod Zoology Book One by Naish, Dr Darren
The Mystery Animals of Ireland by Gary Cunningham and Ronan Coghlan
Monsters of Texas by Gerhard, Ken
The Great Yokai Encyclopaedia by Freeman, Richard
NEW HORIZONS: Animals & Men *issues 16-20 Collected Editions Vol. 4* by Downes, Jonathan
A Daintree Diary -
Tales from Travels to the Daintree Rainforest in tropical north Queensland, Australia by Portman, Carl
Strangely Strange but Oddly Normal by Roberts, Andy
Centre for Fortean Zoology Yearbook 2010 by Downes, Jonathan
Predator Deathmatch by Molloy, Nick
Star Steeds and other Dreams by Shuker, Karl
CHINA: A Yellow Peril? by Muirhead, Richard
Mystery Animals of the British Isles: The Western Isles by Vaudrey, Glen

Giant Snakes - Unravelling the coils of mystery by Newton, Michael
Mystery Animals of the British Isles: Kent by Arnold, Neil
Centre for Fortean Zoology Yearbook 2009 by Downes, Jonathan
CFZ EXPEDITION REPORT: Russia 2008 by Richard Freeman *et al*, Shuker, Karl (fwd)
Dinosaurs and other Prehistoric Animals on Stamps - A Worldwide catalogue by Shuker, Karl P. N
Dr Shuker's Casebook by Shuker, Karl P.N
The Island of Paradise - chupacabra UFO crash retrievals, and accelerated evolution on the island of Puerto Rico by Downes, Jonathan
The Mystery Animals of the British Isles: Northumberland and Tyneside by Hallowell, Michael J
Centre for Fortean Zoology Yearbook 1997 by Downes, Jonathan (Ed)
Centre for Fortean Zoology Yearbook 2002 by Downes, Jonathan (Ed)
Centre for Fortean Zoology Yearbook 2000/1 by Downes, Jonathan (Ed)
Centre for Fortean Zoology Yearbook 1998 by Downes, Jonathan (Ed)
Centre for Fortean Zoology Yearbook 2003 by Downes, Jonathan (Ed)
In the wake of Bernard Heuvelmans by Woodley, Michael A
CFZ EXPEDITION REPORT: Guyana 2007 by Richard Freeman *et al*, Shuker, Karl (fwd)
Centre for Fortean Zoology Yearbook 1999 by Downes, Jonathan (Ed)
Big Cats in Britain Yearbook 2008 by Fraser, Mark (Ed)
Centre for Fortean Zoology Yearbook 1996 by Downes, Jonathan (Ed)
THE CALL OF THE WILD - Animals & Men issues 11-15
Collected Editions Vol. 3 by Downes, Jonathan (ed)
Ethna's Journal by Downes, C N
Centre for Fortean Zoology Yearbook 2008 by Downes, J (Ed)
DARK DORSET -Calendar Custome by Newland, Robert J
Extraordinary Animals Revisited by Shuker, Karl
MAN-MONKEY - In Search of the British Bigfoot by Redfern, Nick
Dark Dorset Tales of Mystery, Wonder and Terror by Newland, Robert J and Mark North
Big Cats Loose in Britain by Matthews, Marcus
MONSTER! - The A-Z of Zooform Phenomena by Arnold, Neil
The Centre for Fortean Zoology 2004 Yearbook by Downes, Jonathan (Ed)
The Centre for Fortean Zoology 2007 Yearbook by Downes, Jonathan (Ed)
CAT FLAPS! Northern Mystery Cats by Roberts, Andy
Big Cats in Britain Yearbook 2007 by Fraser, Mark (Ed)
BIG BIRD! - Modern sightings of Flying Monsters by Gerhard, Ken
THE NUMBER OF THE BEAST - Animals & Men issues 6-10
Collected Editions Vol. 1 by Downes, Jonathan (Ed)
IN THE BEGINNING - Animals & Men *issues 1-5 Collected Editions Vol. 1* by Downes, Jonathan
STRENGTH THROUGH KOI - They saved Hitler's Koi and other stories by Downes, Jonathan
The Smaller Mystery Carnivores of the Westcountry by Downes, Jonathan
CFZ EXPEDITION REPORT: Gambia 2006 by Richard Freeman *et al*, Shuker, Karl (fwd)
The Owlman and Others by Jonathan Downes
The Blackdown Mystery by Downes, Jonathan

Big Cats in Britain Yearbook 2006 by Fraser, Mark (Ed)
Fragrant Harbours - Distant Rivers by Downes, John T
Only Fools and Goatsuckers by Downes, Jonathan
Monster of the Mere by Jonathan Downes
Dragons: More than a Myth by Freeman, Richard Alan
Granfer's Bible Stories by Downes, John Tweddell
Monster Hunter by Downes, Jonathan

Fortean Words

The Centre for Fortean Zoology has for several years led the field in Fortean publishing. CFZ Press is the only publishing company specialising in books on monsters and mystery animals. CFZ Press has published more books on this subject than any other company in history and has attracted such well known authors as Andy Roberts, Nick Redfern, Michael Newton, Dr Karl Shuker, Neil Arnold, Dr Darren Naish, Jon Downes, Ken Gerhard and Richard Freeman.

Now CFZ Press are launching a new imprint. Fortean Words is a new line of books dealing with Fortean subjects other than cryptozoology, which is - after all - the subject the CFZ are best known for. Fortean Words is being launched with a spectacular multi-volume series called *Haunted Skies* which covers British UFO sightings between 1940 and 2010. Former policeman John Hanson and his long-suffering partner Dawn Holloway have compiled a peerless library of sighting reports, many that have not been made public before.

Other books include a look at the Berwyn Mountains UFO case by renowned Fortean Andy Roberts and a series of forthcoming books by transatlantic researcher Nick Redfern. CFZ Press are dedicated to maintaining the fine quality of their works with Fortean Words. New authors tackling new subjects will always be encouraged, and we hope that our books will continue to be as ground-breaking and popular as ever.

Haunted Skies Volume One 1940-1959 by John Hanson and Dawn Holloway
Haunted Skies Volume Two 1960-1965 by John Hanson and Dawn Holloway
Haunted Skies Volume Three 1965-1967 by John Hanson and Dawn Holloway
Haunted Skies Volume Four 1968-1971 by John Hanson and Dawn Holloway
Grave Concerns by Kai Roberts

Police and the Paranormal by Andy Owens
Dead of Night by Lee Walker
Space Girl Dead on Spaghetti Junction - an anthology by Nick Redfern
I Fort the Lore - an anthology by Paul Screeton
UFO Down - the Berwyn Mountains UFO Crash by Andy Roberts

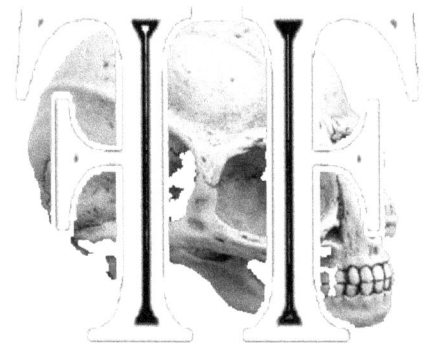

Fortean Fiction

Just before Christmas 2011, we launched our third imprint, this time dedicated to - let's see if you guessed it from the title - fictional books with a Fortean or cryptozoological theme. We have published a few fictional books in the past, but now think that because of our rising reputation as publishers of quality Forteana, that a dedicated fiction imprint was the order of the day.

We launched with four titles:

Green Unpleasant Land by Richard Freeman
Left Behind by Harriet Wadham
Dark Ness by Tabitca Cope
Snap! By Steven Bredice